Franklin Carter

Mark Hopkins

Franklin Carter

Mark Hopkins

ISBN/EAN: 9783337112226

Printed in Europe, USA, Canada, Australia, Japan

Cover: Foto ©Raphael Reischuk / pixelio.de

More available books at **www.hansebooks.com**

American Religious Leaders

MARK HOPKINS

BY

FRANKLIN CARTER
PRESIDENT OF WILLIAMS COLLEGE

BOSTON AND NEW YORK
HOUGHTON, MIFFLIN AND COMPANY
The Riverside Press, Cambridge
1892

The Riverside Press, Cambridge, Mass., U. S. A.
Electrotyped and Printed by H. O. Houghton & Company.

PREFACE.

An estimate of Mark Hopkins cannot be out of place in a series of American Religious Leaders. He belonged among the later religious leaders of New England. His endowments, his attainments, and his long service made him a unique figure among the teachers of this age. But for a complete estimate of him as a man, there is a lack of material. His own letters, with the exception of those written to the late Rev. Dr. Ray Palmer and President Garfield, have been generally lost. His life in a country town was devoid of picturesque and varying incident. He lived one side of the advantages of stimulating society and the intellectual discoveries of his time. The great thrills of modern thought reached him chiefly through newspapers and books. His profound and far-reaching influence in the country was for that reason all the surer testimony to the wisdom and power of his manhood.

It was perhaps not without propriety that I was asked to examine into the elements of his character and teaching, and to compose this book.

I was his pupil, his colleague when he was president, and later his colleague in an inverted relation when I became his successor as president of the college, though not immediately following him in this office. My acquaintance with him was not as lengthy as that of some others, but I knew him from widely divergent standpoints, and only by these later years of the anxieties and cares that belong to the presidency of a New England country college have I come to the full understanding and appreciation of the great qualities which marked his career. The estimate which is here presented is the mature estimate of one who has thus had unusual opportunities of knowing him, and of entering into sympathy with his activities. But this will not compensate for the loss of those expressions of his earlier and later inner life of growth which all who knew him would highly value. Nor will it serve to relieve much the lack of that incident which life in a larger community would probably have supplied. This little book, then, whose writing has been a pleasant labor and the grateful recognition of a large debt, is sent forth with regret that it is not fuller and richer in material, but not without confidence that the judgments expressed in it are accurate, and will be indorsed by those who have penetrated the true secrets of this beneficent life.

FRANKLIN CARTER.

WILLIAMS COLLEGE, *October* 26, 1891.

CONTENTS.

CHAPTER IX.

CHAPTER X.

CHAPTER XI.

CHAPTER XII.

CHAPTER XIII.

CHAPTER XIV.

CHRONOLOGICAL TABLE.

THE principal dates in Dr. Hopkins's life are here arranged in chronological order, In certain cases the invitations to positions in other institutions did not become formal, but I have judged from the correspondence that in all the instances recorded in this list the invitation would have been formally given, if Dr. Hopkins had shown a disposition to encourage the belief that he could be drawn away from Williams College. Doubtless his regular refusal of such invitations prevented even the informal suggestion of many other such offers. But the list is long and varied enough to show the very high esteem in which he was held as teacher, thinker, and preacher by the best informed in our land; it shows also his loyal devotion to his own college.

1802. Born February 2, at Stockbridge, Mass.

1821. Entered Williams College as a Sophomore.

1824. Was graduated as Bachelor of Arts.

1825. Tutor in Williams College.

1827. Delivered the Master's oration on " Mystery."

1829. Graduated in medicine from Berkshire Medical School.

1830. Appointed Professor of Moral Philosophy and Rhetoric in Williams College.

1833. Licensed to preach by the Berkshire Association.

1836. Elected President of Williams College.

1837. Created Doctor of Divinity by Dartmouth College.

1841. Received the same degree from Harvard College.

1843. Elected Fellow of the College of Physicians and Surgeons in New York city.

1844. Lowell Lectures on " The Evidences of Christianity."

1844. Invited to become Pastor of the Plymouth Church, Brooklyn, N. Y.

1847. Elected Bartlett Professor of Sacred Rhetoric in Andover Theological Seminary.

1848. Elected Member of the Board of Visitors in the same seminary.

1850. Offered the Chancellorship of the University of New York.

1850. Appointed Professor of Systematic Theology in Union Theological Seminary.

1851. Called to the pastorate of the Mercer Street Church in New York city.

1852. Urged to accept a nomination to the presidency of the University of Michigan.

1853. Invited to become Pastor of a new Presbyterian Church in Philadelphia.

1857. Received the degree of LL. D. from the Regents of New York University.

1857. Elected President of the American Board of Commissioners for Foreign Missions.

1857. Elected Vice-President of the National Society for Compensated Emancipation.

1858. Offered professorship of Didactic Theology in Chicago Theological Seminary.

1860–61. (December, 1860, and January, 1861.) Lowell Lectures on "Moral Science."

1861. Visited Europe.

1867–68. (December, 1867, and January, 1868.) Lowell Lectures. "The Law of Love and Love as a Law."

1868. Elected President of the Academy of Metaphysical and Ethical Sciences.

1871–72. (December, 1871, and January, 1872.) Lowell Lectures. "An Outline Study of Man."

1872. Resigned presidency of Williams College, but retained the professorship of Intellectual and Moral Philosophy.

1873. Invited to the Chair of Intellectual and Moral Philosophy in Bowdoin College.

1875. Course of lectures before the Yale Theological Seminary on "The Scriptural Idea of Man."

1876. Lectures before the students of the same seminary on "The Scriptural Idea of God."

1876. Invited to the direction of the Post-Graduate Department in Boston University.

1876. Lectures on "Scriptural Anthropology" before the Theological School of Boston University.

1881. A second trip to Europe.

1883. Lectures on "The Scriptural Idea of Man" before Princeton Theological Students. These lectures were also delivered in Chicago, Illinois, and Oberlin, Ohio.

1886. Created Doctor of Laws at the 250th anniversary of Harvard University.

1886. Took position at Des Moines, Iowa, at the annual meeting of the A. B. C. F. M., for the reference to a council of applications for missionary service "in difficult cases turning upon the doctrinal views of candidates."

1887. Died, June 17.

THE EARLY YEARS.

"My parents were professors of religion: and I descended from Christian ancestors, both by my father and my mother, as far back as I have been able to trace my descent. I conclude I and my ancestors descended from those called Puritans in the days of Queen Elizabeth, above two hundred years ago, and have continued to bear that denomination since, and were the first settlers of New England. This I have considered to be the most honorable and happy descent, to spring from ancestors who have been professors of religion without interruption during the course of two hundred years and more: and many of them, if not all, real Christians." — SAMUEL HOPKINS's *Autobiography.*

> "The thought of our past years in me doth breed
> Perpetual benediction: . . .
> . . . for those obstinate questionings
> Of sense and outward things,
>
> .   .   .   .
>
> . . . for those first affections
> Those shadowy recollections,
> Which, be they what they may,
> Are yet the fountain light of all our day,
> And yet a master light of all our seeing:
> Uphold us, cherish, and have the power to make
> Our noisy years seem moments in the being
> Of the eternal silence: truths that wake
> To perish never."
>
> WORDSWORTH, *Intimations of Immortality.*

CHAPTER I.

THE EARLY YEARS.

AMONG the low hills that form the Naugatuck valley in Connecticut, in the year 1677, the actual settlement at Mattatuck, now Waterbury, began. In 1680, Stephen Hopkins, the son of John who settled in Cambridge in 1634, went to Waterbury from Hartford and received a house-lot. He built a mill on Mill, now Mad River, which he probably erected to provide occupation and a livelihood for his eldest son John, and possibly the house-lot was originally secured for him. John Hopkins became influential in the new settlement, and held nearly all the offices which a respected and enterprising man in such a community could attain. He was town clerk one year and tavern-keeper (no mean distinction) for several years, and received military honors. John's second son, Stephen, born in 1689, was also a prominent citizen, and maintained well the dignity of family which his father's services had established.

His third son, Timothy, born in 1691, was probably the most influential man of his generation in the town. He was often constable, selectman, grand juror, and moderator of the town meeting.

He was justice of the peace for eight years, and represented the town many times in the General Court. He was also a man of military distinction, being appointed captain in 1732. He was a man of more than ordinary intelligence, a type of that old-fashioned integrity and religion and authority which was not uncommon in the New England villages during the last century.

One of his sons was Samuel Hopkins, the celebrated divine. The latter alludes in his autobiography to the influences of his childhood in the following appreciative words: —

"I have considered it a great favor of God that I was born and educated in a religious family, and among a people in a country town, where a regard to religion and morality was common and prevalent, and the education of children and youth was generally practiced in such a degree that young people were generally orderly in their behavior, and abstained from those open vices which were then too common in seaport and populous places." He congratulated himself that his ancestors on both sides "had been professors of religion without interruption during the course of two hundred years or more: and many of them, if not all, real Christians."

Samuel's father, Timothy, died in 1749, when Samuel was twenty-eight years old. Samuel had been graduated from Yale, and trained in theology by Jonathan Edwards; became in 1743 the settled minister at Great Barrington, then called Housatonnuc, a parish of Sheffield, in Berkshire County,

Massachusetts. It was while settled over this parish that he first published sermons, three in number, the very title of which seems to transport the reader to the last century. The title runs: "Sin through Divine Interposition an advantage to the Universe, and yet this no Excuse for Sin or Encouragement to it: illustrated and proved: and God's Wisdom and Holiness in the Permission of Sin: and that his will herein is the same as his revealed will shown and confirmed in three sermons from Rom. iii. 5, 6, 7, 8." These sermons were first published in 1759, though there was at least one subsequent edition.

The youngest brother of Samuel was Mark, born in 1739, and ten years old when his father died. The care of three younger brothers devolved upon the eldest, Samuel, from that event; and Mark was taken to his brother's home in Great Barrington and by him fitted for college. He was graduated from Yale in 1758, and was admitted to the bar at the first session of the Berkshire court in September, 1761. He was fitted both by his talents and training to maintain the honorable traditions of his family, and was rapidly advanced through the various public positions to which those serious and stormy times called only able men. The first and most distinguished Theodore Sedgwick studied law in his office. He early espoused the cause of the colonies, and was a delegate from Great Barrington to the county convention convened at Stockbridge July 6, 1774, and became one of the committee who drafted the resolutions passed by the convention on the relations to the mother country. It is not to be forgotten that this convention was the first of the county conventions that assembled in Massachusetts to consider the encroachments of Great Britain, and that the resolutions adopted by the committee of which the first Mark Hopkins was a member struck the keynote of loyalty to the king, but of devotion to the maintenance of the rights of the colonies, which influenced subsequent conventions and led to the Revolution. He was, when the Revolution became actual, a member of the Committee of Safety, and his wise energy was felt throughout the county in giving direction and efficiency to the patriotic movement.

He had, too, like his father and great-grandfather, an adaptation for military command, and was active in organizing and equipping the militia, of which he became colonel. In the summer of 1776 he commanded a detachment of Berkshire militia which had been summoned into the field by General John Fellows, and was stationed for a while at Peekskill. While engaged in the service he was taken with typhoid fever at White Plains, and to prevent his falling into the hands of the British army, who were marching on the place, he was carried from his sick-bed in the arms of a soldier to a place of safety. The excitement and fatigue gave an unfavorable turn to the disease, and he died two days previous to the fight at White Plains, October 26, 1776.

The wife of Colonel Mark Hopkins, the grandmother of President Hopkins, was Electa Sargeant, daughter of Rev. John Sargeant, the first teacher of the missionary school among the Indians at Stockbridge. The conception of this school originated with Rev. Samuel Hopkins, of West Springfield, a younger brother of Timothy, and thus an uncle of the great Dr. Samuel. Mr. Sargeant was a man of unusual talents, of sweet temper, of engaging manners, and was a thorough scholar. Among the books owned by the late Dr. Mark Hopkins is a volume of Livy, with the inscription on the fly-leaf: —

"Iohannis Sargeant, Liber Donum Pupillorum, An. Dom. 1735."

As the Indian school began in 1734, it has been supposed that this book was a present to Mr. Sargeant from the grateful Indians gathered into the school, and that the selection of a classical author was made for them by some scholarly friend of their teacher. But as Mr. Sargeant remained only a few weeks in the school in 1734, and, securing a temporary substitute, returned to Yale College to finish his four years' engagement as tutor, which ended the next summer (1735), there can be no doubt that the volume of Livy was a present from his pupils at Yale. Professor F. B. Dexter, of Yale College, says of Mr. Sargeant: "As a tutor he was one of the most successful holders of that office in the early history of the college."[1] Mr. Sargeant

[1] *Yale Biographies and Annals,* p. 395.

studied the language of the Housatonnuc Indians so diligently that in 1737 he was able to preach without an interpreter, and the Indians were afterwards wont to say, "Our minister speaks our language better than we ourselves can do."

Mr. Sargeant's wife, the mother of Mrs. Colonel Mark Hopkins, was the eldest daughter of Colonel Ephraim Williams. The second Colonel Ephraim Williams, her elder half-brother, was the founder of Williams College. Thus, through his grandmother, Electa Sargeant, Dr. Hopkins had in his veins the blood of the families that founded the missionary school among the Indians at Stockbridge, and the college at Williamstown of which he afterwards became president.

Colonel Mark's eldest son, Archibald, a farmer, a man perhaps of less striking gifts than some of the line, but a true Hopkins, lived and died in Stockbridge, where, on February 4, 1802, his eldest son, Mark, was born. It is his life and thought, which were of great service to the church and to mankind, that an effort is here made to record, not in minute details, for these have been largely lost, but in the strong outlines which his pupils love to honor.

It is a somewhat singular circumstance that nearly all papers relating to the early life of the subject of this study seem to have disappeared. A long life, whose constant residence was in one county, which had intimate associations with the best people of the county from childhood, and

in its influence affected thousands of educated men
throughout the land, seems scarcely to have had
a beginning. As his life stretched over eighty-
five years, those older persons who knew him as
a little boy have long since passed away. To very
few now living was he known in the days even of
his undergraduate life, and the pupils of his connection with the college as professor are no longer
numerous. To all these he seemed to have the
full maturity of manhood from the first. Now that
a complete picture of his career would have great
interest for those who were personally acquainted
with him and for many others, the inability to present some satisfactory account of his boyhood and
youth is disappointing. Perhaps it is this part
of his life which those who knew him in manhood, when the impression of his personality was
so striking and definite, would value most highly.
One would be glad to learn whether the heaven
which "lies about us in our infancy" revealed itself
in any peculiar way; whether the "white celestial
thoughts" that the poets give to childhood were
early soiled, as in most cases they are, by the development of selfishness and passion. His mother,
who was Mary Curtis, of Stockbridge, a genuine
descendant of the Puritans, a woman of large intelligence and force, and a firm believer in the inspiration of the Bible, although she never made a
formal profession of religion, brought up her sons
with scrupulous fidelity to the development in them
of the purest morality. Doubtless from her he and

his brother Albert learned something of that reverence for God's word which manifested itself in their later life with perhaps equal distinctness, but in somewhat different ways. The childhood of these gifted boys (there was a third brother who early died, but not until he had shown unusual talents as a civil engineer, and as an artist) must have had in it much that was vigorous and healthful. The final eminence of Mark as a philosopher, of Albert as an astronomer, and the traces of the genius of Henry, who seems to have had an Italian's love of color and a Greek's perception of form, and to whom the creative touch was not wanting, would suggest rare advantages and incentives. But the father was a farmer, and the boys worked more or less upon the farm, as the district school hours and the seasons permitted. It is hardly to the environment that we must attribute their large development. The beauty of the Housatonic valley was not lost upon Henry, and the love of nature that Albert showed was quickened by the search for and discovery of rare flowers, and by the study of the manifold unity of vegetable and animal life. But Mark, who was also very fond of nature, probably had a deeper tendency to reflection; and while for the coming of all the boys the manly, self-respecting training of several generations had been preparing, in Mark peculiarly the influence of the serious New England thinkers was to be reproduced.

When he first went to the district school, at the age of four, the teacher, taking the reading book in his hand, asked: "And where can you read, my little fellow?" "Just where you please, sir!" was the reply. The teacher found it so. He could read anywhere, and was always at the head of his class.

This incident is suggestive of the care with which his mother had begun his intellectual training. He showed aptitude for learning in all his school years, but was not pretentious, though apparently somewhat ambitious. His brother Albert in later years wrote of him to a friend as follows: —

"Study was more congenial to my brother Mark than to me. He entered upon the pursuit of knowledge, prompted, I think, by a love for it, mixed doubtless with something of a worldly ambition." There was so much genuine humor in the two brothers, who became connected with the college as teachers, that one cannot help thinking that their boyhood must have had in it a deal of robust fun. Mark was fitted for college partly at Clinton, New York, partly by his uncle, Rev. Jared Curtis, who had for a time the control of the Stockbridge Academy, and he was for a little while a member of the Lenox Academy.

Before entering college he taught school in Richmond. A letter from a cousin, the Rev. Moses Ashley Curtis (Williams, 1827), written thirty-five years after, gives some interesting details of the experience. The cousin writes from Hillsborough, North Carolina, and begins his letter with the statement that he, the writer, is officiating as clergyman once a month for a small settlement not far

from where he is writing.   He has recently stayed
with a physician, who asked in the morning as they
were waiting for breakfast, "if I knew a Dr. Hopkins, President of some College at the North.'   I
need not tell you that he brought his eggs to the
right market that time.   'Why,' says he, 'Mark
Hopkins was my teacher, when I was a lad in Virginia.'[1]   The Doctor listened with great interest
to what I could tell him of you, and had to repeat
my information and our relationship to the different members of the family, as they came in.   He
seemed to think that he was rather a favorite with
you, though he says you were much esteemed by all.
He told me of your boxing young Howerton's ears
pretty roundly for a bit of impertinence, when you
took him to task for picking some young kildees
and then setting them to swim in a pond.

"On telling him that I sometimes had communication with you, he desired me to say that he still
holds you in very affectionate remembrance."

[1] It is believed by Dr. Hopkins's family that Mr. Curtis has
here substituted the name of the State, Virginia, for Richmond,
and that the Richmond referred to was not in Virginia, but the
town in Berkshire County lying northwest of Stockbridge, Dr.
Hopkins's native town, where it is certain Hopkins taught.   The
name of one pupil, Speed, mentioned in the letter, was known in
Richmond, Mass., at the time Hopkins taught there.   Howerton
may have been a Christian name.   Another reason for believing
that Richmond in Massachusetts became in Mr. Curtis's mind
Richmond, Virginia, is the statement that Speed made that Hopkins, when traveling as agent of the American Tract Society,
called upon him in central New York, where he was then living.
A migration from Richmond. Virginia, in those days to central
New York was not very likely to occur.

We see here that the young teacher had the same power of attaching his pupils to himself as was later exhibited by the venerable president, and it is interesting to note that this power rested on the same love of manliness and scorn of meanness.

A more interesting picture in the same letter is the reference to the return home of the young Mark Hopkins: —

"I remember your return from that (then) far away country. I was going after the cow at evening, and had just entered the willow-flanked lane below Colonel Dwight's, when I saw you approaching whistling upon a blade of grass between your thumbs *à la grandpa*. I knew you at a distance; but when you saluted me and took me by the hand, in my sheepishness I hung my head, and told you 'I did not know you.' What fools does bashfulness make of children! I did the same thing once by Edwin Dwight. I have not yet got over the shame of such contemptible folly, and I feel *mean*, whenever I think of it. You spent part of that evening at our house by the old burying ground. I remember where you sat and *how* you sat. You can sit so still, sometimes. I know I then thought it a very funny mode. If you have forgotten, I can inform you that you brought from Virginia \$540,[1] as I learned from your own mouth that even-

[1] As Hopkins, when studying medicine, taught in New York city, this amount, apparently too large to be earned in Richmond, Mass., may have been gained there, and the return would be more important, both to the boy Curtis and to the Hopkins family, than that from teaching in Richmond, Mass. It is very probable that

ing, and that you left it, if I am not mistaken (for I am not so certain about this) for some sort of investment in the hands of Harry Sedgwick in New York."

The picture of the young Berkshire student coming home from a few months' work as teacher with an exuberance of spirits that finds expression in whistling on a blade of grass between his thumbs is charming. It is "*à la grandpa*," and he is stealing home to surprise his mother and give her his renewed homage after a long absence. The other picture of his sitting so as to make a deep impression on the mind of a younger boy suggests that already thoughtful study of the grave problems of life had produced an effect upon his manner; that there was something peculiar and striking even at that early date in his personal presence. He entered Williams College as a Sophomore in 1821, and was graduated valedictorian of his class in 1824. A single classmate, the Hon. Harvey Rice,[1] of Cleveland, survives, and he has furnished to me so interesting a paper of reminiscences of his friend, that it is here given entire.

"The late Rev. Dr. Mark Hopkins was one of my classmates in Williams College, and graduated with me in the class of 1824. I think he entered college in advance of the Freshman year. He came

___

the boy received a wrong impression in respect to what was said, but not about what he saw.

[1] Mr. Rice died November 7, 1891, after this manuscript went to the printer.

into the class with the reputation of being a bright
scholar, and continued to maintain that reputation.
We soon became, I hardly know why, mutual
friends. He seemed as remarkable for his modesty
and unassuming manners as for his excellence in
scholarship. He enjoyed the respect of his class,
and was regarded by all who knew him as an ex-
emplary young man.

"He was studious in his habits and scrupulous
in the discharge of his duties, kind and obliging,
and always ready to bestow favors. This he
often did by way of aiding the inefficient of his class
in acquiring their lessons, and in writing the essays required of them as class exercises. He was a
deep thinker, and acknowledged to be the best literary writer in his class. He never indulged in
sports, or frolics, so common among college students, but, in whatever he did or said, he always
observed the proprieties of life. In matters of
serious import he was considerate, and in his religious observances, reverent and sincere.

"Yet he appreciated humor and witticism, loved
to hear and tell anecdotes, and enjoyed a hearty
laugh. He was quick in his perceptions, logical
in his conclusions, and could make a fine point and
see a fine point without spectacles. In the recitation-room he often put questions, arising out of
our lessons, to the learned professor, which per-
plexed him, and then would answer the questions
himself with becoming deference.

"In his course of reading, while in college, he

manifested little or no relish for novels, but seemed to prefer standard authors in literature and science. He soon evinced a decided love for the study of metaphysics, and read all the books on that subject which he could find in the college library, and took great pleasure in discussing the different theories advanced by different authors.

"I well remember that on one occasion, during our Senior year, he read before the class in the presence of the professor an essay on a metaphysical subject. About half the essay was original, and the other half copied from the distinguished Scotch author, Dr. Reid. Hopkins had placed quotation marks on what was original, but omitted to credit Reid. The learned professor who had the class in charge, in criticising the essay, pronounced the quotation all right, but cut and scored Dr. Reid unmercifully. Hopkins said nothing, but doubtless 'laughed in his sleeve.'

"He soon afterwards confided to me the finesse he had practiced on the professor, with the injunction to keep it a secret, lest it might come to the ears of the professor and wound his feelings. I doubt if he ever spoke of it to any one else. I kept the secret for more than forty years, and then disclosed it, for the first time, in a speech which I made at the Commencement dinner, in 1871, when Hopkins was President of the College and presided at the table. The anecdote was received with prolonged applause.

"At graduation Hopkins received the appointment of valedictorian, — an honor justly bestowed and heartily approved by every member of the class. His valedictory was pronounced a literary gem, and was generally admired not only for its beauty of language, but for its elevation of thought. In a conversation with him nearly fifty years afterwards, I happened to remark that I was greatly surprised that the only dullard of our class, in his graduating oration, had manifested a degree of ability and talent which exceeded the expectation of everybody who knew him, and that I was unable to account for it. 'Well,' said Hopkins, 'perhaps I may — now the fellow is dead — explain it. The truth is, I wrote the oration for him.'

"The golden threads which were wrought into the texture of Hopkins's college life seem to have grown brighter as he grew into manhood. They were the elements of his character, — a character that is based on the principles of a true Christian philosophy. The college that educated him did itself honor in bestowing upon him its presidency. I regard it as an honor to have been one of his college classmates."

One gets a hint of how fully he understood himself in the remark made to a college classmate who complained of the difficulty of the Greek lessons: "They are easy. I do not know enough of Greek to make them hard."

The health of the undergraduate Hopkins was the source of some solicitude to himself and his friends. He was absent from college for some weeks at one point in his course, seeking vigor, and then made so deep a study of the claims of Christianity that the questions of its origin and value were for him answered. He settled these questions not mainly on the grounds of external evidence, certainly not on such external evidence as would be necessary to-day to overcome doubt based on external considerations, but on that internal evidence which in every age is the true satisfaction of the soul that hungers and thirsts after righteousness. For him "the life of Christ and his death and resurrection, his whole being on earth and in heaven, as revealed to us in the New Testament — this was an all sufficient self-substantiating evidence and exposition of Christianity — the source of its vitality and the secret of its power."[1] There were other evidences for his mind, as was proved later, but this was enough. From that time his faith in the supernatural, regenerating power of Christ never wavered. There is something very significant even on the intellectual side in this examination and decision. At the age of twenty his hold on the profound principles that underlie Christianity was so firm that the long, deep thought of his later life only strengthened that hold. His views underwent modifications as to certain doctrines and relations, but the grounds on which he first accepted Christ as a Redeemer were unchanged, and amply sufficient through all his

[1] *Catholic Thoughts on The Bible and Theology.* Frederick Myers, p. 262.

thoughtful career. It was the eternal truth he laid hold of, not the temporary props of varying scholarship. And because it was the eternal truth, ever young and ever new, his inspiration as a Christian teacher had in it an uplifting, increasing power "that grew brighter and brighter unto the perfect day."

After leaving college he entered the Medical School at Pittsfield, but taught a part of the year in Stockbridge.

THE PROFESSOR.

" What delights can equal those
    That stir the spirit's inner deeps,
    When one that loves, but knows not, reaps
    A truth from one that loves and knows ? "

TENNYSON, In Memoriam.

CHAPTER II.

THE choice of the medical profession may seem strange to those who knew Dr. Hopkins in the full tide of his career as a philosopher and theologian. He was so eminent a master in these fields that a consciousness of fitness for something else seems singular. He was not a mathematician, but for the other subjects of the college course he seemed to have much more than average abilities. He was probably graduated with far better qualifications for any career not involving advanced mathematics than any member of his class. And the lack of mathematical enthusiasm may have been owing to poor instruction before he entered college. Very possibly the flourishing condition of the school at Pittsfield was one influence that led him into medicine. He must have known a good deal of the school through some of the students, and may have caught the desire for this study from their enthusiasm. But whatever may have been the motives that led him, it is plain now that the training derived from his studies for the profession of a physician became of the greatest use to him in his later life-work. It was the guidance of the higher Hand that was preparing him for a larger career.

Although, as has been said, he settled for himself the validity of the claims of Christ to his allegiance before graduation from college, he did not make a public profession of that allegiance until 1826. The question of becoming a minister of the gospel was probably not very seriously considered, when he entered the medical school. The other profession attracted him strongly. In 1825 he became a tutor in the college. For two years he filled that position acceptably. It was a very different position from a tutorship to-day. There were besides the president, Dr. Griffin, who taught theology and philosophy and rhetoric, but two professors in the college. These were Chester Dewey, who taught mathematics and natural philosophy, and Ebenezer Kellogg, who taught Latin and Greek. Whatever subjects laid down in the curriculum these three men did not teach, or whatever parts of the subjects assigned to the professors they could not cover, fell to the tutors. Mark Hopkins had a classmate, William Hervey, who was appointed tutor the same year. The more advanced subjects were given to Hopkins.

There is a record still existing which testifies to the high appreciation of his first year's services by the class then finishing the Junior year. This class was graduated in 1827, and though numbering but thirty, twenty-three of its members entered the Christian ministry.

The paper is addressed to Mr. Tutor Hopkins, and bears date September 4, 1826. The college year ended at that period early in September. The paper is as follows: —

DEAR SIR. — The Junior class, fully sensible of their obligations to you for your exertions in their behalf, both as it respects their intellectual and moral improvement, and cordially reciprocating every sentiment of esteem, take this method to express to you their gratitude, respect, and best wishes.

The scenes of the year which now closes will ever excite in us a grateful remembrance of your kindness, be a source of pleasure during our collegiate course, and unite our hearts to you, sir, in bonds of affection when we leave these academic walls.

Signed,   A. D. WHEELER.
NATHAN BROWN, } *Com.*
B. PHINNEY,

There can be but one explanation of the "scenes of the year." It was a year of great spiritual revival; considering the number with which the year opened, eighty-five in all, of whom only forty-three at the beginning of the first term professed faith in Christ as the Redeemer, it may be doubted whether a more thorough revival ever took place in the college. When the term ended, there were but seventy-four students actually in attendance. Of the thirty-one who had no personal devotion to the Divine Master at the beginning of the term, twenty-seven, or all but four, had put themselves into an attitude of allegiance to Him. The entire year was one of marked religious activity. There is something at once delightful and prophetic in finding a record that gives to Tutor Hopkins during the first year of his service for the college an honorable share in the direction of the thought of the young men toward Him "in whom are hid all the treasures of wisdom and knowledge."

From 1825 until 1887 the prophecy of the first term of his labor was continually fulfilled. There was never an hour during all these years when the purpose and the expression of his work was not to enthrone Christ in the hearts of the young men committed to his charge. It is easy, however, to believe that the sense of responsibility awakened by his position as a tutor in the college was quickening from the first. His large nature responded largely to these new claims, and, under the influence of that first solemn but beautiful year of service to his Alma Mater, on his return home to Stockbridge in the autumn he took his stand with the people of God, and became a member of the church militant.

In the autumn of 1826, Tutor Hopkins went as agent of the American Tract Society through central New York on horseback, partly for his health probably, and did not return to his duties as tutor until after the opening of the next college year. A sentence in the letter of a graduate referring to this period, and alluding to Tutor Hopkins as "leaving me to the gentle sway of Tutor Hervey," makes the inference of a delayed return unavoidable. But tutorial duties were resumed, if somewhat late, in the autumn. The delicate health which Hopkins contended with as student and also as tutor will perhaps be a surprise to those who knew him in later years. There was something so masculine and robust and even majestic in certain respects in his figure that he was usually regarded as a very vigorous man. He had great powers of endurance, but his long and singularly useful life was marked by the most careful observance of the laws of health, and a strict attention in all his habits to the one great principle of his philosophy that all lower activities should be made subservient to the higher.

The late E. W. B. Canning, of Stockbridge, gives, in a letter received from him a year or two since, a glimpse of the college tutor as the teacher of a Bible-class. He says:—

"My first recollection of Dr. Hopkins was during the spring and summer of 1827, when he was Sophomore tutor, and I was fitting for college at the Williamstown Academy. I was one of ten or a dozen lads who composed his Sabbath-school class. Under his instruction I received my first vivid realization of the paramount truths of the Bible and of my personal responsibility thereabout. He was my ideal of what a Bible-class teacher should be. He left in the autumn of that year, and the final meeting with us was an occasion whose memory of more than sixty years is still tearful."

The tutorship ended at the close of the college year, 1827. The master's oration was delivered by the retiring tutor. Its subject was "Mystery." It was printed in the "American Journal of Science and Arts," in April, 1828, and is the first paper in the volume of "Essays and Discourses" collected and published in 1847. It is impossible to read it without admiration of the clear, manly march of the thought and the purity of the style, characteristics as definitely exhibited in this oration as in the maturest work of his life. The concluding paragraph shows the reverent but philosophic attitude of the writer: —

"Of the essence of mind or matter we have not, and perhaps no finite being can have, the power of forming an elementary conception. But aside from this we see from what has been said, that the intelligence and experience which we may hope for hereafter may enable us to solve all those difficulties which we now term the mysteries of Providence, to reduce every physical fact to its general law (consequently to behold the universe without one anomaly), and to refer all general laws immediately to the volition of the Almighty. That will indeed be a noble elevation of being to attain unto, when, as clearly and as directly as the rays of light emanate from the sun, every being and event shall seem to flow from the energies of Omnipotence and the depths of ineffable love. But though all mystery may thus far be removed, clouds and darkness must still rest upon the existence, creative energy, and attributes of the Great Cause uncaused, and the darkness of 'excessive bright' forever encompass his throne."

In the autumn of 1827 he resumed his medical

studies, and the next three years were spent mainly in their pursuit, although he taught a part of the time as a means of paying his expenses. In 1830 he had completed his studies and was preparing to settle as a physician in New York city, where he had studied for a time, when the professorship of Moral Philosophy and Rhetoric in his Alma Mater, which had become vacant by the death of Professor William A. Porter, was offered to him and accepted.

The feeling was much more general in that early period of college education than now, that a college professor should be a teacher not wholly in the college, but also in the churches. In accordance with this feeling, Professor Hopkins, after three years of study of the subjects belonging to his department, to which theology was closely related, was licensed to preach in the Congregational churches by the Berkshire association, at a meeting held at Dalton in 1833.

He was married on Christmas Day, 1832, to Miss Mary Hubbell, of Williamstown. This marriage was in every way happy, and the ideal relations of family life may be said to have flowed from it. Through a period of over fifty-four years, covering a career of great usefulness and eminence, but not unmarked by trials both of a domestic and personal character, with all his massive strength he leaned in tenderness and trustfulness upon the wife whom he had chosen. He rarely went from home unless accompanied by her, and in all his varied

literary work, her approval and sympathy were to
him the seal of success. She was several years
younger than he, and especially after his form was
bent and his whitened hair had become scanty, she
was now and then when away from home with him
taken for a daughter. This always afforded him
pleasure, and was the occasion of happy repartee.
Ten children were born of this marriage, of whom
two died in infancy, and one, the eldest, Mary
Louisa, in the developed powers of what seemed a
perfect womanhood.

At the age of twenty-eight, then, Mark Hopkins,
doctor of medicine, is professor of Moral Philosophy and Rhetoric in his Alma Mater. An election
to this professorship nowadays would hardly be
given to one whose professional studies had been in
another field. It would be thought necessary that
the incumbent of the chair in a good college should
have made deep studies in this department both in
this country and abroad. But education was less
specialized in those days, and the appointee had
proved himself a consummate teacher. Not by the
study of any systems of pedagogics, nor by any
methods that could be formulated in minute rules,
but by sovereign tact, by genial insight, by practical wisdom, by true interest in each individual
pupil, and steady movement towards definite ends,
his success had already been brilliant. He never
was an enthusiast for pedagogical science, though
he valued the knowledge of educational movements.
He would have said with a recent German that "no

concrete educational questions can be solved in terms of an universally valid science." And that the rules of any system could take the place of that fine tact, the want of which often characterizes men of great power, and the absence of which is never known except in the most general way by those not possessing it, would have seemed to him absurd. Without tact, without the coördinating power that discovers and leads and wins and concentrates the energies of the pupil to an end, perfect mastery of subjects and tremendous force are of no avail. Indeed, transcendent abilities without fine discernment and tact will often present the mournful figure of a man who pipes at a very high key without eliciting a single graceful responsive step, and whose discourse is practically and permanently the "voice of one crying in a wilderness," because no one will give heed. But Mark Hopkins, when teaching lads in Richmond and in Stockbridge, as tutor and Sunday-school teacher, had awakened interest and kindled intellectual life. No one can call in question the solidity of intellectual powers and equipments where such results are attained. "Nothing succeeds like success," and the appointment of young Hopkins as professor was an instance of decision where there could have been no misgiving.

In moral philosophy the text-book used was by Paley. After the lapse of nearly sixty years, one [1] of the class of 1833 recalls distinctly the sharpness

---

[1] Hon. Martin I. Townsend, of Troy.

with which Professor Hopkins criticised the statement of one author that conscience is often "identical with a man's habits and prejudices." He said, "If the man's habits and prejudices were in point of fact identical with his conscience, we may apply to the one what is said of the other. Now how would it sound to say that a man's habits and prejudices are 'seared as with a hot iron'?"

The pupil [1] who gave us a glimpse of Tutor Hopkins as a Bible teacher presents fuller impressions of him as a professor. He says: —

"In 1830, I left college for a two years' interval, and on my return found him installed as Professor of Moral Philosophy and Rhetoric; and as the increasing infirmities of President Griffin not infrequently required a substitute instructor, our class, during both Junior and Senior years, had not only the regular but extra services of Dr. Hopkins, which were duly appreciated. His eminent characteristics as an educator have been so often and so generally treated, as to render it impertinent in me to attempt more in the same direction than to remark that no opinion of his army of pupils, oral or written, however eulogistic, can adequately portray the actual man, the living instructor, in his recitation-room. So apt in illustration, so fertile in collateral resource, so ready on occasion with his spice of humor, so tactful in the adaptation of his questions to the calibre of his respondent, so original and independent in his ideas of the topic under

____

[1] E. W. B. Canning, of Stockbridge, Williams, 1834.

discussion, so skillful in drawing out the thoughts and queries of his pupils, he woke interest in the sluggish and provoked attention in the thoughtless and indifferent. Perhaps all his rare abilities in this regard may be summed up in the expression, — he made men think.

"Sometimes he good-naturedly crushed a captious, self-important, or dissentient student by a quick and timely turn of the remarks of the objector. For example, Dr. Hopkins, one Saturday forenoon, took the president's place at the recitation in Vincent's Catechism, usually regarded as the dustiest lesson of the curriculum; but whose dry bones Dr. Hopkins clothed with life, warmth, and vigor. He was expounding the 'exceeding breadth' of the Fifth Commandment, — its correlated grasp of the care and authority over inmates of public institutions and schools. A bright but erratic student, who had a recalcitrant propensity toward the college Faculty, and had made them great trouble, took occasion to sneer at the latitude claimed in the premises, and scouted the idea of such extension of parental authority. The professor sat, a smiling listener, watching a weak spot in the objector's armor for an effective thrust. It came when an expression of the speaker made it perfectly apt to interrupt him with this inference: 'Hence we see that a father who has an unruly son whom he knows not what else to do with is sure to send him to Williams College.' The critic subsided amid a roar of laughter from his classmates.

and his subsequent ventures in the line of criticism
were few.

"As regards Professor Hopkins's influence in
the *government* of college, it seems to me to have
been eminently one of affection rather than of authority, and that respect for his lovable qualities,
coupled with his mental ability, secured almost universal obedience. Indeed, perhaps he never appeared at less advantage than in the management
of a fractious, incorrigible pupil, utterly unap-
proachable by moral suasion. Punishment was
truly with him 'a strange work,' and seemed to cost
the inflictor more than the recipient. But rare was
the instance where his quiet influence and paternal
counsel proved unavailing."

Rev. William E. Dixon, writing to President
Hopkins from Enfield, Connecticut, in 1868, in
acknowledgment of some kindness, and referring to
his college life, alludes to his dealing with students.
Mr. Dixon was graduated in 1833, and was also a
pupil of Professor Hopkins.

"Always when I was in college, I observed the
great wisdom and tact with which you got along
with the students, not pressing upon them with
severity to kindle anger, but inciting and ruling
them . . . by reason, kindness, and love."

More than sixty years have elapsed since the
election to the chair of Moral Philosophy. Naturally little testimony to the character of the teaching given during the six years that Dr. Hopkins
held the professorship can be received from pupils

of that period. All the testimony that can be secured confirms the sagacity of the appointment and the wisdom of the acceptance. Whatever great things the life of a physician might have seemed to promise and might have accomplished, a careful examination of the actual career and the results leaves no doubt that when he selected the life of a teacher, he chose that for which he was by nature preëminently fitted, and that to which God surely called him.

THE COLLEGE.

" Nature constitutes throughout one intellectual organism: humanity one moral organism; and as God is the informing thought of the one, so is He the spiritual authority of the other. In recognition of the former, we raise the University: as symbol of the other, we dedicate the Church: neither of which fulfills its essential idea, till it places us at an altitude whence the whole domain of knowledge on the one hand, of duty on the other, can be surveyed in its relations, and seen suffused with the Divine and blending light." — JAMES MARTINEAU, *A Study of Religion.*

CHAPTER III.

THE COLLEGE.

By the acceptance of the professorship in 1830, Mark Hopkins identified himself permanently with Williams College. His connection, begun as a student in 1821. continued with two intermissions, one of one year immediately after graduation, and one of three years after the expiration of his tutorship in 1827, until his death in 1887. Of these sixty-six years, sixty-two were years of closest alliance with the college, and for thirty-six of the sixty-two he had the chief responsibility before the world for the direction of its affairs. A connection so close, so vital, and so enduring cannot be shown for any other American educator. There is something wonderful in the simple physical endurance it suggests. When it is remembered that he left college for a while on account of delicate health, and that in spite of his massive frame and majestic figure he was never a robust man, but was always very dependent on sleep, the length of service is still more surprising.

It was the New England college to which this long and enduring life was devoted, and no educator, in this or any of the past generations, can be said to be more fully identified with this peculiar outgrowth of Puritan ideas than Dr. Hopkins.

If the original aim of the New England college, as indicated by the motto of Harvard, founded in 1636, *Christo et Ecclesiæ*, and by the character of the instruction given for many decades, was largely to train men for the ministry, that idea was already growing wider, when Yale was chartered in 1701. Yale was to be a "school wherein youth may be instructed in the arts and sciences, who, through the blessing of Almighty God, may be fitted for public employment both in church and civil state." But when Yale was founded, her trustees were all ministers of the gospel, and no layman was admitted to the corporation until 1792, when a grant of money from the State of Connecticut opened the doors of the corporation to the "Governor, Lieutenant-Governor, and six senior assistants in the Council of the State." In 1819 the words "six senior assistants in council" were changed to "the six senior senators."

Williams College was chartered in 1793, and the majority of her trustees were Yale graduates. The educated men in New England had come to see by the great events of the Revolution, and by the history of the Confederation, and in the conventions and debates that led to the adoption of the present federal constitution, that college-bred men were of immense importance to the state, and that the services that could be rendered by the college to the other learned professions were not less valuable

than those given to the ministry. It seemed wise
to the first trustees of Williams that this wider connection with the state should be fully recognized.
Of the thirteen trustees named in the charter, nine
were laymen, and when, the next year, in accordance with a provision of the charter, three additional trustees were elected, one of these was a layman; so that when the full number of trustees had
been chosen, the clergymen on the board were but
six out of sixteen. As the founder, Ephraim Williams, was a soldier, and the money which he left was
for the establishment of a "free school," it may have
been thought that to give laymen a preponderance
in the corporation would be more in accordance with
his purpose. Out of this "free school" of 1790
grew the college, and this connection doubtless
helped to strengthen the lay element, as the original
trustees were continued in office. The New England colleges at the beginning of this century were
far more alike than they are to-day. They were
all colleges. Divinity students were trained by
settled clergymen. The Andover school was not
founded until 1807. Law students were trained
in the office of eminent lawyers. The medical
were the first professional schools under the shelter
of the colleges, the school at Harvard dating from
about 1783, and the school at Yale from 1813. It
seemed desirable to have this connection both for
the college and the professional school, and even
Williams College had, for a period, an organic relation with the medical school in Pittsfield. The

growth of professional schools about the college has been mostly, and the development of the college into the university wholly, within this century. Sixty years ago, the number of professors in the largest colleges was small, and instruction was given more largely by tutors than at present. The occasion for the establishment of nearly every college founded in New England previous to 1820, except Harvard, was that a large and prosperous region was without the privileges of higher education, and the journey to a college a hundred miles away was costly and difficult. All the New England colleges of the last century except Brown University, founded as Rhode Island College, belonged originally to the Puritans, and conformed to the same general plan, and were regarded with interest and affection by the great body of the New England people.

That traveling should become so easy and cheap; that one central college in New England might be reached in less than one day from the extremities even of new Maine, before the century ended, was not even imagined in 1820. The competition of to-day was still farther from the early conception. The first trustees of Yale were Harvard graduates. A majority of the first trustees of Williams, as has been stated, were Yale graduates, and the territory between Williams and Yale, a hundred and twelve miles to the south, seems by the selection of one of the first trustees for Williams from Norfolk, Connecticut, to have been equally and amicably divided.

The denominational development of colleges was beginning to make itself felt, and besides Rhode Island College, several others, not belonging to the Congregationalists, had been founded in New England when Mark Hopkins was elected professor, and one was chartered the following year. The earliest form of competition was denominational rivalry, but these new colleges followed the same general plan as the earlier. A president, two or three professors, and two or three or more tutors constituted the teaching body. The classes were not large, those in Harvard graduating between 1830 and 1840 averaging about fifty each, those in Williams and Brown during the same period about twenty-five, and those in Yale probably nearer eighty. The religious traditions of the colleges were still potent, and the required religious services were frequent and not always attractive. Even in those colleges where, as in Williams, a large number of trustees were laymen, it was felt, though not always prescribed, that it would be better that the president should be a clergyman. The clerical influence was for that reason alone very large in the board of trustees in most of the colleges. More frequently the professors also were clergymen, as the dominion that belonged to that profession, still somewhat marked, seemed to suit well the professor's position. The students themselves were very largely from religious families, and though, at the close of the last century, skepticism was rife in the colleges, in many of them the tide had turned, and long before 1830 came in full and strong with faith. Those colleges that were favorably situated in large cities or wealthy communities have of late years left behind, with their richness of instruction and variety of equipments and splendid professional schools, the old New England college, but that was and still remains the nucleus and foundation of all the new growth. Its power was immense for good, and for the safe and honorable development of our country the Puritans opened no richer fountain than the New England college. Such presidents as Woolsey at Yale, Wayland at Brown University, and Hopkins at Williams; such professors as Hadley at Yale, honored in Europe for his scholarship and yet condescending to teach Freshmen the dialect of Homer with unfailing patience, or Peabody at Harvard, winning the respect and affection of all the young men and inspiring them with a new conception of learning devoted to Christ, or as Diman at Brown, kindling enthusiasm for academic culture, but making that always tributary to service, — these are types of men not without representatives in nearly every general catalogue, all the products of the old-fashioned college, and handing down unpolluted the precious influences which quickened them. The early college had small equipments, but the narrow and plain rooms in which men were drilled and taught were large enough for great kindlings and for deep and permanent impressions. It is easy for the college graduate of fifty years ago to find in most of the colleges an enormous improvement in technical instruction, but while he is amazed at the fine appliances and at the dexterity with which the young men handle them, he has no accurate instrument to test the breadth and power of personal inspiration which quickened him in his own college years. A few years since, a discussion arose in an assembly of educated men on the decline of the personal influence of the teachers in colleges. There was not an agreement that this personal influence had declined. One distinguished educator held that "there is no personal influence except that of genius, and that there is more genius than there used to be." Some supposed that there is a personal influence from learning when guided by love; from sweetness of nature when inspired by faith; from robust manhood when led to condescension; from a character symmetrical and true, even if genius have not touched the mind with its brilliant and fascinating insight. All these sources of personal influence may not be in one teacher, but the scorn of meanness. and the love of truth, and delight in the progress of one's pupils, may be felt in varying proportions from different teachers. They will be felt as a quickening and formative power, whenever the relations between teacher and pupil cease to be formal; and behind the lucid exposition, or the cogent argument, or the purely intellectual attitude, the warm glow of right affections is perceived, and the instruction is permeated with the subtle influence of a high ideal in life as well as in thought.

Without doubt, when the training is liberal, rather than technical: when it tends to the enlargement and expansion of the entire man, to the harmonious use of all the powers; when it is less for definite utilities and more for the enjoyment that will underlie the entire career, the moral and spiritual resources of the teacher have fuller play. The college has stood for liberal training. That was the aim and the result in the days when the college was simply a collection of young men with their teachers, and the range of studies was narrow and the requirements not severe. That has been the aim until within the last twenty years. Though a larger infusion of technical and special training has come into the college curriculum than formerly, it still remains true that concentration, general power, ability to enjoy society and the thoughts of God, manliness, and gentlemanliness are assumed to be the ends of the college.

For these ends Dr. Hopkins loved the college. He believed that they were realized by the New England colleges when he became connected with Williams, and to their more perfect realization he gladly devoted his life. He felt deeply the dangers that beset young men in the freedom which the college involves. This was increased much from the changes in social conditions during his life. But this very freedom has its advantages. The transmission of enthusiasms from one to another; the self-reliance that is often developed; the watchfulness exercised by companions over one another; the interplay of generous emulations, — these results are greatly fostered by the freedom of college life. Larger learning could undoubtedly have been secured in many cases by the system of private tuition. The very relations of college students have been a preparation for citizenship. and the college training has given force and foresight and wisdom to the leaders in the best movements of our modern period. It has given these qualities sometimes where the attainments in knowledge were not great. and has been a perpetual reinforcement of all that is good and true in official life.

Dr. Hopkins was not a theorist in education. He worked with the material that was given him, and studied patiently to bring the largest results out of that material. He considered questions of education with care, and he loved freedom too ardently to believe that all teachers can use the same method. He thought that the good teacher is not exactly "born," but certainly is not "made," unless he is "born" first. His pupils were always persons, and not simply a group or a class. While he held firmly to the class system, and to the great advantage for the community of the old-fashioned liberal training, he was never absolutely certain that so much Latin, or so much Greek, or so much mathematics was the best management for all classes.

But he never adopted the modern notion that the immature student can wisely decide all the studies that will be most advantageous for his training.

"To decide this point, including the order of the studies as they are related to each other and to the opening powers of the student, requires wide information and sound judgment; and that the college should decide it seems to me due to itself and to the young men who come to it."

These words are a part of the final statement which he made of his views on education in the address commemorative of the fiftieth anniversary of his election as president. And it should be kept in mind that he was far more charitable to new ideas in his last than his earliest years. He grew progressive as he grew old, but on this point he did not waver. He would not admit that a wide range of possible studies is essential to a university. His strong words are:—

"It is a mistake to suppose that by giving a wide range of option in undergraduate studies a college approximates a university. It rather approximates a high-school, and may virtually become one."

With him it was a question of degree, for he was thoroughly friendly to the introduction of certain elective branches in "the later part of the course." Not one of the board of trustees, on which he served from his election as president in 1836 until his death in 1887, more cordially approved the introduction of certain elective studies into the Junior year, which took place in Williams at the beginning of the academical year in 1886. Elective studies had been added to the required work in 1882, but did not reduce the aggregate of such work. The test case was in 1886, when it was proposed to change three eighths of the required work of the Junior year to elective, and that change he wholly approved. That the college authorities should decide all the studies and their order, and the amount of time to be given to each subject in at least the first two and to a large degree in the last two years, and should never omit the study of philosophy and morals, was a strong conviction with him.

His questioning attitude with regard to the proportion of time to be given, for instance, to the ancient languages early bore fruit in the introduction of other studies into the Sophomore year. He felt the immense advantage of interesting students in a country college in nature, and both natural history and natural science have now in Williams College time that in many other institutions, holding to a fixed curriculum, is given to the ancient languages, though for this substitution an offset is found in the electives offered later in the classics. His own enjoyment of the studies of anatomy and physiology had opened his mind to the value of the sciences. He perceived early the very great advantages that arise from an interest in and a knowledge of the natural world in this scientific and practical age. Without hesitation he would say with Herbert Spencer: "To prepare for complete living is the function which education has to discharge: and the only rational mode of judging

of any educational course is to judge in what degree
it discharges such function."

His chosen arrangement of studies in the Senior
year of the course, on which he set high value, was
founded on his conception of this function. He
taught anatomy and physiology partly as a foundation for psychology, but partly that his pupils
might more fully understand the beauty and
symmetry of the structure in which the human
mind is lodged, and might more wisely care for
this structure.

The study of psychology followed upon this physical study of man in his method, partly as introductory to an examination of the moral nature, but
largely that his students might each understand his
own mind, and each know how to make the most of
his endowments. Upon psychology he based the
study of morals, not merely for theoretical knowledge, but that a well-regulated body and a well-un-
derstood and well-trained mind might coöperate,
and their activities issue in a pure and loving life.
All these studies in this order, resembling a pyramid having its broad foundation in the physical, led up to the recognition and reverence of God.
So long as he taught natural theology, it was the
last study of the year. These studies were so
connected that the dullest student saw the oneness
of the system. In an important sense the studies
were a system, and many mature young men, who
had not had the preliminary training necessary for
full membership of a class, resorted to the college

for the instruction which he gave, were admitted as special students, and received great enlargement from his teaching. For those who had had the thorough training of the earlier years, this order of studies was of incalculable profit.

It would be hard to convince any one who had seen the great expansion and quickening of the intellectual and moral powers of students under Dr. Hopkins's training in the Senior year in Williams College that absolutely free choices of studies can so perfectly prepare the average undergraduate for right living. The Senior year under Dr. Hopkins was the old Senior year of the New England college made harmonious and progressive.

The colleges of New England have been the most potent auxiliaries of the Christian faith. Nothing in these colleges is more surprising to the thoughtful foreigner than the loyal devotion of their resources to the honor of the gospel of Christ. Formal religious services have been less frequent of late years, but there is nothing of which these colleges are more jealous than their reputation as related to Christ. There is often restlessness under the mention and maintenance of this allegiance among some students; often a tendency to rebel against it appears among the teachers of a great university: but the college representing what Yale, for instance, was fifty years ago, insists that there is no manhood comparable to Christian manhood, and no hope for the redemption of a lost manhood except in the acceptance of the divine Saviour.

An atmosphere pervaded by these conceptions, where the teachers, eminent for learning and purity of character, do all in their power to enforce these conceptions, embraces the students for four years. The religious influence has not been lessened by petty restrictions. Discussion has been free, but generally only the presentation of the larger doctrines has been favored. Students of all denominations are welcomed by each college, and the offensive enforcement of peculiar tenets is avoided. There is not in the world another gift by any church to the cause of Christ equally as great and beneficent as the great gift of Congregationalism, — the colleges of New England. It may be thought that modern missions are an equally important contribution, but the missions came through the colleges and are the outgrowth of their thoughtful and Christian spirit. No student, however skeptical, can wholly escape the effect of the living enforcement by pure men of the doctrines of the Gospels. No graduate can wholly throw off the influence of these years. There are students in every college who profess an allegiance to Christ that does not control their lives. There are many young men in the colleges to whom these years are years of small intellectual labor, of easy enjoyment, and some to whom they are years of self-indulgence and degradation. Many of them meet obstacles and do not finish their course. Even to the most thoughtless serious lessons are brought home by the influences of the college, and a young man

must be very insensible who is not at some point
of his college life deeply impressed with the significance and scope of Christian character.

There has probably been a decline in the average
ethical standards of the students entering the New
England colleges. The attendance of students of
foreign birth, the less thorough discipline at home
in religious things even among American boys, consequent on the hurry and press of modern business,
may affect somewhat the material the college has
to deal with. But Christian sentiments and traditions and Christian usages pervade the college life
as visibly and really as ever, and the efficiency of
the colleges as allies of the Christian faith has not
been diminished. It was to this side of the college
that Dr. Hopkins was peculiarly attracted, and his
experience as tutor must have made this side peculiarly promising.

The fact that the quickening of foreign missions
in this country dated from a prayer-meeting held
by Williams students under the shelter of a hay-
stack invested the college with a unique and ro-
mantic charm. It is no wonder that large numbers
of men from many classes, under the new inspira-
tions of the opening century, went into the service
of the Christian ministry and Christian missions.
These influences touched the large imagination of
the young and gifted professor, and his mind was
filled with the conceptions of the great things that
the college could do for Christ. He was greatly
blessed in seeing his pupils become on all sides

friends and champions of the Christian faith. There were days when his labor seemed fruitless; when the low standards and lower living of Christians in college weighed very heavily on his heart, but he steadied himself with the assurance that a "thousand years are with the Lord as one day," and labored on.

The unique attractiveness of his brother Albert, who was elected professor in the college before his own appointment, and who was a profoundly religious man, and whose experience seemed to bring back Old Testament traditions and combinations, made the acceptance of the professorship easy for him; and throughout his presidency the presence and companionship of such a brother, perhaps more ardently, certainly more outwardly devoted to the encouragement of Christian living among students than any professor of whom I have had personal knowledge, was an incalculable help and blessing. These two men, the one an Old Testament prophet, and the other an expounder of the relations between the old and the new covenants, a reasoner on the universal presence of God's law, a persuasive advocate of the reasonableness of the gospel, stood together for over forty years, and gave to Williams College a noble individuality as a Christian college. The resignation of the presidency by Mark and the death of Albert were almost synchronous. Those who knew the untiring efforts of Professor Albert for the religious welfare of the college, and the immense support that these efforts gave to the presidency of his brother, will not wonder that, when an alliance so tender and manly, which had endured for more than forty years, was threatened by the failing health of one member, the other, who had borne burdens of colossal magnitude for thirty-six years in conditions of great depression, felt that he could no longer carry on the entire work. The influence of these two men on the New England and hence on the American college will not be lost. Their brotherhood helped to maintain the distinctively Christian character of the New England college. It exhibited the alliance of large endowments and great acquisitions wholly devoted to the kingdom of God. In the shadow of these lives no student could despise Christianity, and no unbeliever, however aggressive, could scoff at the results in character of faith.

When Mark Hopkins accepted the professorship, he could not foresee the brilliant results of his career. But the New England college seemed to him to represent the noblest forces in his country, and having had some experience as a teacher, he knew that success was probable. By accepting the appointment he made a choice worthy of his large endowments and his pure aspirations. The college honored him, but he was destined greatly to honor the college.

THE ADMINISTRATOR.

"Endurance is the crowning quality,
    And patience all the passion of great hearts:
    These are their stay, and when the leaden world
    Sets its hard face against their fateful thought,
    And brute strength like a scornful conqueror
    Clangs his huge mace down in the other scale,
    The inspired soul but flings his patience in,
    And slowly that outweighs the ponderous globe, —
    One faith against a whole world's unbelief,
    One soul against the flesh of all mankind."
                                    LOWELL, *Columbus.*

CHAPTER IV.

THE ADMINISTRATOR.

THE doctor of medicine had not been suffered to establish himself as physician when he was appointed Professor of Moral Philosophy. The professor had scarcely lost the sense of surprise that came with his election, or the feeling of novelty that accompanied his new work, when another promotion came. The Rev. Dr. Griffin, who had entered upon his duties as president at a time when a grave crisis existed, and when the prospects of the college were very dark, and who had put heroic courage and patience and energy into the colossal task of building up the college, began in 1833 to show signs of failing health. Notwithstanding increasing weakness, he continued to discharge his duties until 1836, when it became evident that he must resign his office. There were varying opinions, as always in such an emergency, as to who was best fitted to succeed him. Among the students there was but one sentiment. The young professor, who only six years before had completed plans for the practice of medicine in a great city, but who at the call of his Alma Mater had renounced medicine for morals, had made so deep

an impression on all his pupils that they earnestly
hoped that Professor Mark Hopkins might become president.   He was but thirty-four years
old.   Dr. Griffin was fifty-one when elected president, Dr. Moore was forty-five when he entered
upon the duties of the office, and President Fitch,
the first president, was thirty-seven.   If Professor
Hopkins was only three years younger than Mr.
Fitch when the latter was elected, there was a
great difference in the dignity of the positions to
which the two were called.   Mr. Fitch was elected
to nurse an academy into a college.   But the college
had now an honorable history, an excellent standing, and the certainty of a noble future.   There has
been with regard to many things a singular sagacity
in the management of Williams College.   The constitution of its board of trustees from the beginning recognized the equal value of the relations of
church and state to its prosperity.   It was the pioneer college to admit alumni representation into
this board.   It was the pioneer college to organize an alumni association.   When, in 1836, the
class just graduating, to which Professor Hopkins
had given the instruction usually received from the
president, sent to the board of trustees sitting to
elect a successor to President Griffin a paper expressing gratitude to the trustees for the instruction
which they had received from Professor Hopkins,
and strongly intimating that they would like to
have him elected president, the trustees, under the
lead of Vice-President Shepard, unanimously rati-

fied the nomination. No prominent New England college dating from the last century has until within ten years elected so youthful a president, and no president as yet has filled so long a term of presidential duties. The age seemed far younger then than it does now. Doubtless the successful example of this presidency has done something towards changing the popular conception as to the desirable age for entering the office. In Professor Hopkins's case it may be said that he had the intellectual maturity of middle life at the age of thirty, and the intellectual freshness of thirty when he resigned his position in 1872. He was mature when he was young, and young when he was old. With the ever-increasing complexity of college relations there is a natural tendency to a diminution of the instruction given by the president, and also of the age at which the duties are assumed, but he was the last New England president of the old type, and for thirty-six years gave an amount of instruction probably unequaled by any teacher of his day. If his enjoyment of administrative duties was at times small, and his weariness of that competition which began in his day and has helped to remove from our colleges academical quiet was at times great, he enjoyed teaching, and the most captious critic was ready to admit his transcendent ability as a teacher.

In his inaugural address, delivered September 15, 1836, he puts into words the conceptions of true teaching which he so fully realized in his life.

A sentence or two will give a glimpse into the secret of his success.

"It is far easier for a teacher to generalize a class and give it a lesson to get by rote, and hear it said, and let it pass, than it is to watch the progress of individual mind, and awaken interest, and answer objections, and explore tendencies, and, beginning with the elements, construct together with his pupils, so that they shall feel that they aid in it, the fair fabric of a science with which they shall be familiar from the foundation to the top stone." The laboratory method, so popular now, was his conception from the beginning.

"He who carries the torch-light into the recesses of science, and shows the gems that are sparkling there, must not be a mere hired conductor, who is to bow in one company and bow out another, and show what is to be seen with a heartless indifference; but must have an ever-living fountain of emotion, that will flow afresh, as he contemplates anew the works of God and the great principles of truth and duty."

The position of college president when Professor Mark Hopkins was elected to the presidency of Williams was quite other than it is to-day. Good teaching seemed then the primary, almost the only element necessary for the success of a college. The sciences were, so to speak, in their infancy, and the appliances necessary for the exposition of the leading principles were not numerous. Undoubtedly there was always a tendency in Dr. Hopkins's mind to set a very high value on principles and character, and to disparage mere externals both in religion and education. Even to the very end of his life, though as to refinements and luxuries there had been a striking change in the habits of our society, elegancies made little difference to him. There was in him something of the simplicity and severity (towards himself especially) of the great Lord Lawrence, of whom it is related that, in the last days of his life, when, tired and thirsty and feverish, he passed a shop-window in which fine strawberries were displayed, and felt a desire to taste them, he entered the shop and asked the price. On learning that each box cost ten shillings, he replied, "Why, I never spent so much on myself in my life," and turned away. This noble simplicity in Dr. Hopkins was partly the result of Puritan training, and partly the outgrowth of earnest thought. It belonged also with the period, and enabled him as president to concentrate his energies without any misgiving on the personal training of his pupils. "Plain living and high thinking," in the truest sense of those words, marked his life, and his conduct of the college led to the same lofty simplicity in others. The situation of the college, its remoteness from any large city, advantageous in many ways for the ordinary work of the college, made it harder, when an imperative want arose, to find the means to meet the exigency. There were neither the persons near to know of the want, nor those with large means to meet it. In such a condi-

tion the severe simplicity of his life often led to
the sternest self-denial. When he began his work
as president, he had already arrived at the belief
that a successful study of the intellectual nature
of man could not ignore the physical. He decided to begin the instruction of the Senior class
with lessons in anatomy and physiology, for which
his own training had given him peculiar fitness,
and to develop from this knowledge the study of
the mental and moral life. For this purpose he
early perceived the value of one of the illustrating manikins which had come into usefulness and
renown in France. In 1841 one had been im-
ported into this region, probably by Dr. Arms-
by, of the Albany Medical College, but for some
reason was offered for sale. Its price was several
hundred dollars. As the funds of the college did
not warrant such an expenditure, and he felt that
the manikin was indispensable for his work, assuming the responsibility of the purchase, he gave a
note for the amount of the price, and determined
to pay for it by giving lectures. This was a bold
venture, but he had great faith in the attractiveness of the paper-man as an accompaniment to
lectures, and this was to be the drawing-card by
which the lectures were to be made profitable.
The manikin was to pay for the manikin.

It was in December when the president started
out with his manikin carefully packed in the box
to go to his native town, Stockbridge, and there to
lecture to secure money wherewith to pay for his

apparatus. It was good sleighing, but the box so filled up the sleigh that the lecturer had to ride with his feet hanging outside of the vehicle. It was not a dignified or comfortable position for a college president, who was to drive thirty miles on a cold day, but at this distance of time there is something impressive in the picture. That lonely ride, with its stern purpose, is the expression of the solitude and earnestness that marked his career as college president. It is an epitome of many long years of patient self-denying devotion to the institution to which he had given his life, and to depart from which flattering calls to positions of comparative ease did not seem to tempt him.

The construction of an astronomical observatory, the first in the country permanently connected with a college, begun at Williams in 1836 by his brother, Professor Albert Hopkins, and largely paid for from his resources, is another illustration of the self-effacing spirit in which the early professors in our colleges devoted themselves to the organism.

It is pleasant to find a record of the success of the lectures in Stockbridge. This success can be regarded as typical.

A letter from Mrs. John Z. Goodrich, then Mary Hopkins, a cousin of the lecturer, written in January, 1842, gives some account of the compliments that were paid to the lecturing president.

"How you did run away from us without ever bidding us 'good-by.' We gave you credit for

the best intentions, however, and concluded that
you did not get through packing up that interesting figure until you thought it too late to call. I
had a dozen things to say to you, to tell you the
compliments all the ladies paid to you, to in part
recompense you for the labor and fatigue you had
undergone for our instruction and entertainment.
There never was anything that took so well as your
lectures here. 'No man but Mark Hopkins could
have effected such a thing. It has advanced us
one grand step in intellectual matters, and swept
away prejudices that have hedged us about ever-
more,' said one. 'In interesting us in his paper-
man, Mark Hopkins has attached us to himself.
We had no idea he was so charming,' said another. The young gentlemen say: 'It is too bad.
Here we have been exerting our bones, muscles,
and mind to boot for years to excite interest in the
minds of the fair maidens of Stockbridge, and after
all this paper-man in one week's time has engrossed
more thoughts and obtained more attention than we
with all our devotion have been able to win.' A
lady says: 'Well, for my part, I think Dr. Hopkins has given a fine blow to our vanity. Whenever I see a fine countenance and a graceful person,
I shall only think that the possessor has a particularly well-disposed set of muscles under his command.' The lectures are the topic constantly discussed and always approvingly. You have done a
great deal of good, and given me personally an immense deal of pleasure and information. I am

quite willing to dispense with my usual quantum of voice for a few weeks for the gratification I enjoyed and do still enjoy from those lectures."

Thus it appears that the lectures were successful so far as the satisfaction of the audience was concerned, but how much threatened still to come out of the president's salary, at that time about $1,100, to pay for the manikin does not appear. From Stockbridge the medical lecturer went to Boston, but whether to deliver more lectures and thus reduce farther the deficit remaining on the cost of the precious manikin is uncertain. There is on the records of the trustees of the college a vote passed August 16, 1842: —

"That the note of President Hopkins for $600, given for money to purchase the manikin, be cancelled, and the property in the manikin be vested in the trustees."

From this it appears that even after the college had assumed the note, and the property in the manikin had been vested in the college, President Hopkins felt so keenly the embarrassment to the treasury caused by the purchase that he endeavored by most self-denying work to diminish the amount taken from the funds of the college.

It is not an unnatural suggestion that the heroic effort to pay for the manikin is a symbol of Dr. Hopkins's presidential career. With kingly gifts, with an equipoise of imagination and insight, consciously capable of large giving and of large doing, it was more natural for him to rely upon his own powers than to appeal to others for aid. It seems unreasonable, at this period, that a college with five hundred living graduates, whose president was the peer of any president, should permit its head to resort to itinerant lecturing in order to pay for the apparatus needful for his college work. It is probable that there were friends ready to relieve him of such labor by generous help whenever they should know of his embarrassment. He preferred to earn the money for the equipments necessary rather than call upon others to assist him, and he went noiselessly to the work. There is something magnificent to one reviewing his thirty-six years of presidential office in the self-reliant, quiet, uncomplaining movement by which he gave and gave, and never asked for help except in the extremest necessity. Nor is it any discredit, but rather the highest praise, that begging was utterly distasteful to him, and that it was definitely understood at his election that he was not to solicit funds for the support of the college. He was willing to undertake the management, with the very loftiest aims definitely presented before himself and plainly announced to his constituents, but the resources for his great work were in himself, and it must be understood that he could not collect money for the college. The years slipped by, and the seed that he had sown kept bearing fruit. New England families sent to his care boys grounded in sound morality. Boys came from Troy and the central cities of New York, attracted by his reputation. The good name of the college traveled to the growing West, and the college among the Berkshire hills became, as he hoped it might be when penning his inaugural, "a safe college;" a place of "health and cheerful study and kind feelings and pure morals." It became also a national college, flourishing in numbers and in reputation, everywhere honored. Probably its situation in the midst of the mountains was not an unfavorable element in the growth of that period. Its guardians, influenced partly by the effect on their own mature minds of occasional visits to the delightful scenery that environs the college, and in many cases by the affections born in their own college life, have been inclined to emphasize the beauty of its surroundings and the purity of its atmosphere. It has seemed to them in the light of revived sentiment an unusually favorable place for study, where it would be easy, —

> "to lure the eye
> To sound the science of the sky,
> And carry learning to its height
> Of untried power and sane delight,"

but it is a wiser view that the growth of any college must depend in the long run on the educational advantages which it offers and the thoroughness of its work. And honorable as was the self-reliance and majesty with which Dr. Hopkins carried on the college, and phenomenal as was its success for many years under his guidance, it was not possible for it to maintain its prestige against increasing competition, if any great change should occur, without a large increase of pecuniary resources. If there was no one to foresee that Dr. Hopkins's massive powers would need reinforcement, and to secure that reinforcement so early and so fully that adverse influences could be overcome, his colossal labors might suffer loss. When the Confederate insurrection came, and many of his students entered the Union army, the crisis so long possible became actual. The numbers in the classes diminished greatly, and there were no funds to make up for the loss of tuition. At last, in 1868, through the influence of Marshall Wilcox, then of Lee, and Samuel W. Bowerman, of Pittsfield, both graduates of the class of 1844, and at that time both members of the Massachusetts Senate, and through assistance rendered by Joseph White of the class of 1836, at that time Secretary of the Massachusetts Board of Education, and others, and through Dr. Hopkins's personal attention, the Commonwealth of Massachusetts by its legislature, recognizing the honorable history of the college and its peril, promised to aid the college to the extent of $25,000 a year for three years, provided a like sum was raised each of the three years by the friends of the college. The State of Massachusetts had made grants to the college in its earlier history, and like assistance had been rendered to other institutions. The invested and productive funds of the college in 1868 were about $100,000. By that act of the General Court there was a possibility that the resources of the college should be more than doubled within three years. The passage of this act was joyfully hailed by all true friends of the college, but the collection of the conditional $75,000 meant no child's play for the president, whose instruction still extended from September until June, and whose labor as pastor of the college church covered every Sunday of the college year. Alexander H. Bullock was Governor of Massachusetts the year of the passage of this act, and the following graceful letter was received from him in response to an invitation from Dr. Hopkins to be present at the Commencement in the summer of the year when the act was passed.

WATCH HILL, R. I., *July* 26, 1868.

Your favor of the 21st instant, inviting me to attend the Commencement Exercises of Williams College on the 29th instant, finds me at an out-of-the-way seaside spot to which I have sought a brief resort for relaxation. The necessity of a little respite from labor at this season must be my warrant for asking to be excused from the journey necessary to bring me to your college on Wednesday.

I should for many reasons like extremely to be with you at your pending anniversary. My visit at Williamstown, two years ago, was enjoyed so greatly that I could wish to repeat it. But more especially would I be pleased to have the opportunity of congratulating the guardians and friends of Williams College for her present advanced stage of prosperity and renown. As the executive representative of the Commonwealth I am happy and proud to have had a hand in this. The bill which appropriated seventy-five thousand dollars to the college, passed by the present legislature, was so consonant with my judgment and feelings that my approving signature was appended to it within one minute after it had been laid before me. Not only my connections, but all the emotions of which my heart is capable, were condensed in that signature. To be an instrument in thus promoting the interests of good morals and sound learning is a pleasure that will abide with me through all the pathway of my remaining life. I beseech the public, the lovers of our State, the patrons and the alumni of Williams, to see to it that their part be quickly performed to the end, that your honored institution may take a fresh start at once on a new and grand career.

I desire, also, in behalf of the people of Massachusetts, to thank you, Mr. President, for the long, patient, and beneficent service you have rendered to the republic of letters. If the time shall come when any of us must believe you to be an old man, — that time is not yet, — it will be to us all a source of pride and solace that we may claim your long life as a glorious part of our moral public riches.

And now, my dear sir, although this communication contains a passage which my acquaintance with you tells me you would gladly suppress, I must request that you will do me the favor to read it to the alumni at the Commencement dinner. For, believe me, it is not a letter designed for personal tribute so much as for justice to Williams College, and to the service rendered by her in the cause of religion, and virtue, and knowledge.

I am, my dear sir, with fresh and enduring sentiments of esteem and honor,

Faithfully yours,   ALEXANDER H. BULLOCK.

The complimentary words to Dr. Hopkins were warmly received by the alumni, as such words always were. Professor Lowell, of Cambridge, in 1885, in a private note to me expressed the same sentiment that the above letter contains of pride in the life of Dr. Hopkins, "whose personal character is a possession valued by all his countrymen." No words could more fitly describe his career as administrator than the quotation from Lowell at the beginning of this chapter. It was preëminently a career of "endurance," of that "patience" which is "all the passion of great hearts;" of that "faith" which is the "assurance of things hoped for, the proving of things not seen."

Additions to the funds of the college had previously come into the treasury slowly as the unsolicited result of his long and eminent services. In 1867 William E. Dodge, of New York city, who had long been associated with Dr. Hopkins in the missionary work of the American Board of Commissioners, gave to the college $30,000 in seven per cent. bonds, of which the interest was to go towards Dr. Hopkins's salary as long as he was president or taught in the college. After his retirement from all college work the income was to be devoted to his personal support during his life.

In the autumn of 1868 occurred the most remarkable rebellion in the history of the college, of which a complete account must be given in a separate chapter. It caused Dr. Hopkins much distress of mind, and did not promise to make his duty in raising the money necessary to secure the gift of the State any easier. However, the labor of the first year was carried through without great depression. For the second and third years a gift of $10,000 each year towards a professorship, by Orrin Sage, of Ware, was of much assistance, yet the difficulty of securing the remainder was great each year, but was finally surmounted, and $150,000 added to the resources of the college. Nearly all the large gifts that had previously encouraged Dr. Hopkins came by the simple attraction of his power. When East College was burned in the autumn of 1841, and it became necessary to erect new dormitories, the present East and South colleges, subscriptions to the amount of over $8,000 were secured, and an unexpected gift of $5,000, in January, 1844, from Amos Lawrence, nearly covered the deficit. Mr. Lawrence continued to show kindness to the college until his contributions amounted probably to $35,000. Another warm friend to the college during Dr. Hopkins's administration was Nathan Jackson, of New York city. Philip Van Ness Morris, of Cambridge, New York, Alfred Smith, of Hartford. Connecticut, William J. Walker, of Boston, David Dudley Field, of New York city, John Z. Goodrich, of Stockbridge, were the other gentlemen whose appreciation of the value of Dr. Hopkins's influence and whose esteem for the college led them to put large gifts at his disposal for the great work of establishing and strengthening the college. At the date of his resignation in 1872, the invested funds of the college amounted to about $300,000. The Astronomical Observatory, East and South College, Lawrence Hall, Kellogg Hall, Jackson Hall, the Chapel, Goodrich Hall, and College Hall were erected during his presidency. Indeed, the only halls that remained from previous administrations were old West College and Griffin Hall. But the feeling was universal, when he resigned the presidency, that his work had not gone into buildings and land and equipment, or into the acquisition of wealth for the college, but into the minds and hearts of those whom he had taught; that he had moulded invisible forces with great power.

Speaking of the graduates, his own pupils, he himself said, when his successor was inaugurated: "Not in the increase of buildings, or grounds, or funds, but in these is my pride. In respect to character, position, or influence they have nothing to fear from a comparison with an equal number of graduates from any other institution."

It required the eye of a large faith to see that the forces he employed for the college could not fail to find expression in abundant material prosperity, but he lived to see the dawn of brighter days, and to know that his heroic labor had not been in vain. General Garfield, then a member of the national House of Representatives, gave expression to the almost unanimous feeling of the graduates, when at the inauguration of Dr. Hopkins's successor he spoke these words to the new president: —

"We recognize the difficulty of the work you undertake as the head of the college — a work always great, always difficult, but now made doubly so by the example of him who has so long and so nobly trodden the path which you now enter. We will not ask you to bend the bow of our Ulysses. Let it here remain unbent forever, as the sacred symbol and trophy of victories achieved."

Few knew in the face of what pressing offers he had remained faithful to the trust committed to him in 1836, and even after his resignation as president frequent invitations came to him to teach in other institutions.

A partial record of these invitations will disclose how widely he was known and how universally he was honored. This may be found in the Chronological Table,[1] which does not, however, include an account of the large number of invitations to preach on special occasions and before distinguished audiences. When we consider the location of the college, the want of any peculiar denominational support, the absence of any state pride in the college, the fact that no fitting-schools were subsidiary to it, and that President Hopkins never knew from where his students were to come, his career as administrator, teacher, author, and example, leading the college to success and honor for thirty-six years, stands without a parallel in the history of American colleges.

[1] See pages ix–xi.

THE REBELLION OF 1868.

CHAPTER V.

In the autumn of 1868 a rebellion occurred among the students of Williams College which was, without doubt, the most serious affair of the kind in the history of the college.

There was at the time a very able body of professors in the conduct of the institution. Such men as John Bascom, at that time Professor of Rhetoric, Arthur L. Perry, Professor of Political Economy, Charles F. Gilson, in the Chair of Modern Languages, Sanborn Tenney, Professor of Natural History, and Arthur W. Wright, Professor of Physics, and later of Yale College, and William R. Dimmock, Professor of Greek, and afterwards Head Master of Adams Academy at Quincy, were among the truest men and the most conscientious teachers to be found in any of our colleges. They were men to whom the work of the college was of the first importance, and who could not be satisfied unless each student was profiting by his work and showing daily the increasing knowledge of the subjects taught. There grew up in the minds of these men and others a feeling that their efforts to secure the best results for an entire

class were in danger of being thwarted by persist-
ent and unnecessary absence on the part of a few
students. I was a member of the faculty at that
time. Having been prepared for college under the
stern requirements of Dr. Samuel H. Taylor, of
Andover, and having had my first experience of
college life at Yale when the numbers were so
large as to make the strictest rules necessary, I
had both as student and professor at Williams a
feeling that there was more absence allowed than
was necessary or advisable. Dr. Hopkins was not
a believer in rigid rules. I think there never was
a time during my acquaintance with him, when
such matters were under discussion, that he did not
express himself frankly in favor, for a small college,
of a more personal and a more flexible system of
government than most of us advocated. He dep-
recated that antagonism which rigid and minute
rules were, he thought, sure to engender. He believed fully in the general influence of a faithful
and earnest body of teachers, and thought that
young men could be far more effectually guided
to true manliness by an example of kindness and
patience than by formal restrictions or constant
intimations that they were under authority. He
was, I think, equally opposed to any very definite
system of penalties. It was offensive to his ideas
of proper training to treat all students in exactly
the same way. His conviction was strong that all
students are not precisely alike in their training,
or tendencies, or abilities. This feeling used to

show itself often and strongly in the discussions that arose in regard to students whose work was deficient. It was a frequent remark of his, that "some one must be at the foot of the class." He did not deny that human government was compelled to allow but narrow range in penalties and practically to treat offenders with uniformity. But he had an idea that college government might have something nobler in it than social government could have, that it might have a good deal of the divine element of mercy, or at least 'of fatherly kindness.

The two opposing theories briefly hinted at here have at different times occasioned more or less collision in our colleges. To give students fuller liberty and appeal to their honor, or to put rigorous requirements upon them and hold them to definite duties and attainments are the two conceptions that still differentiate the New England colleges. There can, of course, be no question which of the two methods is nobler, if students were all actuated by high principle, and were all aiming at a high ideal. There can be, on the other hand, no doubt which method would be necessary, if the majority of the students were inclined to make their life as easy and self-indulgent as possible. Because these two classes of students exist in colleges in ever-varying proportions, and especially because most students have in them the two opposing tendencies in varying strength, there will always be an opportunity for good arguments in favor of each method of government. The more generally popular theory in the New England colleges during Dr. Hopkins's administration of Williams was probably somewhat opposed to his views, but that there has been a movement if not precisely towards the acceptance of his theories, at least in that general direction in later years, hardly admits of a doubt.

These two theories are always more or less in conflict in individual minds, and are both pretty sure to find expression in the same college faculty. There had been for a year or two previous to the autumn of 1868 a growing impression among the students of the college that the more liberal view, that which would govern by influence rather than by rules, was giving place to a closer watch and a more stringent requirement. When, accordingly, the question of absences was discussed by the faculty, and a series of rules was promulgated with the definite purpose of restricting the amount of absence, the students felt that here was another movement towards the introduction of what they called "school-boy methods." There were one or two things particularly unfortunate about the change. One was, that although the committee of the faculty was appointed at a meeting at which the president was present, the committee reported and the rules were adopted during Dr. Hopkins's absence. The students learned this, and at once jumped to the inference that the president would not favor these rules, and that they had been adopted in his absence without regard to his wishes.

They heard in some way the substance of the rules before they were definitely adopted, and believing them to be capable of unjust application by unfriendly or indifferent instructors, they were extremely restive. After the formal approval of the rules by the faculty they called for an immediate repeal.

The rules were as follows: "Each absence from any recitation, whether at the beginning of or during the term, whether excused or unexcused, will count as zero in the record of standing. In cases, however, in which attendance shall be shown by the student to have been impossible, each officer shall have the option of allowing the recitation to be made up at such time as he shall appoint; and no mark shall be given to such recitation, unless it shall amount to a substantial performance of the work omitted."

The ideas in these rules were approved by the faculty at their regular meeting on the evening of November 4, 1868, and some professor stated the substance of their purport to his class the next morning. So far as I can ascertain from the records, the rules were more definitely presented and fully discussed at a special meeting held on the evening of November 5. They were formally communicated to the students the day after their adoption. These rules are substantially the same that had been for many years operative in Yale College, but the insertion of the statement that no mark should be given to the recitation made up, "unless it shall amount to a substantial performance of the work omitted," was quite unnecessary, as each officer without such statement would mark the recitation according to his estimate of it. Furthermore, this definite statement seemed to the students to be an offensive assertion of power to deprive a delinquent of the small recognition that might be justly due him. There was also a feeling that not to allow a student to make up an omitted lesson, unless attendance was shown to be *impossible*, would often result in hardship, where a student might be in circumstances such that attendance would be very difficult, or at least require the neglect of some important duty, and yet be possible.

Against these two points, or rather against the extreme form of power apparently given to any professor to reduce the standing of a student, the students revolted almost unanimously. I venture here to record the statement that at the meeting of the faculty on the evening of November 5, at which the rules were presented in their final form, one professor expressed the opinion that the rules could not be executed in the existing state of things. He was answered by one of the professors on the committee that "the rules would execute themselves."

On the evening of November 6, the day on which the rules were announced, the entire college assembled in Alumni Hall, and unanimously adopted the following preamble and resolution: —

"Whereas, the faculty of Williams College have

imposed upon us, students of said college, a rule to the effect that each absence from recitation, excused or unexcused, shall receive a zero mark in the record of standing; and it is left with each officer of the college to act his option as to whether he will hear necessary absentees in their lost lessons; and said officer shall act his option as to giving any credit for such recitation; and

"Whereas we, students of Williams College, regard the imposition of this rule as a blow aimed at our personal honor and manhood, therefore

"Resolved, That we students of said college protest against said rule, and call upon the faculty of Williams College to annul it."

This paper was presented the evening of its adoption to the officer of the Senior class, but was regarded by him and by other members of the faculty as much too imperious in tone to permit any hasty reconsideration of the rule.

Probably the wisest course would have been for the faculty to suspend the enforcement of the rules until the return of Dr. Hopkins and to discuss the matter carefully with him. But there was a belief that the conflict was "irrepressible;" that the question now was whether the faculty or the students should determine the policy of the college; and that the students' attitude made it impossible for the faculty to do otherwise than stand by the rule. Accordingly, although the committee of the students not merely delivered the resolutions that evening, but the next day visited the Senior class officer, who was looked upon as the real head of the faculty in Dr. Hopkins's absence, and urgently pressed him to call a faculty meeting for the consideration of the situation, and especially urged that the enforcement of the rule be delayed until the president's return, by general consent of the professors, a policy of inactivity was adopted.

The students regarded themselves as entirely in the right, and while there was much excitement, no general disturbance of the peace occurred. The student committee sent to each class the following notice: —

"The committee will report on Tuesday evening next, before which time they earnestly recommend that there be no individual or concerted action. November 7, 1868."

This notice is dated the 7th, which was Saturday. The most active Christian men in the college were heartily enlisted on the student side of the matter. Saturday, Sunday, and Monday, the students were discussing the question what their next move should be, if the faculty would not at least suspend the rule. On Monday evening the committee came to the decision to recommend to the entire body of students to withdraw from the college, and to remain aloof from it, until the rule was repealed. This decision was made known to the classes on Tuesday morning, that every student might have the day for consideration, and deliberately making up his mind might go into the college meeting appointed for Tuesday evening and act intelligently, and "not feel that he had been dragged along by the spirit of the meeting."

The meeting was held, and the following preambles and resolution were unanimously adopted: —

"Whereas, The faculty of Williams College have imposed upon us, students of said college, a rule that 'Each absence from any recitation whether at the beginning of or during the term, whether excused or unexcused, will count as zero in the record of standing. In cases, however, in which attendance shall be shown to have been impossible, each officer shall have the option of allowing the recitation to be made up at such time as he shall appoint, and no mark shall be given to such recitation, unless it shall amount to a substantial performance of the work omitted;' and

"Whereas we, students of said Williams College, regard the imposition of this rule as a blow aimed at our personal honor and manhood; and

"Whereas, our petition presented to the Faculty of said Williams College, November 6, 1868, for the repeal of the above-mentioned rule, has been disregarded, therefore

"Resolved, That we students of said Williams College declare our connection with said college to cease from this date, until the authorities of said college shall repeal the above-mentioned rule."

The following resolution was also unanimously adopted: —

"Resolved, That we, as a body of young men, agree to remain in this neighborhood and abstain from all objectionable conduct, until the final settlement of our difficulties."

The paper, ending with the declaration of the students that their connection with the college had ceased, was handed to the Senior class officer that evening, November 10. It was a dark and stormy night, and I remember that, as the committee passed my house carrying the paper down to the acting head of the college, they raised a sort of exultant shout that seemed to intimate that, at last the faculty were defeated and the students had manfully maintained their rights.

I had not believed in the possibility of successfully enforcing the rules as worded, and although I did not know certainly, I had reason to suppose that the meaning of the shout was that practically the entire college would be absent from exercises the next day. An hour later the majority of the professors had convened, and under the guidance of Professor Bascom a brief circular was prepared, containing a fair statement of the situation for publication and communication to the parents. The statement contains in addition to the rules and the two sets of resolutions by the students the following paragraphs: —

"As very unusual action has been taken by the students of the college, we have deemed it desirable that a statement of the occasion of that action be made to the public.

"We are by no means unqualified in our support of the marking system, but have used it hitherto as

a disciplinary means of reaching young men, many
of whom are not disposed to improve their opportunities. One form of neglect has long embarrassed us and limited the value of our institution.
Many students on slight and insufficient grounds
have been repeatedly and protractedly absent from
college duties and thus from recitation, much of
the value of which depends on consecutive attendance."

The circular then recites the new rule, and is
followed by an explanation saying: —

"It was our intention in all cases, in which the
claim was just, to accept cheerfully the labor of
extra recitations, and to allow the standing of the
students necessarily absent to be regained. We
deem it, however, eminently fair that absence in
other cases should carry with it the presumption of
ignorance of the ground passed over, rather than
the opposite presumption of knowledge, and that it
should therefore affect the standing of the absen-
tee."

The first set of resolutions adopted by the students in which the faculty are called upon to annul
the rule is then given as on page 85, and the following comment is added: —

"Deeming this paper objectionable in form and
spirit and also embarrassed in our action by the
absence of President Hopkins, who was not present at the passage and promulgation of the law, we
declined to give their request final consideration
before his return." Then the additional paper con-

taining the declaration by the students that their
connection with the college had ceased is given, and
the circular concludes with the statement that: —

"The action of the faculty in this matter has
been unanimous, and believing that far more important issues in the government of the college are
involved than those relating simply to the maintenance and wisdom of a single law, we submit this
statement to the public."

This circular was signed by the secretary of the
faculty, and was printed and mailed November 11,
the day after the students withdrew, to all the leading newspapers in New York and Boston, and to
the father of each student concerned.

The circular as mailed to a father had the additional statement that his son was concerned in the
action, and his immediate attention was invited to
the son's position.

At the first meeting of the students after the new
rules were announced, in addition to the resolutions
calling for a repeal of the rules a series of resolutions was passed denunciatory of the marking system. There can be no doubt that some of the leaders in the movement believed seriously that they
were engaged in action of great significance in regard to that system. They expected or at least
hoped to effect its abolition in the college, and that
this issue would result in a new order of things in
the colleges generally. They said: "We are convinced that the system of marks and prizes defeats
the end for which it was established: first, by call-

ing the mind of the student from the great aim of education to petty and selfish ambition for honor, thus destroying the very germ of manhood which it is the aim of education to develop; second, by leading those desirous of maintaining a good stand to indulge in deceitful practices and thus essentially teaching dishonesty, when it should be the aim of education to teach a strict morality." And it was by this moral enthusiasm that was awakened in the minds of these earnest reformers and in the minds of those to whom they unfolded their hopes that so many were led into the rebellion. There were many, doubtless, to whom the whole movement was a great lark; who believed that where the most eminent students and Christians of the college were leading, no great disaster would befall those following, and who joined in the movement with a sort of cheerful faith that some pleasant excitement would result from it.

The next morning after the passage of the resolutions of withdrawal there were three students at prayers, two Freshmen and one Senior. It was my duty to hear the Freshman class recite, and after prayers I repaired to my room with the two Freshman pupils, and went through the lesson as usual. I believe the Senior had no instruction that morning, and the recitation with two Freshmen was not repeated. The college came to a perfect standstill. Everything was quiet about the town. The weather was ordinary November weather. Some who could afford it enjoyed driving; many resorted to the halls of the two literary societies and spent the time in discussing the situation and playing cards. Every word from a professor was reported among the students. Every conversation between a student and a professor (and there were many of them) was repeated in its details among the professors. The professors were the more anxious party, because they understood more fully the significance of such a movement and the far-reaching consequences that a direct antagonism and a complete disregard of all obligations to the college might have.

Both parties awaited President Hopkins's return with interest. The students undoubtedly believed that he would not have consented to such a rule. The professors felt that only he could set the machinery of the college into operation again, but saw no way open for such a result except by an absolute submission of the students.

The absence of Dr. Hopkins was caused by his acceptance of an invitation to preach the sermon on the quarter century anniversary of the Society for the Promotion of Collegiate and Theological Education at the West. This sermon was preached at Marietta, Ohio, November 10, the day of the final action of withdrawal by the students.

Probably the first intelligence that Dr. Hopkins received of the fact that the college to which he had given as president thirty-two years of most laborious toil had been deserted by the one hundred and sixty students whom he had left satisfactorily

at work a few days before, was the announcement
of the circular published by the faculty. It could
not have been a pleasant surprise. He returned to
Williamstown on Saturday, November 14, after an
absence of nearly two weeks, and preached Sunday
morning to such of the students as chose to come to
the chapel. That must have been an anxious Sunday. It is impossible now to recall the circumstances without admitting that his position was most
trying. The friends of some of the students had
appeared here, and many of the absentees had received positive orders to return to their duties.
The combination was somewhat weakened, but it
still presented a perfectly solid front, and no exercises could be held until some had come forward to
acknowledge that they had taken a wrong position,
and were ready to resume their places as loyal students in the college. Dr. Hopkins, whose return,
it was felt by all parties, must in some way contribute to a solution of the grave and difficult problem
existing, invited the students to meet him in the
chapel on Monday morning, and nearly all the college accepted the invitation.

It may be questioned whether he ever faced an
audience more intent on hearing every word than
that which was gathered in the college chapel on
Monday morning, November 16, 1868. Nor can
it be said now that the presentation which he made
of the situation lacked fairness, or candor, or sympathy. The college paper, reporting the meeting,
said that "he spoke in behalf of the faculty, the

members of which were present." As I remember the address, it was a plain statement of the situation. It began with the announcement that the position taken by a resolution that declared the "connection of any student with the college at an end, until the new rule was repealed," was not tenable; that no student could thus dissolve his connection with the college. He then proceeded to show that when a student was dissatisfied with any arrangement made by the authorities of the college or any rule imposed, the only way of withdrawing from the college was by seeking an honorable dismission, and that such letters would be given to any one who, after a return to duty, should ask for a letter in a proper way.

Having made it clear that the students who had signed the paper declaring their relations to the college at an end were still in the college and under its government, he said that the faculty ruled the institution, and must rule it, and that any combination against their authority was inconsistent with the signing of the pledge at the time of matriculation. He said of the rule that, if it was not the best rule that could be devised for the regulation of the evil arising from too frequent absences, it might be repealed, and that at all events the authorities of the college wished the best rule possible; one that would effectually reduce absence and be perfectly fair in enforcement. The address did not seem to effect much at once, but it may be doubted whether any presentation could have been loyal to the authority of the faculty and have been immediately effective. The college paper of the date of Saturday, November 21, says that the address "did not accomplish much except the part which intimated that we could secure letters of dismissal upon our return to duty." The address was, however, an important element in altering the situation. It was made clear that the president would not favor any concession to the students inconsistent with the maintenance of the authority of the college, and at the same time the statement that the authorities wished the best rule possible gave the students an opportunity to believe that reason and not arbitrary will would finally determine the exact wording of the rule. The address must have been somewhat chilling to the more conscientious students who had been the leaders from the beginning. It doubtless enforced strongly in the minds of many the doubts that had arisen in respect to the wisdom of their action.

The college paper adds that "In the afternoon matters took a different turn. Dr. Hopkins, who has the affection as well as the respect of every one who knows him, appeared in the street and conversed freely with the students. He said that the law did not have his approval, would be reconsidered, and he promised to use his influence in getting the rule changed or rescinded."

This statement of the students' paper is not perhaps wholly accurate, but it was perfectly reasonable for Dr. Hopkins, who had been absent when the law was passed, to state that he did not approve of the wording of the law. This statement had doubtless a great influence on the minds of some. Other influences had been at work, and some affected by personal appeals, made by friends who came on, and some stirred by letters from parents, and convinced that they had made a mistake in their action, decided to go back to their college duties at the four o'clock recitation. The rest, I think a majority, unwilling to be left in the more marked attitude of insubordination by not attending the exercises, if exercises were to be held and others were to attend, agreed to return to duty "under protest." In my recitation that afternoon, which was for the Sophomore class, the largest in the college, many answered when the roll was called, "Here under protest." When this was reported to Dr. Hopkins it displeased him exceedingly. He said that a student was either in college or out of college, and that no student could be in college "under protest." He went in with me to my class the next afternoon, and made some forcible remarks with reference to the matter before the roll was called, giving the students to understand in the plainest way that no student could remain in the college and announce "to any professor in the class-room that he was here under protest." He then asked me to call the roll, and it appeared that the *protestants* had all become good catholics. Nothing more was heard in the college exercises about attendance under protest. The rule was afterwards slightly modified, and no student left the college in consequence of disaffection arising from the adoption of the rule.

It has seemed best to give a somewhat minute account of this rebellion, as it was called, because it was one of the gravest crises in Dr. Hopkins's administration of the college, and because, looked at dispassionately after the lapse of many years, it is impossible to deny to him the honor both of great wisdom and of perfect loyalty to his faculty and to the best interests of the institution in the entire management of the affair. So far as I know he never uttered in public one word of condemnation of the precipitate action of the faculty, or of their misreading of the student mind in the promulgation of this rule during his absence. With heroic patience and consummate skill he faced the difficulties that confronted him. The world about him was ignorant of what a burden of anxiety he carried in those days. A few extended to him sympathy and kindly help, but the loneliness of his responsibility on learning in New York that the college exercises had been suspended for days, and the intenser consciousness on that Sunday when he preached to the few who, having declared their connection with the college at an end, chose to come into the chapel and hear him, that he alone could reknit the broken threads of college life, must have awakened all his energies. For meeting such an emergency his great powers and solid training and the wisdom learned from long experience and shrewd tact were all needed. When the sun went down on Monday, and he knew that the college, after five days of interruption, had through his intervening influence once more settled down to work, there was some relief of the strain, but there was still the certainty present that weeks and months must elapse before the asperities of such a crisis could be removed, and that it must depend largely on those whom he had selected for helpers, and who had precipitated this crisis, whether similar hostilities might not recur. There is one who did not and could not appreciate then the greatness of his burdens and anxieties, who would pay the tribute of honest admiration and reverence for the qualities displayed in this emergency. However different the tendencies which two minds may represent, what candid mind is there that would withhold from Dr. Hopkins unstinted praise for his conduct in this delicate and dangerous crisis, or deny the calmness, patience, tact, wisdom, and manhood that established peace between the widely separated faculty and students?

THE TEACHER.

" Love is his bond, he knows no other fetter,
    Asks not our all, but takes whate'er we spare him,
    Willing to draw us on from good to better, ·
                        As we can bear him.

" When he comes near to touch us and to bless us,
    Prayer is so sweet that hours are but a minute;
    Mirth is so pure, though freely it possess us,
                        Sin is not in it.

" Thus he conducts by holy paths and pleasant
    Innocent souls, and sinful souls forgiven,
    Towards the bright palace where our God is present
                        Throned in high heaven."
            CARDINAL NEWMAN, *St. Philip in his School.*

CHAPTER VI.

THE TEACHER.

AFTER Dr. Hopkins became president the instruction in Intellectual Philosophy was a part, and a large part, of his duty. He used as a text-book Stewart's "Elements of Intellectual Philosophy" for twenty-five years, as appears from the record of the catalogues.

With the class of 1862 he substituted for Stewart the abridgment of Sir William Hamilton's lectures on Metaphysics. He was not wholly satisfied with this book, and made trial of various other books until he published his own, "An Outline Study of Man," in 1873.

His sympathies were with the Scottish philosophy from the first. He was trained in that school, and it is probable that he made a greater impression in favor of the ideas represented by this philosophy than any other thinker America has produced. Other eminent thinkers have had larger classes and have published fuller treatises built upon the Scottish ideas, but Dr. Hopkins had the rare faculty of interesting the dullest mind in the laws of its own being and in the deep questions which the study of philosophy opens. The characteristics of the Scottish school were in accord with his own habits of thought. A philosophy based upon careful observation was the only philosophy that could appeal to him. The farthest remove from his thought was the speculative or dogmatic method. Nothing was more deeply impressed upon his students than the truth that facts arrived at by careful observation are and must be the beginning, and must guide to the end in all psychological study. Self-consciousness was to be interrogated on every definite question, and when its answer was clear and distinct, that became a starting-point. For every individual his own self-consciousness should be the constant "instrument of observation;" and what self-consciousness yielded was not to be set aside. He believed fully in the universality of mental laws, but admitted freely that on certain points the more cultivated intelligence would give the more trustworthy answer. He held indeed that it was possible for the investigator to be deceived in regard to the content of his own consciousness; to mistake an inference for an intuition, or a generalization for a self-evident regulative principle. He taught too that much might be learned from the habits of men, and from language, but the first and final instrument in the hands of a clear thinker was self-consciousness. So he says in the introductory lecture on Moral Science: [1] —

"If a man cannot know what he is conscious of,

[1] *Lectures on Moral Science,* p. 27.

it would seem that he cannot know anything. And yet the whole question between Reid and Hamilton on the one side, and the great mass of philosophers on the other respects simply the fact whether there is or is not given in an act of consciousness both a subject and an object that are not in the last analysis identical. What consciousness testifies to must be accepted. This all allow. Not to do it would be suicidal even to the skeptic; for he would have no ground for affirming that he doubted. The only question is what it is that consciousness gives. If we say that it does give both the subject and the object, that simple affirmation sweeps away in a moment the whole basis of the ideal and skeptical philosophy. It becomes as the spear of Ithuriel, and its simple touch will change what seemed whole continents of solid speculation into mere banks of German fog."

If Dr. Hopkins affirmed that "all allow that what consciousness testifies to must be accepted," he was not less certain that the actual testimony of consciousness is to the existence of certain principles in the mind prior to and independent of experience, though developed in experience. His philosophy rested on these intuitional principles, and by the presence and power of these principles he taught that all rational thought is guided, and that by their help all rational progress is made. Holding to an immediate knowledge [1] of the external

[1] *An Outline Study of Man*, p. 99.

world as given in the act of perception under the
clear light of these principles

" that shine aloft like stars,"

his philosophy led directly to the fundamental truth
of religion, the existence of a supreme personal
reason whose thoughts are expressed in man, nature, and history. The pillars on which his faith
rested were solid because pillars of reason.

Hamilton's doctrine of the contradictory alter-
natives had not the least fascination for him. He
discerned at once the fallacy underlying the two
uses of the term "inconceivable," and did not for
an instant regard the delivery of consciousness as
inconsistent. Kant's antinomies from which this
doctrine took its origin were antinomies only because thesis and antithesis were applied to different
objects of thought. I am sure none of the more
thoughtful members of the class with which he first
used Hamilton as a text-book can ever forget the
calm but earnest words in which he repudiated
Hamilton's statement that "faith is the organ by
which we apprehend what is beyond our knowledge." Faith to him was the trust of the whole
soul reposed in a person. To claim that faith is
an "organ" or a "faculty" seemed to him to introduce utter confusion into the study of mind and
moral relations. Nothing was more averse to his
method, and as he felt to the method of the Scottish
philosophy, than to adopt the principle that the
study of consciousness leads into contradiction or
confusion, which faith as a sort of *deus ex machina*

should disentangle. This would be like discerning a rainbow on a sky so dense with clouds that no ray of sunlight could possibly penetrate them. It was not often that he interrupted the Socratic method of teaching with a long discourse. But on meeting in the class-room this statement by Hamilton in regard to faith, he spoke in refutation of it for nearly half an hour in his own masterly way. It was perhaps the most impressive incident of my college life.[1]

Undoubtedly to some the publication of "The Law of Love" seemed to mark a departure from the old Scottish philosophy. But it was a departure only from the later Scottish writers on the nature of the idea of right. The Scottish philosophers generally believed in right as an intuitive idea. Dr. Hopkins believed in *rights* and obligations as primitive ideas, not in right. He held that "We are never under obligation to do an act as morally right for which there is not a reason in some good besides its being right and on account of which it is right." This doctrine, so closely connected with the philosophy of ends, was the result of long and patient study. He was indeed a "self-contained" thinker, and his promulgation of this doctrine, which he did not derive from any wide reading, but from the faithful use of self-conscious-

---

[1] The discussion of this point, which was given to the class of 1862 in an informal way, is presented with great clearness and fullness in the second lecture on the *Scriptural Idea of Man*, with special criticism of certain expressions made by Professor Calderwood in his *Philosophy of the Infinite*.

ness, from profound examination of the moral constitution of man, showed his perfect independence.
But the philosophy remained essentially Scottish,
and probably this departure from the views of
Stewart did not lessen, but rather promoted the
influence of these ideas in this country.

The Scottish philosophy has been called the
philosophy of " common sense."   This phrase,
which had been employed before Reid, caused a
good deal of discussion relating to Reid's usage of
it.   Dr. McCosh has pointed out the ambiguity
of the phrase.   If used with the meaning of good,
practical sense, it cannot have high authority in
philosophy.   It has always been in the name of
common sense that new discoveries and theories
arising from them have been resisted, and whatever
worth we assign it in practical affairs, it must not
be exalted to the disparagement of mathematical
demonstrations or the inductive proof that certain
long-established opinions are incorrect.   In the
other sense of original principles in the mind it
comes very close to the chosen instrument of the
Scottish philosophy.   The difference between what
consciousness delivers to the closest, most careful observer and thinker and what the ordinary
man accepts as the dictates of common sense will be
found to be very great.   There may be, therefore,
little attractiveness in such a term as "common-
sense philosophy" for the philosopher who knows
how far removed uneducated judgments are from
necessary, and how deep and embracing the mys-

tery is that envelops the simplest mental operations. But it cannot be denied that Dr. Hopkins,
who expressed his philosophical thoughts in simple
language, and had small patience with pretentious
terms, and turned away with positive aversion [1]
from those definitions and phrases which have been
invented with elaborate abstractions in order to
eliminate all trace of personal intelligence behind
nature, seemed in his teaching to present his philosophy as a sovereign common sense. Difficult
problems were not avoided, but were made simple,
and however the student ambitious of wide learning in philosophy may be inclined to look upon his
text-book as a mere primer, it may be safely asserted that for the general purposes of a liberal
education, for the opening of the average mind
into the secrets of its own being, no better hand-
book has been written than "An Outline Study of
Man," published in 1873.

It is, of course, impossible for the reader of the
book to get any idea of the power of the teaching
that accompanied its use; of the cautious, suggestive way in which each topic was opened; of the
subtle and yet genial path by which the unwary
student who had made some rash statement was led
to retract it; of the broad light which long experience with young men and long study of their differences made it possible for the teacher to throw over
a difficult question so that the student seemed to
himself to master the difficulty. An acute thinker,

[1] *Scriptural Idea of Man.* p. 53.

a graduate of one of our best universities, who had followed the required course in philosophy under a distinguished scholar in his own student life with interest, after attending one of Dr. Hopkins's examinations remarked, as he came out: "There was more teaching in that single exercise than in all the exercises in philosophy that I attended when in college."

The atmosphere of a class-room is a subtle, hardly describable thing. It is determined by the wisdom and the power of the teacher and the diligence and receptivity of the pupils. The elements contributed by the teacher gain in richness with each receding year up to a certain point in the life. The materials in the pupils vary from year to year, according to previous training and native endowments. Very bright students may have had little severe training, may have grown up in enervating surroundings, and yet have slipped through the examinations of the earlier years. These will be likely to contribute pride and indocility, restlessness and reluctance, to the influences affecting those whom the teacher of a Senior class has to lead into the study of the profound questions of philosophy.

Dr. Hopkins was accustomed to give early in the first term of the year an hour each day for a week or more to the instruction of the Freshman class in the laws of health. He used as a text-book Combe's "Health and Mental Education," but enriched the instruction with the stores of knowledge accumulated by his own studies. By giving this instruction he gained a closer knowledge of each student from the beginning of his course, and an impression was thus made in the minds of some that prepared the way for a strong personal influence.

There has been an opinion that the students of Williams College were, during Dr. Hopkins's administration, largely of the maturer, self-supporting, earnest types. There were many such, and he fully understood that they were likely to reflect great honor upon the college. He answered their letters when writing in advance to state their needs with patient minuteness and kindest promises. For while he walked with stately steps along the flaming bulwarks of the universe, he bent kindly down to recognize the upward movement of the humblest being those bulwarks were erected to defend.

But there were many young men under his guidance in the years when I knew the college who belonged to families where abundance, not to say luxury existed. Many such were sent to the college in the belief that its remoteness from city life would guarantee freedom from certain temptations. Some of these came to the college against their will. A few were never reconciled to the quiet "monastic" life, as they termed it, and in every class elements of the most diverse character were found. Generally these elements were fused into more or less unity by Dr. Hopkins's instruction, but each succeeding class presented new and difficult varieties of the genus student.

It was in no small degree dealing with these difficult cases and teaching them to think that added each year increase to his power. His form so large and massive, his keen, kind eye, his persuasive voice, however little appreciated in their distinctiveness, were, when taken together, of great advantage in his first relations with pupils. The increasing calmness and benignity of advancing years added also with each new year impressiveness to his presence and words.

> " We see thee standing there,
>   The tall form gravely bent:
>   The thin and silvery hair
>   O'er the lordly dome besprent;
>   The keen uplifted glance :
>   The long arm's curving sweep:
>   The serious countenance
>   Where the merry twinkles sleep :
>
> " We hear thee speaking now,
>   Each weighty word well weighed —
>   Simple and clear and slow —
>   No rattling fanfaronade
>   Of words, but a master's thought,
>   Untainted by sneers or gibes,
>   Like His who the people taught
>   With authority, not as the scribes." [1]

A faithful record of the brighter sayings of the teacher and pupils in Dr. Hopkins's room for a single year would be an instructive revelation of his power. No such record exists, and the understanding of his eminence as a teacher must be

---

[1] Rev. Dr. Washington Gladden's poem at the Williams alumni dinner, June 29, 1887.

far inferior to what such a record for the fifty-six years of his instruction would give.

His skill in answering questions was not inferior to his skill in asking them. His own enjoyment of his sallies and of the effect which they produced on the class was perfectly unrestrained and natural, and seemed to bring him into closer sympathy with his students. But there was never the slightest sacrifice of dignity, or loss of control. He would sometimes tell an old story, but however old it was, it always had a sharp application. Very few reminiscences of his quick perception or ready wit have been preserved.

It was his custom, as has been already said, to begin the instruction of the Senior year with Anatomy and Physiology, to form the base of the pyramid to which he likened the studies which he taught. Upon that base of man in his physical nature was raised the structure of the intellectual and moral and religious studies. It was man as a whole that occupied his time for nine hours each week during most of the Senior year when I was a student.

I remember that one of our brightest men was once questioned in regard to the sensitiveness of the patient during the amputation of a leg. He was asked if he supposed that any pain was felt from the cutting of the bone. He replied that he had always supposed that there was. "And the most acute pain when the knife goes through the marrow?" interrogated the president. "Yes, sir," was the reply. "Well, there is no sensitiveness whatever in either of these two formations," answered the president. I remember thinking at the time that perhaps the leading question was misleading, but the lesson was taught that we were not to have an opinion on a question of fact unless we had data for the opinion.

One of the keenest of Dr. Hopkins's retorts was made when he was nearly seventy years of age. The distinction between man and the lower animals was a favorite subject of discussion with him, as it was of the earlier Scottish philosophers. The point had been made that man is the only animal that laughs. "As he alone laughs, so I think he alone has the perception and feeling involved in that."[1] A student who had perhaps more personal acquaintance with dogs than the president raised his hand on hearing this statement and said: "Dr. Hopkins, I have a little dog at home. When I am there, he sometimes runs up to me and puts his forepaws on my knees, and looks up into my face, and I really think he laughs." Dr. Hopkins turned and looked at his pupil and replied: "When a man laughs, he generally laughs at something. What do you suppose your dog was laughing at?"

When I entered the Junior class in Williams College in the autumn of 1860, Dr. Hopkins was fifty-eight years old. He was then in the zenith of his powers. His hair was already somewhat whitened, and was mostly gone from the high crown of his head. The occasions when I used to see

---

[1] *An Outline Study of Man*, p. 11.

him were the Sunday morning preaching service in the chapel, which he conducted, and the daily evening prayer. It is of the latter service that my recollections are most distinct. There was a reverence and a dignity in his conduct of the service that greatly impressed me. The Scriptures seemed to him to be such a reality; to open such direct communication between him and the Supreme Being, and there was such an uplifting power in his prayers that admiration was from the first kindled within me for his lofty personality. The silvery touch of age had not diminished the strength of manhood, but had added a soft beauty to the lines of power. The form was bent a little, but the strong definite features indicated a marked individuality. Up to that time no teacher, although I had been fortunate enough in different institutions to attend prayers conducted by eminent men, had ever impressed me in the same way. Several members of my class, which had a large number of well-trained and refined minds, used to speak together of these exercises. Evening prayers were not irksome to some of us, and are remembered still with affectionate gratitude. In any reasonable estimate of Dr. Hopkins's influence on college students, I think the evening prayers must have a place.

One of his most distinguished pupils writes: —

"His conduct of evening prayers was very nearly his greatest service to the students, if I may judge others by myself. I shall never forget his reading of the fifteenth chapter of the First Epistle to the Corinthians one hot summer afternoon, just after we had been discussing in his recitation-room Butler's chapter in which he touches upon immortality. As he read the words: 'When this corruptible shall have put on incorruption and this mortal shall have put on immortality,' his utterance of the word immortality was absolutely sublime."

He was particularly fond of those lofty passages in Isaiah which treat of God's majesty, and some of those noblest verses always carry me back to my seat in the chapel that first year in Williams College.

His sermons Sunday mornings were for the most part on doctrinal theology, and were the outline of a system. These were always clear and cogent, and sometimes eloquent. It is probable that the occasional repetition of a noble strain of prophecy in the sermons had something to do with the permanent association in my mind of the sublime language of Isaiah with his ministrations in the college pulpit. In the lectures by Dr. Hopkins on the "Evidences of Christianity," which was one of my text-books the first term of my student life at Williams, reverential words from Isaiah are also now and then quoted, and I cannot but feel surprise now, as I look back and note how largely my first term of study in the college was stamped by the influence of his mind, and how very largely not merely religious, but also Scriptural that influence was. Certainly I did not then realize how pervasive in the atmosphere his thought was, but I see now that the permanent impression of that first term, the opening of my mind to the sublimity of God's government as seen both in nature and the Scriptures, was the work of this one man. Many men, as boys more thoughtless than I was, must have since been awakened to the fact that Dr. Hopkins's influence was the constant environment. I am sure that, whether they confess it or not, his noble reverence for God and his Holy Word has been an effective power in keeping the look of the graduates of this college directed to the higher and better things that concern us, or, if I may use language of which he was so fond, "to the everlasting hills from whence cometh our help."

It seems altogether fitting that this chapter should contain extracts from various letters written by Dr. Hopkins's pupils, conveying their testimony to the influence exerted upon their lives by his teaching. From the great number of such letters which were found among his papers only a few extracts can be given.

Israel W. Andrews, a member of the first Senior class, that of 1837, which came under Dr. Hopkins's tuition as president, writes from Lee, where he was teaching, October 9, 1838: —

"It is my intention to devote the little leisure time I have to theological studies, and I should be much gratified if you would advise me respecting the course. Conscious that I have received more instruction (in Whately's sense) from yourself than from any other one, I know of no one to whom I could better apply for instruction."

Mr. Andrews, who had a distinguished career as a teacher, chiefly in Marietta College, where, after having been tutor and professor of various subjects, he became finally a succesful president, was deputed by the Williams men in attendance at the National Educational Association in Topeka, Kansas, in 1886, to convey congratulations and kind remembrances to Dr. Hopkins. He writes: —

"I am sure no one of those present at Topeka, and I may say no one of all the alumni of Williams, can cherish a profounder respect or warmer love for yourself than do I. As General Garfield said at the inauguration of President Chadbourne, 'Dr. Hopkins will always be our president.' No one has greater cause of gratitude to you than myself, and if I have been of service in any degree as an educator, it is because of your instructions and of your recommendation of me to my field of labor."

Two letters written on the same day, June 6, 1859, one from the Andover Theological Seminary by a graduate preparing for missionary work in India, and the other by the Rev. Dr. Corwin, then pastor of a church in Honolulu, are a striking evidence of grateful appreciation of his inspiration to the noblest life.

The letter from Rev. Dr. Corwin begins with these words: —

"Your kind note with many others reached me as a most acceptable New Year's present on the morning of the 1st, and nothing could have been more acceptable than its familiar, cordial tone, which left me no room to doubt that I was very kindly remembered by one who has done more to shape my destiny than any other man.

"Senior year was to me the butt end of the college course. It was a time when I could feel myself grow. The studies of the first three years were for the most part pursued from a sense of duty. Senior studies were a pursuit of pleasure."

The other letter was written by David C. Scudder, of the class of 1855, whose brief life as a missionary has been told by his brother Horace: "I write to request you to forward to the Mission House at Boston a testimonial respecting my fitness to become a missionary. I cannot let this occasion pass without expressing my thankfulness to God that he sent me to Williams. I knew nothing of the college when I entered, except that a friend of mine had been converted there a year before, and I wished to be converted also, and therefore went. During my second term, through the kind attention of Professor H., I was induced to consider the subject of religion. I did so, and as with me becoming a Christian and becoming a foreign missionary were one and the same thing, committing myself to Christ, I also committed myself to his service abroad. I shall ever look back to my college life with pleasure and yet with regret. . . . But I feel peculiar regret, when I think how poorly I appreciated the studies of Senior year.

"Still, though I accomplished so little, I shall always be thankful, as every other pupil is, that I was brought under your tuition. If I learned nothing from your words, I did much from your example; and although I never was reprimanded that I remember, a look which I thought was intended for me has often recurred to me when tempted to live at ease.

"I hope, sir, that you will excuse these perhaps to you foolish words, for I felt that I could not refrain from expressing though in crude language my esteem for your instructions, my admiration of your example, and my affection for yourself."

A distinguished clergyman, whose name would at once suggest very great services to the church, wrote to Dr. Hopkins from Bennington in 1851 as follows: —

"And let me speak of one more instance of kindness on your part, my dear sir, among the many, as one for which I am deeply grateful, and one that has, I hope, had its influence for good forever upon me. You once addressed words on the subject of religion, to me, when I called on another errand at your study. You were not displeased or wearied when I told you of my doubts and troubles, but conversed with me till half my load was gone. And as we went together to your evening meeting, by some strange coincidence, or in kindness, you took up the course of our conversation in your lecture just where we left it. Never did all seem so clear to me as you made it that night. I found those same thoughts always in my mind, whenever I recurred to the subject. And a few months afterward, when I hoped I had found peace in believing, and a change in intention, in hope, and in feeling had come over my life, I traced many of the influences that pressed most earnestly upon me to the words you gave me that night. I have often wanted to tell you of this, sir, but I never have had the opportunity till now. You have probably forgotten it all long since, but it is among my most cherished and most holy remembrances. Why I never became a Christian in the midst of all the religious association that gathered around me in Williams College I cannot now understand. But to yourself and your sincerely respected brother, Professor Hopkins, who one time also almost kindled me to life, do I trace influences which under the power of God, as I hope, afterwards. brought me out into the light of his truth, and which now give me life and hope and joy in believing."

Titus Munson Coan, the well-known writer of the class of 1859, sent in 1881 a warmly appreciative letter, of which these words are most interesting: —

"I have long meant to tell you with what pleasure I remember my Senior year, 1859. It gave me the impulse to the life of study which I have lived for the most part since then; and I look back to the little country town and to your class-room in the old chapel as to a spring of intellectual and moral energy. Those were formative days, and second only in importance to those of the earlier life at home, and I hoped to thank you for them this summer by word of mouth."

In the later years of his life few class meetings occurred at which his service not merely to the world at large, but in the training of individual lives, was not discussed, and often the pleasantest words of grateful recognition were conveyed from such meetings to him. In 1883 the class of 1863, of which twenty-two members were present, adopted these resolutions:—

"On this the twentieth anniversary of our graduation the undersigned, members of the class of 1863, extend to the venerable and beloved President Hopkins our warmest greetings!

"Having tested the value of his instructions during a score of years in various spheres of thought and of action, and having found them, under all circumstances, helpful for guidance and for inspiration, of immense worth in the working out of our career and the moulding of character and life, we come back and lay at his feet the tribute of our gratitude and affection.

"We rejoice in his convalescence, and cherish the hope that his precious life may long be spared to the college which his name has made illustrious."

The following letter from Rev. Dr. Gladden, of Columbus, Ohio, is another testimony to the value of his teaching:—

COLUMBUS, *February 5, 1884.*

MY DEAR SIR, — I have asked my publisher to send you a volume of sermons, which I beg you to accept with my grateful remembrance.

It would be quite unfair to hold you responsible for the doctrines taught — (though I strongly hope that you will find in these far more to approve than to condemn) — but if there is anything of skill or success in the *methods* of presenting truth, or anything of philosophical breadth and candor in the manner of dealing with it — these qualities are largely due, I am sure, to impressions made on my mind when in your classes, twenty-five years ago.

General S. C. Armstrong, whose work for the negroes and Indians at Hampton, Virginia, has been so eminently conducive to the welfare both of his pupils and through these of our country, gives this testimony not in a letter, but in his "Twenty-two Years' Work of Hampton Normal and Agricultural Institute:" "Let me say here that whatever good teaching I may have done has been Mark Hopkins teaching through me."

Professor William D. Whitney, of Yale University, writes in the preface to the "Forty Years' Record of the Class of 1845:" —

"It remains only to speak of our venerable and venerated president, Mark Hopkins. We had from him, even during our Freshman year, a few lectures on anatomy illustrated by the manikin; then during Senior year he was almost the only one with whom we had to do. Senior year was the time looked forward to with eager anticipation all the way through college, as giving us the privilege of his instruction, and on that account 'going to be worth all the rest of the course,' as it used to be said; and like other classes before and after us we were not disappointed. References here and there in the biographies will show how strongly he impressed us."

In the autumn of 1883 an effort was made to raise $25,000 toward the endowment of the college pastorate, to which the Rev. John H. Denison of the class of 1862, a son-in-law of Dr. Hopkins, had been appointed. The professor was to be called the "Mark Hopkins Professor of Divinity." On the occurrence of Dr. Hopkins's birthday, February 4, 1884, the money had been raised. I was not able to attend the company given at Dr. Hopkins's house, but sent a letter containing the announcement that the professorship was secured. The letter was read aloud to the company by the Rev. Edward H. Griffin, D. D., then Professor of Rhetoric in Williams College, now Professor of the History of Philosophy in the Johns Hopkins University. From this letter a few sentences are given: —

"More fortunate than Woolsey in still imparting order and life to expanding minds; more fortunate than McCosh in being relieved from the pressing responsibility of executive details, long may you live to continue to open to us all the deep lessons of patience, benignity, and serene faith!

"It is now over fifty years since you became professor in this college. Griffin, Denison and I, members of the class of 1862, were not born when you became president in 1836. Through all these years you have watched and nourished and loved this college.

"You cherish, I am sure, no desire that it should become a university or even a great college, but I believe that you cordially sympathize with its present self-denying, harmonious officers (not less self-denying, nor less harmonious, nor less able than any body that has preceded them here) in their efforts to make this the best college of its size in New England; to render, while holding character of supreme importance, the instruction and equipments so excellent and the scholarship so thorough that there shall be no question as to the value of our degree, nor any as to the meaning of membership in our classes."

Dr. Hopkins was agreeably surprised by the main fact communicated by the letter, and made one of his happy extemporaneous speeches to the delight of all present.

Resolutions adopted by the Senior class, the class of 1884, presented the same evening, are an illustration of the feeling that each succeeding class cherished and was pretty sure to express on the birthday of the eminent teacher.

"To our beloved and honored Dr. Hopkins.

"We take great pleasure on this the eighty-second anniversary of your birthday in offering you our congratulations. We rejoice greatly that God in his goodness has allowed us to sit under the instructions of one whose teaching for more than half a century has prepared so many young men to take a useful and honorable place in the work of the world. We appreciate better than we can express the inestimable privilege which we enjoy, and heartily hope that you may be spared to see many more of these anniversary days, and be permitted to guide many classes of young men by your experience and counsel.

"As you said to us in our late affliction,[1] so now we say to you, 'May God bless you!'"

Horace E. Scudder, of the class of 1858, sent in 1884 a copy of the school-book "A History of the United States," which he had just published. In the letter accompanying the book these sentences occur: —

"I am afraid that none of us say enough of our obligation to you. There is a shamefacedness which belongs in the New England character, I think, and I am one of those who feel very deeply their indebtedness to you for the early formation of habits of thought. I was immature enough in my Senior year at college and unable to make the best use of it, but I am confident that but for the kind of training which I there received this book would scarcely have been written. So you see you are receiving your own again."

[1] The sudden death by an accident when coasting of Nathan Gest, of Illinois, a member of the class.

In the same year Lavalette Wilson, of the class of 1856, sent an appreciative letter, from which a few words are taken: —

"It is true that your pupils collectively have often expressed their indebtedness to you, but I know from my own experience as a teacher how pleasant it is when old pupils come individually in after years and show their appreciation of past labors.

"At this late day, then, my dear and much loved Dr. Hopkins, let me express to you my thanks for your valuable instruction and uniform kindness during my college course, and at the same time tender to you all the good wishes which are appropriate to this season of the year."

These testimonies might be indefinitely extended. Dr. Hopkins kept all the letters which were addressed to him that were not mere business forms, and the number of kindly greetings and grateful acknowledgments that flowed in upon him during the last years of his life was astonishing. Clergymen, teachers, jurists, authors, among his pupils, and eminent men not his pupils, were constantly sending messages of respect and love. Classes, alumni associations, bodies not connected in any organic way with the college, sent telegrams and congratulations with each returning birthday.

The delivery and publication of the address in 1886 on the fiftieth anniversary of his election to the presidency of the college was the occasion of the reception of many letters, expressive of indebtedness for moral and intellectual inspiration. Each of these letters has its individual character, and though all of them are in general similar to those from which quotations have been given, the record would be incomplete without adding two or three illustrations from this fresh harvest.

The following letter from an eminent professor in a theological seminary, Rev. Dr. George Mooar, of Oakland, California, was called out by the announcement that the commemorative address would be delivered at Commencement.

"I note that at the approaching Commencement the chief matter of general interest to the Alumni will be the completion of your fifty years of service in connection with the college. I feel impelled to offer you my congratulations in your having been allowed of Providence to continue so eminent a service for the half century. I desire also to express to you my personal gratitude in memory of what you did for me in the four years which closed thirty-five years ago. It was much to me to have your wisdom in the class-room and your kindness and patience in private counsel. May I refer to one occasion which was to you but an ordinary incident, probably, but became to me no doubt of very great importance. Our class had been down the street on some joviality, and returning we were supposed all of us to smoke on our way back to the college. I had not formed the habit prevalent in the class, but had occasionally tried my capabilities and joined the rest. Soon after, being in your library,

you gently referred to the fact, and advised me not
to form the habit, which you said would, to one
of my sedentary tendencies, prove very injurious.
That advice touched me deeply and reinforced my
conscience and will. Now, after thirty-five years, I
find myself dwelling on this friendly service. You
will receive loftier tributes, and I, if I were to say
anything in public, should have as much occasion as
any one to speak of my indebtedness as to clearness of thought, insight of principles, and ideals of
life. But just now in this informal way I am
moved to speak of this incident in your personal
helpfulness to my own conduct."

Another letter well worth preservation in this
record is from a professor in a theological seminary, who was not a graduate of Williams: —

"I have read with great pleasure your address at
Williams College during Commencement week. A
graduate of Williams who had been taught in your
own class-room could scarcely have had greater
pleasure in reading it than myself. The truth is
that your students are not limited to the Williams
Alumni. These are scarcely a tithe of the entire
number of minds that you have quickened and
directed. As one of these, I beg not only to offer
you my congratulations on your possession of the
physical vigor required for the delivery of such an
address, but also to thank you for your defense of
a liberal course of education, and for your contention that its scope and main elements should be
determined by the educating body rather than by

the unformed pupil.　Your strong and timely words will, of course, be eagerly and widely read, and cannot fail to do great good."

The following letter is from a pupil in the ministry, Rev. Dr. Addison P. Foster, of Roxbury:—

"I shall never cease to be thankful that God in his goodness permitted me to receive training at your hand.　Next to my sainted father, whose influence on me to the day of his death was constant and most helpful, I owe more to you than to any other man.

"Not long since a gentleman remarked to me, 'All Williams men have a family resemblance. They all bear the mark of the same master mind.' I have heard this remark more than once.　I am thankful that I can call you my mental father.

"Years since, when I entered Princeton Theological Seminary and attended Dr. Charles Hodge's lectures in theology, I found to my surprise that my theological system was already outlined, and that it did not at all agree with his; and when I came to reflect upon it, I saw that your Saturday morning lectures on Vincent's Catechism had determined the matter.　The working theology of my ministry was given me by you."

One more letter, addressed to the writer of this study, may be added to these.　It is from the Rev. Dr. John Tatlock, of Hoosick Falls, N. Y. Two or three admirable letters written by him to Dr. Hopkins are preserved, but this letter is eminently fit for publication, as it contains the matured judgments of an earnest and acute mind that has been for thirty years successfully devoted to the work of the ministry: —

"Referring to your favor of the 30th ult. I remember one or two letters to Dr. Hopkins, written under the impressions made upon me by his later works, but of course cannot recall, at this distance in time, the sentiments they expressed. As, however, my judgment of him, as a thinker and teacher, has not changed, except as experience and reflection have made it stronger and more discriminating, I shall find little difficulty in conveying it.

"I understand that what you desire is not so much a critical estimate of Dr. Hopkins and of his philosophy as a statement of my indebtedness to him in my own intellectual life, and to this therefore I shall confine myself.

"In the first place I owe very largely to Dr. Hopkins whatever power of clear and discriminating thought I may possess. He incited his pupils to think, and taught them how to think. He instructed them in the nature of the mind and in the proper mode of using it. He made the impression that the thinker is more than the thought, and truth less valuable than the ability to discover it. I recall distinctly my intellectual awakening in his class-room, and the peculiar feeling of delight I experienced on finding that I had a mind of my own.

"I have never forgotten some of his definitions and distinctions: and these have served me, not more by their intrinsic importance, than by their confirmation of the habit of distinguishing between things that differ.

"By his admirable method of educing the powers of his students, by treating them, in a sense, as his equals in the field of discussion, he evoked the consciousness of an independent and vigorous intellectual life, of more worth than the most perfect system of philosophy.

"But while I place this consideration first, I must also confess my indebtedness to him for a scheme of thought, deep, and wide, and fruitful, satisfying at once, in its main features, the demands of the reason and those of the moral nature. From him I first learned the meaning of the word 'universe,' and under his guidance began the life-long work of bringing its three great divisions, nature, man, and God, into intelligible and harmonious relations.

"More particularly I desire to bear testimony to the immeasurable advantages I have derived from his 'doctrine of ends.' I do not suppose that Dr. Hopkins is to be credited with the discovery of this form of philosophy, for, on the supposition of its correctness, it must have been practically assumed in all ages, and have been at least implicitly recognized and admitted by many writers. But to him belongs the high honor of having clearly formulated the doctrine, elaborated a system upon it, and defended it from the gross imputations of utilitarianism. At any rate, Dr. Hopkins was

the first to open up this doctrine to me, and to secure my profound and unwavering acceptance of
it, and I can truthfully say that no philosophical
principle with which I am acquainted has been of
greater service to me in the field of theology, both
speculative and practical; casting light upon dark
places, and cutting paths through the thickets.

"I could write much more upon this fruitful and
pleasing theme, but as a personal testimony from
one of Dr. Hopkins's most grateful pupils what I
have written will be, I presume, sufficient."

Perhaps the most striking testimonial to his
power as a teacher is the hall dedicated at Williams
College to the honor of his memory three years
after his death. This fine building, almost wholly
devoted to purposes of instruction, representing a
cost of nearly $90,000, permanently identifies his
name with the teaching of the college. It is not
the idea that its massive walls typify the solidity
of his character, or that its abundant windows suggest the openness of his mind to light and the clearness with which he saw and enforced the truth, that
is most affecting to one who knows the history of
the building. It is the thought rather that there
went into its construction a multitude of small sums
from teachers, ministers, and men in humble relations, most of them his pupils, whose lives had been
made brighter by his words, and into whose hearts
had passed the inspiration won by his own endurance and self-denial. The small subscriptions represent equally with the largest the consciousness of

a debt which cannot be paid.   The building is the chorus of many voices saying in harmony: —

> " To thee it was given
> Many to save with thyself:
> And at the end of thy day,
> O faithful shepherd ! to come,
> Bringing thy sheep in thy hand."

THE AUTHOR.

"No wild enthusiast of the right,
Self-poised and clear, he showed alway
The coolness of his northern night,
The ripe repose of autumn's day."

WHITTIER, *Rantoul.*

CHAPTER VII.

The important books of Dr. Hopkins are not numerous. They were, singularly enough, all of them called out by invitations to deliver a course of lectures. Four of the five were given as courses before the Lowell Institute, and the substance of the fifth was delivered before the students of several theological seminaries. But these books contain matured thinking, and are the outcome of the long and careful study required for his constant teaching of the subjects discussed. He had taught morals more than thirty years before either of the books on morals was written, and intellectual philosophy thirty-six years before he published "An Outline Study of Man." A volume of "Miscellanies" made up of various addresses was published in 1847, and a collection of the baccalaureate sermons was made in 1863. Another collection of these sermons appeared with the title "Strength and Beauty" in 1874, and an enlarged edition of this was issued in 1884, but the title was changed to "Teachings and Counsels." A large number of addresses and sermons and review articles were printed in his long life, some of which are of great

value but are not contained in either of the collected
volumes.   As perfect a list of these as can now be
made will be found at the end of this book.

The lectures on the " Evidences of Christianity "
delivered in January, 1844, the first important book
of Dr. Hopkins, bear clear marks of the great influence that Bishop Butler had exercised upon his
mind.   It seems at first thought singular that the
" Analogy," which was written with special reference to the unbelief of the last century, and had
been published over a hundred years when Dr.
Hopkins delivered these lectures, should have kept
so firm a grasp on religious thought, and should
leave its indelible marks on minds so different as,
for instance, that of Cardinal Newman and that of
Dr. Hopkins.   There was indeed a certain affinity
between these thinkers.   Both were born almost
at the beginning of the century, Newman in 1801
and Dr. Hopkins in 1802, and the lives of both
stretched on through the most varying changes in
the intellectual world.   They certainly lived to witness the effect of discoveries and conceptions that
do to a large degree lessen the cogency of Bishop
Butler's argument, but apparently neither of these
would ever let go of two immensely significant
principles which the " Analogy " teaches: namely,
first, that the things that are seen have counter-
parts in things unseen; and secondly, the com-
mon-sense and wholesome belief that probability is
and must be the guide of life.   The one was indeed
a Puritan, the other a Romanist.   The one believed

in the smallest amount of machinery in religious
things and in the fullest liberty for a local church.
The other was carried by his processes of thought
to the acceptance of authority, to a profound hatred
of schism, and to a fervent attachment to what he
held as the one original Christian church. When
Dr. Hopkins in conversation with one of the college
professors regarding Robert Browning said, "I too
am a mystic," he expressed the affinity that he had
with all the great spiritual teachers of the age; and
though he would have rejected with disdain much
of Newman's sacramentalism, he accepted him as
a brother in the higher region of spiritual thought,
and with him emphasized always the immediate relation of the soul to the things unseen. No work
of Newman's shows more plainly or more beauti-
fully the far-reaching effect of the great "Analogy"
than these lectures by Dr. Hopkins on the "Evidences of Christianity."

The lectures from the third to the eighth inclu-
sive are simply the carrying out with fine and yet
powerful strokes suggestions that might well arise
from the study of the "Analogy." Of this there
is an abundance of evidence. The following statement from the "Analogy" finds reproduction in
the third lecture: —

"The natural world, then, and natural government of it being such an incomprehensible scheme,
so incomprehensible that a man must, really in the
literal sense know nothing at all, who is not sensible of his ignorance in it; this immediately sug-

gests, and strongly shows the credibility, that the moral world and government of it may be so too." [1]

The third point in the third lecture on the "Evidences" opens as follows: "I observe that there is an analogy, both in their kind and in their limit, between the knowledge communicated by nature and that by Christianity."

Under the fifth head in the same lecture reference is made directly to the fourth chapter of the second part of the "Analogy."

The seventh point in the same lecture is introduced by quotations from the chapter in the second part of the "Analogy," on "the appointment of a Mediator and Redeemer," and is quite covered by the quotation. [2]

The following extract shows plainly the potency of the analogical argument for Dr. Hopkins's mind: —

"I observe that there is an analogy between the laws of nature, as discovered by induction, and the moral laws contained in the New Testament, not only as implying the same natural attributes in God, but as they are carried out to the same perfection. It is the great and sublime characteristic of natural law, especially of the law of gravitation, that, while it controls equally the minutest

----

[1] Butler's *Analogy*, part i. chap. vii.

[2] It is farther proof of Butler's hold on Dr. Hopkins that he quotes from the Sermons, in the controversy with Dr. McCosh, to the effect that there need not be inconsistence between holiness and happiness, and calls Butler "the highest English authority in morals."

particle that floats in the sunbeam; and that, however wildly that particle may be driven, — wherever it may float in the infinity of space, — it never, for one moment, escapes the cognizance and supervision of this law. It never can. This implies a minuteness and perfection of natural government, of which science, as known in the time of Christ, could have given no intimation. But now, how natural does it seem that the same God, who, in the universal control of his natural law, no more neglects the minutest particle than the largest planet, should also, in his moral law, take cognizance of every idle word, and of the thoughts and intents of the heart! Yes; I find, in the particle of dust, shown by the greatest expounder of God's natural law to be constantly regarded by him, and in the idle word declared by Christ to come under the notice and condemnation of his moral law, — I find, in the minuteness and completeness of the government of matter, as revealed by modern science, and even shown to the eye by the microscope, and in that interpretation of the moral law which makes it spiritual, causing it to reach every thought and intent of the heart, — a conception of the same absolute perfection of government, both in the natural and moral world; and I find the same infinite natural attributes implied as the sole conditions on which such a government in either of these departments can be carried on.

"This idea of the absolute universality and perfection of government in any department — the only one, however, worthy of a perfect God — is not an idea, especially in its moral applications, which I should think likely to have originated with man. In the department of nature we know that he did not originate or suspect it till it was forced on his observation. And how comes it to pass that this absolute perfection of moral government, this notice of the particle of dust there, this judgment of every idle word, of every secret thing, of the minutest moral act of the most inconsiderable moral being that ever lived, should have been discovered and announced thousands of years before its more obvious counterpart in the natural world was even suspected?"[1]

The third lecture from which this passage is taken, and which presents many suggestions of Butler's influence, is more distinctly an argument from analogy than most of the lectures, but not more really so than some of the others. For instance, in the fifth lecture on Christianity and its adaptation to the intellect and the affections, the argument from analogy is constantly appearing.

Probably no lectures that Dr. Hopkins ever wrote had a greater effect on the audience or appealed more strongly to the general reader. The subject is not treated from a theologian's standpoint, but from that of an ordinary intelligent thinker, and the treatment is at times plain, but always dignified; at times admirably eloquent, but never extravagant. I remember distinctly the im-

[1] Lecture III. p. 83.

pression produced on my mind by some of these passages, when as a student I read this book. It was like being led up to a lofty standpoint, where one could take a wide view and note how solid and grand the buttresses on the great mountains are, to have the righteousness and love and reason of the revealed God distinctly exhibited as sustaining his throne. It was impossible for a thoughtful student not to feel that his previous conception of the system of nature as related to the system of Christianity had been very imperfect, and that his ideas of the unity in God's kingdoms were very rudimentary. The strange sensation of enlarging views that may come with the first mastery of a principle in arithmetic or algebra or language, but whenever it comes in any department of knowledge suggests a prophecy of endless attainment, came to me at times over this book.

There is perhaps more of a glow of eloquence in these lectures than in any other of his writings. They were, in the first place (and this often seems to imply freshness and vigor), the first important production of the author. There is often much in a first book that is germinal, that finds ample fulfillment and development later; but when for the first time a thoughtful mind that has had long training, and has pondered life or moral truth, or has made a solution for itself of some deep question, seeks utterance, there may be a warmth and power that find quick entrance to the popular heart. It would be easy enough to name poets, novelists, and moralists whose first publications have at once obtained and never lost popularity, a popularity often greater than that vouchsafed to their subsequent writing. It has already been stated that at a certain point in his college course young Hopkins, compelled by physical weakness, went home to Stockbridge for rest, and while at home applied his mind to the study of the Christian evidences. He came to the perfectly definite conclusion that Christianity is a supernatural revelation from God, and from that position, as, at the age of eighty-three, he stated to the students in the college chapel on the day of prayer for colleges in 1885, he never in the least wavered. That was probably the first great subject with which he grappled. There can be none more momentous, and in that deep pondering doubtless some of the admirably clear and convincing thoughts of these lectures first crystallized. They were ripened and developed by subsequent thought, but the lectures exhibit the strength of the young man, the glad movement, the exuberance and vigor of illustration that belong with the first utterance of symmetrically developed power.

In the second place the lectures were written in a brief period of time. It does not seem that Dr. Hopkins ever had the love of authorship for authorship's sake. He had accepted the vocation of teaching. The allotment of regular tasks often induces the disposition to regard these of supreme importance. In his case these were numerous enough and various enough to absorb his entire

time for many years after he became president.
He could not work upon these lectures which he
had been invited to deliver before the Lowell Institute during the college session.　When in the autumn of 1843 the college year ended, he found it
impossible to force his mind to undertake the labor
of writing.　He dropped everything and went into
the woods for three weeks, and on his return took
up the work with ardor, and wrote the twelve lectures in a few weeks.　They have the dash and
glow that belongs with rapid composition.　They
are less elaborate, but more spontaneous than much
of his published writing.　A notable but friendly
critic [1] took exception to two or three inconsistencies
of thought and to a haziness in certain passages.
So far as there was any justice in the criticisms,
the inconsistencies and lack of clearness so rarely
found in his writings had their origin in the rapid
composition.　For the general reader we may, however, well question whether the rapidity of composition did not secure a freedom of movement and a
persuasiveness in presentation that more than com-
pensates for the presence of here and there an idea
not perfectly thought out, or the introduction of an
occasional question not definitely settled.

Lectures on moral science were originally written
soon after Dr. Hopkins's election in 1830 to the
chair of Moral Philosophy and Rhetoric.　After
his election as president in 1836, the duties which

[1] Rev. Dr. Noah Porter, afterwards President of Yale College;
see vol. iv. of *The New Englander.*

he had to discharge were so onerous as to leave little room for the writing of lectures. He taught
Anatomy, Intellectual Philosophy, Moral Philosophy, Natural Theology, Butler's Analogy, and such
Doctrinal Theology as was involved in Vincent's
Questions on the Catechism. Up to the year
1855 he taught also Rhetoric. The correction of
compositions and the criticism of declamations
were a part of his duties. If we add to this long
catalogue the preaching at least once every Sabbath, there can be little doubt that no New England college president was doing the same variety
and breadth of work. For distinction and eminence among his contemporaries, for a visible, permanent record of his great intellectual and literary power, one may be tempted to regret this.
When one recalls the clear flowing words of the
lectures on the "Evidences," and is uplifted by the
sweep of the thought, or perceives the admirable
and subtle analysis of the lectures on "Moral
Science," one cannot repress a feeling of disappointment that so potent a master of English, and
so exact and penetrating a thinker, should not have
left more abundant records of his unique powers
as a writer on the lofty subjects with which his
thought was always conversant. This feeling is
deepened somewhat by the remembrance that his
article on "Mystery," which was published in the
"Journal of Science" in 1827, was marked by the
same high qualities that characterized his last
course of lectures on "The Scriptural Idea of Man,"

published in 1883. He continued to teach until 1887, the year of his death.

This period of sixty years was filled with pure and ennobling thoughts on the highest subjects, and many of these thoughts are written only in the minds and memories of his pupils. Reflection leads to the conclusion that, by making his paramount duties those of the class-room, he contributed more effectually to cleanse and ennoble the thought of his generation than if he had sought for influence chiefly or largely as a writer. It was not an auspicious fate that put the teaching of so many subjects and the upbuilding of the college all on one man. What a college owes first and always to its pupils is the inspiration of good teaching, the example of manly, courteous, broad intellectual activity in the class-room. This Dr. Hopkins always gave. In the days of his darkest fears for the college (and there were many dark days) the steady patience and kindliness and incisiveness of his teaching never revealed in the least the anxieties that beset him. It would have been easy enough for some men to say, "I cannot carry this heavy burden of teaching; I must have time for reading and writing," and there would have been reason in the appeal. But regarding his life as consecrated to the college, and conscious that nothing could ever stimulate and mould the young men gathered in the college like the personal influence of conscientious teachers, he gave to the Senior class his efficient guidance from the beginning of the year to the end. It was in one sense the Christian, self-denying course, but it was also the wisest course. He might have been recognized in England and Germany and France as a discoverer of truth and an illustrious writer. He chose to be remembered by his pupils as the humble teacher who held their hand in their early halting and uncertain steps. The seed that he sowed was germinating through all the lives, especially in those who became teachers and preachers of righteousness. The loyalty of the many alumni to the college became something both higher and deeper than it could have been had it rested simply on pride in distinguished achievements. It was enkindled by a personal relation; its foundation was gratitude for intellectual and moral awakening; for an opening of the mind to the universal in the individual, and to the beautiful harmonies of the universe. Wherever the graduates of the college went, they carried something of his breadth with them. When one considers the location of the college, its great remoteness during most of his presidency from the world's activities, the centralizing tendency that swept the best prepared young men into the larger colleges from the centres of culture, one must admit something unique in the results of his training. The college might be called provincial. Its equipments were meagre. For a considerable period of his hardest labors notes of provincialism were perceptible among the diverse college utterances. Some of the students from the cities remarked these notes. For all that, when the Williams graduate went out into the world, whether he came originally from a retired farm or from a city home, he went with a good understanding of himself, with a clear idea of his relations to the world, and with a much broader conception of the universe and its harmonious adjustments than characterized the graduates of some larger colleges. He may have known less Latin, less Greek, less history, and less literature, but he knew quite as much about man in his essential, fallen, but divine manhood; about the laws of his being and their relations to one another; about the universal principles of God's natural and moral government. It was the peculiarity of this teacher that he gave this stamp of universal relations in conditions largely provincial, and thus struck the keynote for many noble careers. For, whatever was provincial in any feature of our college life when I was a student at Williams, there was nothing provincial about Dr. Hopkins. Wherever he went, he was and he looked a citizen of the world, one might rather say a king of men, and this was preëminently true in the class-room. Whether he spoke, or prayed, or was silent, the observer knew that that massive head carried wisdom; that those eyes had looked into secrets of the widest range and application. This universal element in his teaching and his character is nowhere more evident than in the lectures on "Moral Science," which were revised between 1858 and 1861. A good illustration of this element is found in the discussion of glory at the close of the fifth lecture: —

"Our constitution does not deceive us. Its tendencies need guidance, not eradication. This part of it is a striking indication of the greatness of our nature and of its capacity of being put into relation with vast numbers and great interests." "Regarding ourselves not merely as citizens of this world, but of the universe, and knowing that God is over all, and that there is somewhere a vast assembly of the good to whom our conduct either now is or shall be known, we may give to this principle of action free scope!"[1]

So in discussing the law of limitation which has so much and such apt efficiency in his system, he strikes again and again the broad universal note, if I may say so. "The law applies universally so long as there is a good, that is, conditional for one above it, — so long as there is an end, there is also a means. But when we reach the highest and supreme good, as that is conditional for nothing beyond itself, there can then be no excess. That is infinite! it is the ocean without a bottom or a shore." Aristotle makes virtue and good consist in proportion, in the golden mean of activity for our appetites and desires. Dr. Hopkins says directly after the above passage, "We may now see how far Aristotle was right. His system had a basis, and not a narrow one. Much of our good is the result of proportion and limitation, and of finding the

---

[1] *Moral Science*, Lecture V. p. 128.

golden mean. He was right as far as he went, but he needed the law of limitation, and he did not see the ocean."[1]

The value of a system of intellectual philosophy may be said to be tested by the clearness and force with which the contents of consciousness are revealed and discussed. Moral systems are differentiated by the treatment of conscience and the foundation of obligation. In these lectures as revised and published in 1863, having been delivered before the Lowell Institute the previous season, there is clearly presented the doctrine that "obligation" to choose the higher good is intuitive and ultimate, and that the "right" itself is not an intuitive idea, which found its fuller treatment later in "The Law of Love." This doctrine, which, if not original with Dr. Hopkins, was at least discovered by him, and which for him set the moral into new and more perfect harmony with the other departments of man's nature, was really the outgrowth of that quality in his mind which sought unity in diversity, and was never content until it apprehended the universal. This quality gives a large part of the charm to his writing, and it is evident enough that the claims of Christianity to our acceptance rested for him in part on the harmony between nature and revelation (considering man here as a part of nature), and found here a basis which seemed increasingly solid. It will be better to discuss later the peculiar doctrines in morals which gave such

---

[1] *Moral Science*, Lecture III. p. 73.

comfort to his own mind, and have found increasing
favor with earnest thinkers of our country of late
years.   There are certain passages in the lecture
relating to "Personality and Conscience" that illustrate both the beauty and the scope of his
thought and the exactness with which he pursued
every thought and analogy to its innermost secret.
The poetic power of the following words serves to
introduce in a general way the importance of the
analysis of conscience: "There is no beauty of a
ship with every sail set, speeding its way over the
subject element to its haven, that can be compared
with that of the organized power of man acting in
harmony, — those ruling that ought to rule, and
those serving that ought to serve, and all conspir-
ing to their destined end ! nor is any storm in nature
so sublime as the conflicts that may arise, when
temptation and opposition come between a true-
hearted man and the attainment of his end."   Dr.
Hopkins does not here identify conscience with the
entire moral nature, but makes its action a function
of the moral reason.   The whole moral nature consists "of those powers whose activity gives the moral
quality, and also of those which judge of the moral
quality, and are affected by it, and it would conduce to perspicuity if the term conscience could be
confined to the latter."[1]   The relation of the will
to conscience makes the advantage of this distinction clear at once.   The will is certainly essential
to a moral act.   There can be no moral act with-

[1] *Moral Science*, Lecture VII. p. 172.

out an exercise of choice and of free choice. The will is then a very essential part of the moral nature, but the conscience affirms obligation to choose, and issues an order to the will to choose and to act under that choice. The will does not always obey. If the conscience was coincident with the entire moral nature, how could the will disobey?

It is in this lecture that Dr. Hopkins reaches what is highest in man and finds his true good. "We now reach a form of activity that is a condition for nothing within the system above itself, which has in itself and in its results not only *a* good, but *the* good and the supreme good for man, and which can therefore be subject to no law of limitation." "What, then, is the highest form of activity of which we are capable? By a fair analysis this has been shown to be love. What are the appropriate objects of love? They are God and our neighbors. What is the highest possible *degree* of this love? It is the love of God with all the heart and of our neighbor as ourselves.

"Here then do we have, after as full and fair an examination as I could give it, the human constitution itself uttering the substance of that law which was spoken in thunder four thousand years ago, and uttering, because it is impossible to find those more appropriate, the very words of Him who spoke as never man spoke, when He gave a summary of that law. Wonderful is it that his words should be the exact formula for the expression of the highest possible activity of the highest powers.

"Thus as in a former lecture we found that the teachings inwrought into the whole framework of nature were in perfect harmony with the constitution of man, so do we now find that the teachings of that constitution are themselves in perfect harmony with those of the revealed word of God. So it is that 'deep calleth unto deep.' So is man the connecting link between that which is lowest and that which is highest."[1]

It is, of course, open to some to say that the feeling for universal relations which exists in every mind had been developed by this great teacher into a passion, and that such a passage as the above only shows how self-deluded an intellect once calm and cool may become. There will be no danger that any student who came under the influence of Mark Hopkins as a teacher will ever believe that the cautious, steady, penetrative, luminous intelligence with which he examined every subject ever became tainted with delusion, or charged with bias. The accusation would come with strange impropriety from those for whom the materialistic doctrine of evolution derives its main support from universal relations. As a matter of fact, one of the most eminent advocates of evolution (but not of materialistic evolution) in this country, and one of Dr. Hopkins's pupils, has admitted that Dr. Hopkins's method of looking at nature and man had been of immense service to him in coming to his conclusions as a man of science.

---

[1] *Moral Science*, Lecture VII. pp. 179, 180.

But with all Dr. Hopkins's love for universal relations, with that master power which he evinced in treating every subject of reaching out into vast spaces and exhibiting the grand affinities of the humblest thing, he drew back from evolution. His philosophy was full of gradations. It was a philosophy of gradations. It connected the lowest atom with divine intelligence. Bird and beast, star and sun, flower and angel, were parts, orderly parts, and graduated parts for him as for Plato of that system which included man and began and ended in God. But differentiations no less, perhaps even more, than affinities were valid for his mind. It was as true for him that moral nature is the highest thing in the universe as that man is subject to gravitation. "The beauty of the ship with every sail set" speeding to its goal across tempestuous seas was incomparably inferior to the march of the martyr to the stake.

In the first of the lectures of "The Scriptural Idea of Man," published in 1883, which had been delivered before theological students at New Haven, Boston University, Chicago, Oberlin, and Princeton, the statement that "God created" brings up this question of evolution. Dr. Hopkins does not regard the term "evolution" as applicable simply to a process, but would make it cover causation, the cause of the evolutionist being an unconscious impersonal force. It is thus set directly against the Scriptural account of the origin of man. His reasoning is cogent and conclusive against that atheistic conception, but the possible truth in evolution as the mode of God's creation and as thus presented, certainly involving nothing more atheistic than the law of gravitation, is not considered. This many Christian theologians accept, recognizing points of transition, large additions to matter and organized life in its different states by a personal God.

It seemed to Dr. Hopkins as to Agassiz that there was an inevitable tendency in Darwin's doctrine, when it was first put forward, to reduce mind to matter, will to a blind *nisus*, freedom to necessity, and to obliterate the pervasive and sublime manifestations of intelligence in nature. The writer well remembers how one of Darwin's illustrations of the possible transformations of animal forms was read from the desk in the chapel one Sunday morning by the president, then in the manliest majesty of age, soon after the book on the "Origin of Species" was published, and what impatience and scorn were expressed for the illustration. The statement was made that it was too early to pronounce positively on a theory apparently supported by a vast body of facts. But it was plain enough that the far-reaching mind of the preacher discovered at once the immense impetus that would be given to materialism and atheism by the adoption of Darwin's views. They would tend to the elimination of the evidences of design from the universe, which was afterward the effect on Darwin himself, and which has been a marked result of the wide acceptance of the theory.

"The field which we took to be thickly sown with design seems under the light of Darwinism to yield only a crop of accidents." [1] Because, in part, of his keen foresight of the natural results of Darwin's teachings, he continued to emphasize differences to the end of his life. I once remarked to him that Professor Gray had asserted that it was impossible to make a clear line of demarcation between the animal and the vegetable kingdoms. His reply revealed the absolutely essential importance for his mind of maintaining fundamental differences. "I do not doubt there is a distinction, though it may not be discovered." The distinction is at least practical, if not scientific, and will probably never be lost from common language. For his mind this difference was the result of additions from a power above, and to reduce all these additions to imperceptible growth from within seemed to deny that there was any uplifting from without.

Evolution meant at first and equally for him at last the obliteration of design, the elimination of a personal God. He did not call a believer in development as to the method of God's creation an evolutionist. To evolution as he defined it he was inflexibly hostile. The gradations of his philosophy had causes and ends. Because they were gradations, because they denoted differences. because they marked additions for ends and expressed the intentions of a superintending mind. he would not abide their reduction to nothingness, or the

---

[1] Professor Asa Gray, *Natural Science and Religion*, p. 85.

reduction of their causes to a blind *nisus* or an unknowable force.

He did not, as has been seen, object to the recognition of affinities between man and the lower animals, or indeed to affinities between man and the clod on which he walks. Indeed, he always emphasized those affinities. He would have been perfectly willing to adopt the words of Faust in regard to nature, —

> " Before me thou dost lead her living tribes,
> And dost in silent grove in air and stream
> Teach me to know my kindred."

"Let the naturalist," he says, in "The Scriptural Idea of Man," "bring man into as close affinity with nature and with animals as he pleases! the closer the better, if it be but distinctly seen that he is capable of dominion and priesthood. Give us these, or the possibility of these, in man, and we ask for no wider ground of separation between man and the brutes ! for of dominion, in the proper sense of that word, dominion over itself, over nature, or over its fellows, no brute can know anything, nor can it know anything of an intelligent mediation between nature and God."[1]

Because of the immense sweep of this difference, Dr. Hopkins did not wholly approve the emphasis with which the Duke of Argyle in the series of papers on the "Unity of Nature" insisted on classifying man with nature. For him the freedom of choice of his own end lifted man into the realm of

[1] *Scriptural Idea of Man*, p. 103.

the supernatural, and he preferred to classify him by his highest affinities rather than by his lowest.

It may be said that Dr. Hopkins was not quite patient enough with the newer theory of man's origin, and it is true that, in "The Scriptural Idea of Man," more than once he speaks of the view of Darwin as representing man as having ascended from the ape.

On page 8 he says, "They who hold that man did thus come up, also hold that the first man was but slightly above the ape." Again, "That a being creeping up by insensible degrees from ape-hood should ever have reached, and especially at that early period, the conception of himself as in the image of such a God, and as rightfully endowed with such a dominion, is impossible." [1]

The Darwinists have objected to that form of stating their theory. For instance, Professor Gray, of Cambridge, who was a devout theist, but a strong believer in the laws of Darwin, says in the lectures on "Natural Science and Religion," published in 1880, "Sober evolutionists do not suppose that man has descended from monkeys. The stream must have branched too early for that."

But it may be said that if the stream did branch behind or below the apes, no great exception can be taken if the opponent to evolution speaks of a connection for man with an animal higher than the one from which the bifurcation begun. Darwinism would seem to claim at least that the ape is

[1] *Scriptural Idea of Man*, Lecture I. p. 8.

higher. It does not seem that this reference is unfair.

Again, it may be said that Dr. Hopkins does not fairly admit the teachings of observed facts with respect to variation. He says: "It is generally supposed that the doctrine of Darwin on the origin of species gives support to the theory of evolution — it tends in that direction, and may do it on two conditions. The first is, that there be produced at least one well-established instance of the origin of one species from another. That has not been done. Varieties within a species, as of pigeons, there are without limit; but there is no instance of the change of a pigeon into an eagle, or of any tendency in that direction."[1] Probably all Darwinists, even those who insist on the reality of spiritual forces and deny that the methods which they bring forward to account for biological changes are adequate to produce the higher faculties of man, would object to Dr. Hopkins's way of stating the significance of the facts of variation. They would not admit that the fact (if it be a fact) that the pigeon has not varied towards an eagle goes far towards settling the question. They have perhaps not claimed, that special variation. But such writers as Wallace, to whose acute mind the variations in nature had suggested the main features of Darwin's laws before they were published by Darwin, would and do claim that "the greyhound and the spaniel were variations from the same animal pro-

<hr>

[1] *Scriptural Idea of Man*, Lecture I. p. 15.

duced by man's selection." They do claim wide and abundant variations as still manifest in nature, and that the evidence for man's descent from some ancestral form common to him and the anthropoid apes is overwhelming and conclusive. It did not appear so to Dr. Hopkins, and he had given the matter careful consideration. Whatever may be the final and decisive verdict, we can have no doubt that those distinctions which he insisted upon as dividing man from all beneath him are shown to be genuine distinctions; features which have nothing answering to them in the lower animals, that self-consciousness, the power to form abstract ideas, the deliberate choice of an end, and the moral nature in man are not the outgrowth of any rudiments found in the animals. That a pure scientist, uninfluenced by theological bias, may come to the fullest acceptance of the theory of natural selection and still maintain that the origin of the noblest features of man's nature is spiritual and not material is proven by the positions taken by Dr. Wallace. His last utterance assures us that in his deliberate judgment, "the Darwinian theory, even where carried out to its extreme logical conclusion, not only does not oppose, but lends a decided support to the spiritual nature of man."[1]

It is important to note, in concluding the discussion on Dr. Hopkins's attitude in respect to this subject, that his method was wholly in sympathy with that of the evolutionist. He looked for uni-

[1] *Darwinism.* p. 479.

versal relations, and also for differentiations, and all his teaching was an exposition of progressive order in nature and in man. Uniformities of process and of law pervade the universe because it is a universe, the work of one author. While drawing back with earnestness from atheistic tendencies, and possibly treating the arguments of some writers with small consideration because of these tendencies, his teachings as a whole contributed to the acceptance by Christian thinkers of the conceptions upon which evolution is based, and which it confirms. His disagreement with the theistic evolutionist was mostly a disagreement in definitions. It is perhaps just to say that the positions taken on this subject in "The Scriptural Idea of Man" do not seem to correspond fully to the general method and scope of his philosophy.

"The Law of Love and Love as a Law" was published in 1869. In it is found the clearest and best statement of the views in morals to which Dr. Hopkins came after years of study. These views, it is worth while to note again, were not derived from any previous philosopher, but were his own solution of the deepest problems in moral philosophy. Similar views had been held by other thinkers. Among the earlier writers who had in a measure anticipated the system of Dr. Hopkins were Shaftesbury and Hutcheson. Hutcheson's views in morals, which Dr. McCosh regards as largely derived from Shaftesbury, have striking resemblances to those of Dr. Hopkins. He does not formally work out the doctrine of ends, but moral excellence consists in "benevolence," and the love "of moral excellence and love to the mind where it resides with the consequent acts of esteem, veneration, trust, and resignation, are the essence of true piety toward God. We never speak of benevolence toward God, as that word carries with it some supposal of indigence or want of some good in the object. And yet as we have benevolence toward a friend when he may need our assistance, so the same emotion of soul or the same disposition toward him shall remain when he is raised to the best state we can wish: and it then exerts itself in congratulation, or rejoicing in his happiness. In this manner may our souls be affected toward the Deity without any supposition of his indigence by the highest joy and complacence in his absolute happiness."[1] From all this it is very plain that Hutcheson would wholly agree with Dr. Hopkins that we should love God, not "because it is right," but "because He is wholly worthy of love."

A passage like the following contains implicitly Dr. Hopkins's doctrine of "the conditioning and the conditioned," and can be almost literally paralleled by sentences from "The Law of Love" and "The Scriptural Idea of Man:" "The selfish affections are then only disapproved when we imagine them beyond that innocent proportion, so as to exclude or overpower the amiable affections, and engross the mind wholly to the purposes of selfish-

---

[1] Hutcheson's *System of Moral Philosophy*, vol. i. p. 70.

ness, or even to obstruct the proper degree of the generous affections in the station and circumstances of the agent." [1]

Notwithstanding the close resemblances in these systems, it does not appear that Dr. Hopkins had made a study of Hutcheson. The fact that he does not mention him among the authors whose theories on the foundation of "obligation" he discusses in the introduction to "The Law of Love" plainly precludes his acquaintance with him. His fuller analysis and development of views presented by one who has been called "the founder of the Scottish philosophy" is extremely interesting; it is all the more so, because it is wholly independent of the earlier author. Several distinguished writers contemporary with Dr. Hopkins published treatises that present fundamental conceptions quite the same, as, for instance, Janet in France, and Martineau in England. The doctrine of ends is as old as Aristotle. Dr. Hopkins was primarily a thinker and not a reader, and the value of his solution is greatly enhanced by the fact that the steps which led to it were, so far as he was concerned, along a path absolutely new. That to reach his final conclusions he gave up the doctrine of right as ultimate, which he had long held, attests the candor and earnestness of his thinking.

Soon after the publication of the book, a review of it appeared in the "New York Observer" from the pen of the Rev. Dr. McCosh, of Princeton,

---

[1] Hutcheson's *System of Moral Philosophy*, vol. i. p. 65.

New Jersey. It was courteous, but plainly charged the doctrine of the author with utilitarianism or at least with eudæmonism.[1] The article was courteous, but probably all of Dr. Hopkins's pupils felt that the introductory remark that the "reading of Dr. Hopkins like that of Edwards seems confined, and confined to rather commonplace works," was somewhat one side of the points at issue. There was a feeling, too, that Dr. McCosh could not well appreciate the burdens which Dr. Hopkins had had to carry in the management of the isolated college, burdens that were pressing upon him at that time with peculiar weight, and that there was a note of insular pride in the remark quoted above not quite worthy of the high discussion. However that may be, Dr. Hopkins's reply to this remark was in the best of taste, and was at the same time quite pungent. He says: "While I acknowledge fully the want of reading referred to by Dr. McCosh and regret it, I may be permitted to say that on this subject he has presented no point that I had not seen, and has raised no objection that I had not considered."

The main point at issue between these two eminent thinkers was the foundation of the obligation

---

[1] A criticism by Dr. McCosh on Hutcheson's system may be well quoted here as showing the same tendency in his thought as in that of Dr. Hopkins. Dr. McCosh says: "Hutcheson's theory of virtue thus comes to be an exalted kind of eudæmonism, with God giving us a moral sense to approve of the promotion of happiness without our discovering the consequences of actions." *The Scottish Philosophy.* p. 80.

to do right felt by every thoughtful mind. With Dr. McCosh, in the search for a foundation there could really be no answer to the question, "Why ought I to love my fellow-men? Why ought I to love God and to love Him more than I love even my fellow-men? To *us*, whatever there may be to higher intelligence, there can be no answer but one, and that is, that I ought to do so. And if any one puts the other question, 'How do I come to know this?' there is but one answer, and this is that it is self evident." In other words, "an action is right because it is right, and that is the end of it."

Dr. Hopkins was not contented with that view. He had long held it, and pleasantly says to his former pupils in his introduction to the "Lectures on Moral Science:" "When the lectures were first written, the text-book here and generally in our colleges was Paley; not agreeing with him, and failing to carry out fully the doctrine of ends, I adopted that of an ultimate right as taught by Kant and Coleridge, making that the end. If, therefore, any of you still hold that view, as doubtless many do, it is not for me to say that you have not good authority for it, or to complain if you object to that now taken."

Working out his doctrine of the "conditioning and conditioned" under the principle that all rational action is for an end, he came to the position that "a reason can always be given why an action is right, and that without a sensibility the quality of right in an action regarded as moral could not exist." "In seeking the foundation of obligation, I suppose moral beings to exist. As having intelligence and sensibility, I suppose them capable of apprehending ends good in themselves, and an end thus good that is ultimate and supreme. In the apprehension of such an end, I suppose the moral reason must affirm obligation to choose it, and that all acts that will, of their own nature, lead to the attainment of that end are right."[1]

Dr. McCosh took exception to Dr. Hopkins's position that because "a good" or "the good" results from right action, or, in other words, because all action arising under the choice of an ultimate and supreme end would issue in the highest good to the individual choosing and to all others, that therefore the good is the highest ultimate end. There was to him a savor of low origin to a good that would in our language express both enjoyment and blessedness. Nor will he judge Dr. Hopkins free from a taint of "utilitarianism," though Dr. Hopkins affirms that he does not mean our own good exclusively, but "that of all conscious beings." Dr. Hopkins repels the significance of that charge adroitly. For him there is nothing objectionable in the thing utilitarianism, "unless it opposes self to love and happiness to duty." He does not mind being called a utilitarian, if only he is clearly understood to require disinterested love, supremely that of God and the love of the neigh-

---

[1] *Law of Love and Love as a Law,* first edition, p. 26.

bor as ourselves; provided also it is seen that he holds it "absurd to suppose that anything could excuse a man from doing what he ought to do." Having, then, shown that in his view of love and also of duty there is no "objectionable" utilitarianism, he proceeds to show that his system in which these two, love and duty, are married, is also free from the taint. He insists, however, on returning to the main question, which is not about the categorical imperative: "Not at all about uncompromising obedience or duty, when that is made known, but whether the very idea of duty is possible except through that of a good from the sensibility and so of a possible love." He laments the lack in our language of a word that shall compass the whole range of feeling, but will not budge one iota from his position that "sensibility is the condition precedent of all moral ideas." He seizes Dr. McCosh's illustration that seems intended to prove that there may be virtue without sensibility, and finds it a *reductio ad absurdum.* Nor can any one deny that his treatment of the illustration is perfectly fair and just. Dr. Hopkins says, referring to Dr. McCosh and quoting his very words, "He puts the case that God creates an angelic being with high intellectual endowments, but without sensibility, and then affirms and founds a principle on it, that such a being would be under obligation to be grateful to God, while yet gratitude is a form of the sensibility, and obligation itself cannot be conceived of without it."

Dr. McCosh seems to see the point on "sensibility" and "gratitude," for in his next paper his "intelligent being" is endowed at the outset by God with "lofty reason, pure fancy, and rich emotions." This intelligent moral being should cherish "gratitude and love towards his benefactor."

After Dr. Hopkins has thus defended his own theory, he proceeds to attack that of Dr. McCosh, and to assert that the system based on an ultimate right is not consistent with the Scriptures. Taking the law of love, he affirms that "the love is to be a simple primitive act in view of the object as worthy of love." Dr. McCosh denies this, and asserts: "We regard God as having a claim upon our love, because it is right and men see it to be so at once." "No," says Dr. Hopkins, "we do not love Him because it is right, but because He is worthy of our love." "If we love God not for his own sake but for the sake of the right, we put right above God." Then growing warm in his attack he adds: "I have seen quite enough of this abstract, hard, godless. loveless love of right and virtue, instead of the love of God and of men." "Wherever this system has been fully received, it has tended to fanaticism."

Hereupon he makes an assertion that Dr. McCosh seems in his reply to disprove. In his absolute faith in the reasonableness of his doctrine and its harmony with the Scriptures he says: "The Scriptures nowhere command me to do right because it is right." "Do they not?" says Dr. McCosh.

"Does not Paul say, 'Children, obey your parents in the Lord, for this is right,' just, due?" But perhaps the appearance here is only an appearance. Dr. Hopkins replies: "The passage quoted by Dr. McCosh is the only one in the Bible that seems to say we are 'to do right because it is right,' but that does not say it, and scarcely seems to. If it said that, no further question could be asked. The theory of morals would be settled. What it does say is, that children should obey their parents because it is right, and that leaves the question, why is it right to obey parents? where it was before." Dr. McCosh had made the words "just," "due" the equivalent of "right" in the text quoted. Was it quite fair to intimate that "just" and "due" had the same meaning as "right" in the discussion? If so, it would seem that every other apostolic adjective expressing what is praiseworthy is equally tantamount to "right." "Honest," "lovely," "pure," of "good report," are these too "right"? If so, on Dr. McCosh's principles we can give no analysis of these virtues, what is right is right, what is honest is honest, and "that is the end of it."

Dr. Hopkins appeals to the whole tenor of the Scriptures. "Our Saviour opened the Sermon on the Mount and every beatitude by speaking of blessedness." On the whole, the appeal to the Scripture seems to support Dr. Hopkins, but Dr. McCosh, in his final allusion to this point, insists that "the word of God in its spirit and letter opposes that theory which makes man's highest end to be enjoyment." Did Dr. Hopkins ever say that man's highest end is enjoyment? Is it a fair inference from any of his statements, even in the first edition of the book (in the revised edition such an inference is most carefully warded off), that the end, the highest end, of man is sensitive enjoyment? Does not the following passage, candidly considered, render such an inference impossible? "I will only add that where moral order reigns, good from all forms of sensibility is distributed according to character; that though a man may be called to oppose for a time his moral convictions to all that he can suffer through natural sensibility, yet that this cannot be permanent under a righteous moral government; and that the good of each is so a part of the whole that obligation on the part of any individual to sacrifice his own highest good for the sake of the whole is not only impossible, but, as impairing the very ground on which obligation is affirmed, is absurd."[1]

How can a man "oppose for a time his moral convictions to all that he can suffer through natural sensibility," if his highest end is sensitive enjoyment?

At the close of Dr. McCosh's second paper there are very grave intimations of heterodoxy in regard to the doctrines of eschatology as flowing from the theory which he is combating. They are intimations only, as "it would weary the readers of a pop-

---

[1] *Law of Love and Love as a Law*, first edition, p. 121.

ular newspaper" to have these consequences fully unfolded. But inasmuch as the requirement of unhesitating obedience, the moment obligation is affirmed, is insisted upon by Dr. Hopkins, and as "justice that has its basis in love justifies itself to itself even in becoming indignation and wrath," it is somewhat difficult to see how these departures from orthodoxy are a necessary outgrowth of the theory. While Dr. Hopkins would not shrink from discussing consequences, if anything were to be gained by such discussion, he prefers once more to call his opponent back to the real point. "Let the question be decided on its merits, that is the only fair way; and to aid our readers in doing that has been my endeavor in the preceding discussion."

In Dr. McCosh's final summing up he makes six points of difference between himself and Dr. Hopkins. The first refers to the relation of an end to the sensibility. Dr. Hopkins had said that "if we suppose the sensibility excluded, the conception of an end is impossible." This Dr. McCosh denies, but admits that "holy enjoyment" may be a supreme end. As Dr. Hopkins notes, there can be but one supreme end, and if Dr. McCosh allows that "holy enjoyment" may be a supreme end, his antagonism to Dr. Hopkins on the first point is essentially modified.

The second divergence relates to the mode of settling the question. Dr. McCosh says that it must be settled "by an inquiry into the mental and moral nature," and thinks Dr. Hopkins does not admit this, and leaves out the higher nature, the moral reason, in attempting to solve the problem of ethics. But he returns to the first point, and expresses new amazement at Dr. Hopkins's statement that "apart from sensibility the conception of an end is impossible."

The second point is not essentially different from the first.

The third point of disagreement is that Dr. Hopkins gives a "confused place" to the moral reason. Dr. McCosh's position "makes the sense of duty to enter into the virtuous act and become part of the end." Dr. Hopkins makes the sense of duty "enter into the act to give it quality, but not as a part of the end." Dr. Hopkins's claim that "the end must be known before the sense of duty can be originated" may give the moral reason a "confused place" for one who believes in "ultimate right," but the making of right a part of the end as "the supreme end" will not seem less "confused" to one who has really grasped the complete harmony which follows the acceptance of "the supreme good of all" as the end of virtuous action. It may turn out that the benevolence of God can only be maintained under this theory.

The fourth difference relates to the quality of an action as a ground of obligation to perform the action. Do we perform a just action simply because it is just, or is there underneath the obligation a perception that the doing of justice will promote always and everywhere the best good of all? It is the application to practical action of the main point at issue.

Under the fifth point Dr. McCosh admits that "we are bound as much as within us lies to promote the happiness of all beings capable of joy or sorrow." But he says there is a moral element in this "we are *bound*," and revolts at the idea of loving God "in the view of the capacity of God and other beings for enjoyment." Dr. Hopkins replies with great energy to this that "if God were as incapable of sensibility as a rock and so incapable of enjoyment, it would be impossible for us to love Him with the love of benevolence, the only love commanded."

To the final point made by Dr. McCosh, which is that the Scriptures are on his side, Dr. Hopkins replies with great earnestness, as it is his final word. Several of the sentences are worth quoting: "In immediate connection, Dr. McCosh speaks of *sensitive* pain and *sensitive* enjoyment, as if they were the basis of my system. I trust I have said nothing to justify this. I am no sensationalist, but a believer in the highest form of intuitional and spiritual philosophy. I am no utilitarian. I believe in a good that is good in itself and to be sought for its own sake! and in disinterested love of beings who are capable of happiness, quite as much, too, as if they were not. In my two books I have examined the constitution of man in its relation both to nature and the Bible. I have found from that, that the law of the constitution is the law of the Bible. That law — *the law of love* — I accept and endeavor to enforce, simply that. I build no half-way house. I bring in nothing 'surreptitiously.' I steal no element. I do not subordinate virtue to happiness, but find a harmony between them. . . . I simply find the moral law, the one law for myself and for all others, impersonal and impartial, and have as little to do with this terrible enjoyment as is possible under a law that requires me to promote it in its purest form and in the highest degree." [1]

The debate excited great interest, and was in every way worthy of its subject and of the disputants. It was upon the theory of virtue, between two thinkers who had spent a great part of their lives in the noblest efforts to train young men to the acceptance of Christianity and to the exhibition of Christian character. It was perhaps regarded by the pupils of each as ended to the advantage of their own teacher. The progress of truth is always attended by controversies, and it is fortunate indeed when, as in this case, each of the disputants can recognize from the beginning to the end of the conflict the honorable motives and lofty purposes of the other. The acceptance of the doctrine of ends as here applied is probably becoming more general, and the wonder may yet be that a doctrine so simple and so harmonious with the other facts of man's nature should ever have been difficult of

---

[1] This discussion is published as an appendix to Dr Hopkins's *The Law of Love and Love as a Law*, revised edition.

acceptance for minds of philosophic power. The tenacity with which the ablest minds cling to a position once assumed illustrates at once the strength and the weakness of human nature. A fundamental opinion enters into all other opinions, and gives color and coherence to the general thinking, and this coherence reinforces the fundamental belief.

In the preface to the revised edition of "The Law of Love and Love as a Law," published in 1881, Dr. Hopkins speaks of the changes introduced into the book, and assigns reasons for them. One of these reasons rested upon a desire to bring the book into greater harmony with "An Outline Study of Man," which had been published since the first edition was issued. Another reason for some changes arose from the conviction that the method of teaching by diagrams which had been adopted in later years in the psychological work might profitably be carried over into moral science. He adds a third reason, a wish "by giving the system more unity to state it, so that it might be more readily apprehended."

In spite of this definitely formed purpose some will be inclined to doubt whether the foundation of the system is made clearer in the revised than in the first edition. To the chapters on "obligation" in the first edition, any one who wishes an understanding of the initial principles may well be referred. The cogency with which the sensibility is presented as underlying all moral ideas, and with

which a good, as an end, is shown to be a condition
for obligation, is not surpassed, if equaled, in any
of the subsequent discussion of the questions involved.

The criticisms of Dr. McCosh did not in the
least affect his confidence in the truth of the system, and probably did not affect his presentation
of it. But the fine passage on the marrying of
"Love and Law," quoted by Dr. McCosh from
page 108 of the first edition, loses something of its
freshness in the revised edition. The revision
made the system more systematic, a completer,
rounder whole, but scarcely more winning or more
convincing to the beginner. For the readers who
gained by long acquaintance with Dr. Hopkins
insight into the movement of his mind and increasing admiration and affection for the solidity
of his character, there is scarcely any book of his
making so interesting, and scarcely any that exhibits so distinctly, that combination of intellectual
sharpness and conciseness and enthusiasm which
marks his best writing as the first edition of this
treatise.

"An Outline Study of Man," published in 1873,
like Dr. Hopkins's other books, grew directly out
of his teaching. The substance of it had been delivered as lectures before the Lowell Institute the
previous year. These lectures were given in an informal way, and a phonographic report formed the
basis of the book. It illustrates more perfectly,
perhaps, than any other book the method of his

teaching. By short, concise definitions and differentiations perfectly simple and clear, he made the progress of the pupil easy and sure. This book more than any other exhibits a resemblance in mind and character that has seemed to me to exist in him to the German Lessing. Lessing was a great teacher. The debt of the Germans to him for services in giving correct canons for language and literature is immense. Dr. Hopkins cannot be regarded as a pioneer of influence anything like so vast, and was greatly inferior in learning. But he went on his own feet in a straight path, as did Lessing, and accepted the tenets of no master. He had the luminous intelligence that comes from the pure reason, and it was the play of this that made his discourse so convincing and satisfying. Something of what Lowell says of Johnson and Lessing was also undoubtedly true of Dr. Hopkins. "Both had something of the intellectual sluggishness that is apt to go with great strength; and both had to be baited by the antagonism of circumstances or opinions, not only into the exhibition, but into the possession of their entire force. Both may be more properly called original men than in the highest sense original writers."

Dr. Hopkins had a spiritual insight that lifted him into a region whose air Lessing did not breathe. Lessing did not concern himself with man as a fallen being, but chiefly with literature and art. For all that his thought was so largely of the beautiful and the true, the general impression of his character, while thoroughly manly, was not so beneficent as that of the simple college president.

In the "Outline," the discussion of Perception and Consciousness, the distinction made between the natural and the supernatural, that between the supernatural and the miraculous, and the division of the necessary products into three classes, those arising in the intellect alone, those resulting from the combined operation of intellect and feeling, and those from intellect, sensibility, and will, are among the newer points of the book, and show well the author's power of illumination. The diagrams in the book, and particularly that at the end, were of great value in his judgment, and are extremely interesting as presenting the absolute definiteness with which man's nature and powers were graduated in his mind. The wide use of the book in schools and colleges, especially in those institutions where students not highly trained by severe discipline undertake the examination of the mental constitution, attests the great clearness of the presentation. Its brief examination of the body as the dwelling-place of mind is the author's anticipation of the modern "Physiological Psychology." The book does not leave the student in the fog that accompanies so much of the learned teaching of intellectual philosophy. A thorough mastery of this treatise has been of immense service to many college graduates, and though it may be said that Dr. Hopkins's students did not many of them become specialists in philosophy, it has not been said that they did not become men.

From "The Scriptural Idea of Man," the last important work published by Dr. Hopkins, quotations have already been given. This book is his final contribution to the exhibition of the harmony of Scripture with reason, and is the ripest fruit of his thinking. It has a unique value, and to it the student of his thought may be referred for proof that he, like Lessing, was ever advancing and gaining new apprehension of many-sided truth, but that, unlike any mere metaphysician or scholar, he had early found in the revelation culminating in "the man, Christ Jesus," such perfection of wisdom and reason that all growth meant simply a fuller apprehension of the divine Master. To this book further references will be made in a later chapter.

Before Dr. Hopkins left New Haven after the delivery of the lectures on "The Scriptural Idea of Man," the faculty of the Theological Seminary invited him to give another course of lectures the following year. After some hesitation he accepted the invitation, and prepared and delivered six lectures on "The Scriptural Idea of God." These lectures, dealing with the most profound questions, are equal in scope and power to any of his earlier work. They were, however, never published, as there were certain points which he planned to develop more perfectly, and thus to give the series a more symmetrical unity. Perhaps the fact that certain points of the discussions appear in some of his other works tended to delay the revision. It will be naturally a source of regret to all Dr. Hopkins's pupils that the lectures are not accessible as a companion volume to "The Scriptural Idea of Man," and a final expression of his views on the nature and attributes of God.

> " As snow those inward pleadings fall,
> As soft, as bright, as pure, as cool,
> With gentle weight and gradual
> And sink into the feverish soul."
> CARDINAL NEWMAN, *St. Philip in his God.*

THE PREACHER.

" The riddle of the world is understood
      Only by him who feels that God is good,
      As only he can feel who makes his love
      The ladder of faith, and climbs above
      On th' rounds of his best instincts ; draws no line
      Between mere human goodness and divine,
      But, judging God by what in him is best,
      With a child's trust leans on a Father's breast,
      And hears unmoved the old creeds babble still
      Of kingly power and dread caprice of will,
      Chary of blessing, prodigal of curse,
      The pitiless doomsman of the universe.
      Can Hatred ask for love ?   Can Selfishness
      Invite to self-denial ?   Is He less
      Than man in kindly dealing ?   Can He break
      His own great law of fatherhood, forsake
      And curse His children ?   Not for earth and heaven
      Can separate tables of the law be given.
      No rule can bind which He himself denies ;
      The truths of time are not eternal lies."

WHITTIER, *In Quest.*

CHAPTER VIII.

DR. HOPKINS early learned to think in the presence of an audience. His preaching in the college chapel was uniformly extemporaneous, and was often strikingly effective from the combination of close logical thought and apt illustration. Some of the students, when I was in college, took notes of his sermons, which were then quite uniformly doctrinal, and wrote them out fully. Doctrinal preaching for undergraduates seems now less suitable than formerly, and it was certainly an evidence of great power that Sunday after Sunday Dr. Hopkins, when president, preached a solid, logical sermon, and kept the attention of the students. Those sermons were an education to some of the maturer boys, and now and then an impression was made that was never forgotten. The critical and skeptical books of the time were often touched upon, not always by name, but always with a keenness that excited discussion among those who understood the allusions. His written sermons, of which the best examples are those preached before the graduating classes, are among the finest illustrations of his skill as a writer and his power as a thinker.

The baccalaureate sermon has been a distinctive

feature of the New England college, and of the colleges modeled after it. As it has commonly been preached by the highest officer of the college, and is the last formal act of instruction given to a body of young men who have spent together four formative years in liberal study, it has served to mark the high estimate put upon religious instruction by our fathers, and to exhibit in a concrete way their purpose to subordinate all training to Christian doctrine and life. Few scenes are more impressive than when, even though a graduating class is not very large, a president, eminent for learning and glowing with love for the divine Master, whose daily life has been among and in his pupils, having put into one compact utterance some deep lesson suggested by the studies of the year, delivers this lesson on the last Sunday of the academical year to his retiring pupils, and enforces it by a personal and practical charge to conform the life to its meaning. Such a sermon is almost certain to issue in an exaltation of the divine Christ as the true friend, example, and Redeemer. The momentous possibilities lying before the young men, the throng of memories for them from the past, the near dissolution of precious companionships, the pathetic significance of what might have been, touch the imagination of the observer, and give for all to the last lesson great dignity and tenderness.

The delivery of one of these sermons by Dr. Hopkins was always an event of great interest to those who had once heard him in this relation. In this act he seemed to gather up and concentrate his greatness, and to become an incarnation of the highest ideal of the wise teacher.

The gradual transformation of the presidential office into a career of simple administration may sweep away much of the Christian influence of the old New England president. In no feature is the loss to be more marked than in the substitution of some distinguished pastor for the counselor and guide of the Senior year, in this last solemn act of instruction.

There was a calmness and dignity, an equipoise of intellect and emotion, in the baccalaureate discourses delivered by Dr. Hopkins that made them strikingly effective. The perfect taste and keen perception of beauty that tempered the sterner logical processes of his mind never shone out more clearly than when he was delivering these last words to a company of his pupils. The symmetry of his nature found perhaps its freest expression in these sermons, and they will give to one who carefully studies them a good idea of his intellectual and moral insight. They were highly intellectual: but they exhibit intellectual elements of the highest order, gaining effectiveness for the reason that these elements were charged with love.

In the sermon delivered to the class of 1855 on "Perfect Love" are the following words, that give in no uncertain tone the secret of his own power as an investigator and teacher: —

"It is a prejudice, as disastrous as it is unfounded, that there can be a schism between the heart and the intellect to the advantage of either. The world is not ready to receive it, but it lies in our structure, and must ultimately appear that the love of God is the highest ground of enthusiasm, not only in the study of his word, but of his works. They may indeed be studied from curiosity, from ambition, from a desire even to disprove the being or the moral government of God; and thus we may have sharp disputations, dogmatical partisans of theories; but the genial, patient, comprehensive, all-reconciling thinker will be most often found where the pale and dry light of intellect is tempered by the warm glow of love. How can he who has no love interpret a universe that originated in love? The works of God are all expressions of his attributes, and thoughts, and feelings. Through them we may commune with him. So far as there is thought in the works of God, it is his thought. He it is that through uniformities and resemblances and tendencies whispers into the ear of a philosophy, not falsely so called, its sublime truths: and as we begin to feel and trace more and more those lines of relation that bind all things into one system, the touch of any one of which may vibrate to the fixed stars, this communion becomes high and thrilling. Science is no longer cold. It lives and breathes and glows, and in the ear of love its voice is always a hymn to the Creator."

It has been a tenet of scientific thinkers, enforced especially in the last decade or two, that the clear light of intellect is to be brought to bear upon the problems of life and mind and society without any intermixture of feeling. It has been claimed that all judgments, to the formation of which feeling has contributed, are of doubtful value, not to say valueless, and that the dry, cool intelligence, utterly dissociated from preferences and satisfactions, is the only fit guide in the labyrinth of modern investigation. The breathing of this rarefied ether is possible indeed for few, but those few, unaffected by the weaknesses of common men, unmoved by sympathies that are incipient prejudices, are the only true leaders for the race. The passage above quoted illustrates how far removed from such thought, how anticipative of its influence, and how distrustful of its hardness was the mind of Dr. Hopkins. To the question, "How can he, who has no love, interpret a universe that originated in love?" he knew that the agnostic would answer, "How do you know that it originated in love? This is the point at issue." To him Dr. Hopkins would have replied: "Your difficulty is in your philosophy. The dry light of intellect cannot be employed, purified of all feeling; it cannot be employed successfully, defecated of all admiration of beauty, or reverence for goodness. If you make your search through nature and human society and history, inspired by those feelings, you will reach results, and know realities." "He that loveth not, knoweth not God, for God is love."

The sermon on "Spirit, Soul, and Body" was not

written until 1869, but it is a more perfect development of the ideas that underlie the discourse from which the quotation just given was taken. In this sermon he lays down with great clearness the doctrine which he believed that he found in the Pauline epistles, that the immediate knowledge of moral law and a personal God is gained by distinctly spiritual apprehension. He held that the soul with its recognition of the truths of reason, with reasoning power, with the wonderful advantages given by language, is that part of man's nature by which progress in arts, in sciences, in literature, in civilization, can be, under favorable conditions, rapidly made. Under the guidance of the soul science may be both empirical and rational, but cannot be theological or, more exactly, spiritual. Art and literature may reach an almost or quite perfect condition, as seen in Greek sculpture and poetry, but it may be questioned whether even into the best examples of their perfection something of a religious nature from the spiritual realm is not introduced.

Certainly, religion as such, having in it such dependence on higher being as shall involve faith, worship, and the regulation of conduct, requires a personal relation to a person. What takes the place of religion in those nations and individuals who do not develop the spiritual apprehension, but direct their energies to the tracing simply of the natural man, the soul, is finely exhibited in the following passage. "Religion: what need have

we of that? God: what need of Him? Have we
not force, uniform force, and do not all things continue as they were from the beginning of the creation, if it ever had a beginning? Have we not the
τὸ πᾶν, the universal all, the soul of the universe
working itself up from unconsciousness through
molecules, and maggots, and mice, and marmots,
and monkeys to its highest culmination in man?
Certainly, no God is needed; a miracle is impossible; or if possible, it cannot be proved even by the
senses, and the idea of a revelation is absurd. If
the religious nature must find some resting-place,
let it make the unconscious universe with its sleep-
ing capabilities its god: or let it frame to itself
the conception of a god whose work is finished, and
who is enjoying himself in everlasting repose.
This is indeed just what those who practically ignore the spirit have always done and are doing now.
Yearning and groping after something higher, yet
recognizing only necessary relations as in mathematics and the uniform and unconscious forces of
nature, they transfer what they thus find, and only
that, over to the infinite. Of this the result may
reveal itself in different forms and under different
names. In India it may be Brahminism or Bud-
dhism. In Germany it may be transcendentalism,
or positivism, or pantheism. In this country it
may be a humble imitation and jumble of them all:
but the thing itself and its paralyzing effect on the
religious character will be essentially the same,
whether at Benares, at Berlin, or at Boston."

The themes of these discourses were always lofty, and the hearer was never allowed to lose sight of the loftiness of the theme. Nor did he ever feel that the treatment was not wholly worthy of the theme. In the passage first quoted the glory of nature is asserted to reveal itself to the loving intellect. In the following passage from the discourse on "Strength and Beauty" the transcending charm of the affections is emphasized. The elements of beauty in character have been given as "spontaneity," "moral rectitude," and "symmetry." "With these elements individual mind possesses a beauty far transcending that of nature, and if this be so in a single individual, how much more in a spiritual system, where every relation is responded to and every duty met! What is the harmony of music to the concord of souls in true affection? What is the breaking up of light into its seven colors, as it meets with the surfaces of matter, compared with the modifications of benevolence, as it meets with the varying forms of sensitive and intelligent life? What is the beauty of natural scenery, with its clustering objects, and contrasted flowers and trees, compared with the meeting of a family, upon no member of which a stain rests, and where you see the gray hairs of the patriarch, and the infant of the third generation? What is the beauty of satellites circling around primaries, and primaries around the sun, compared with the order of families and the state — compared with the order of that moral government, of which

God is the centre and sun, and of which a holy love is at once the uniting force and the glory and beauty?"

The following passage from the sermon to the class of 1862 is closely related to the passages already quoted. It presents the true object of God's creation both of matter and of mind, that He might have conscious subjects in loving obedience to himself and in active coöperation with Him in promoting righteousness. "This life is in Christ. He is 'the life.' This bond is from Him. In Him are condensed all human relationships as of 'brother and sister and mother:' and to these, higher and holier, that of Saviour is added. In Him, as the second Adam; in his matchless character, human, yet divine; in his all-embracing and self-sacrificing love; in Him as the champion of humanity in its weakness and guilt, able and willing to bring succor in the hour of its direst need and to raise it up from the darkness and the dust of death, there is every requisite for a centre of unity for the race so that 'all things which are on earth' as well as 'those which are in heaven' may be gathered together in one, even in Him." In this, in this only, is there an object worthy of God. He has created worlds, and families of worlds of mere matter, and given them a unity of unspeakable grandeur; but without sensation or recognition, without enjoyment or praise, what would they be worth? Nothing. No, the only work worthy of God is one crowned by creatures made in his image, with their vitality from Him, and himself the centre of their unity — unity in love, fitly represented by the marriage union. This work, we believe, will correspond in its vastness to that of the stellar hosts, and as far transcend them in glory as mind transcends the inanimate clod. It will embrace all orders of rational intelligences, in all worlds; sin and its consequences will be eliminated, and it shall stand in its glorious order forever. The promised new heavens and new earth do not so much respect any new combinations and unity of matter as of conscious agents; and they will be such that all that has gone before in the works of God will be as nothing. 'For behold,' says God, 'I create new heavens and new earth; and the former shall not be remembered nor come into mind. But be ye glad and rejoice forever in that which I create; for behold I create Jerusalem a rejoicing and her people a joy.' "

As the final words to his classes, whose characteristics from year to year were somewhat similar, and yet always more or less different, but whose moral character was always the matter of the deepest solicitude to him, he never failed to make these discourses vigorously ethical. Eloquent passages of ethical import are found in them, which cannot fail to have remained in the memory when much of the discourse was forgotten. In the sermon on "Strength and Beauty," from which a quotation has already been given, there is a striking passage on the impotence of high gifts to dignify or palliate badness of character: —

"The distinction is that between the agent and the instrument, between a person giving direction and that which is directed. The relative place of these is to be carefully noted, because of the peculiar difficulty there is in the present moral state of the world in combining talent and genius with a high and reverent regard for duty. This is not that there is any natural opposition between them, but because the administration and influence which are so dear to men possessing talent and genius are expected to follow them without much reference to moral integrity. Now what we say is that we are not to overestimate the mere instrument, however brilliant. We say that our chief regard is due to that sacred personality, that moral presence, which has both the power and the right to direct talent and genius, and before which it is their place to wait and to bow. We say that in any other relation talent is a curse, and that the light of genius can only 'lead to bewilder, and dazzle to blind.' We would honor genius and talent as gifts of God; we would make large allowance, if they must have them, or think they must, for their peculiarities, their idiosyncrasies, their weaknesses even; but when those who possess them would regard themselves, and be regarded by others, as privileged persons, whose moral delinquencies are to be allowed or winked at, and that, too, on the very ground that should be their highest condemnation, we would utter our solemn protest. We say that the influence of no other men can be so hostile to the best interests of the community, if they be public men, to the liberties of a free people. We say that no rebuke can be too prompt or severe, when any man would practically dignify or even palliate meanness, or trickery, or falsehood, or profaneness, or licentiousness, or corruption, by associating them with high intellectual gifts."

In the sermon to the class of 1864 occur the following solemn, noble words on the intimate relation between character and destiny. "Settle it therefore, I pray you, my hearers, once and forever, that as your character is, so will your destiny be. Whatever capacities there may be for enjoyment or for suffering in this strange being of ours, and God only knows what they are, they will be drawn out wholly in accordance with character. There shall be no inheritance of possessions, or felicity of outward condition, no river of life, or gate of pearl, or street of gold; there shall be no serenity of peace, or fullness of joy, or height of rapture, or ecstasy of love; there shall be no hostile and vengeful element, no lake of fire, no gnawing worm, no remorse or despair, that will not depend upon character."

In the last baccalaureate that he preached, in June, 1872, the year when he laid down his presidency, there was a peculiarly touching appeal for fidelity in the discharge of humble duties. This passes over into an affectionate entreaty to follow Christ, and is enforced by a tender reference to the death of his brother Albert, which had occurred the previous month. The subject is "The Circular and the Onward Movement."

"What man is this who is so earnestly at work in the very humble employment of making a fine powder still more fine by constant attrition? It is Michael Angelo, grinding the paints with which he is to paint for eternity. The humble duties must be done; the paints must be ground; but they will be ground all the better, if we feel that we are to paint for eternity with them. There are duties towards God, indispensable, the highest of all, but they can never be performed in the willful disregard or neglect of any duty toward man. You are never to forget that the best preparation for heaven is in that character which will fit you for the greatest usefulness on earth.

"Since, then, the problems — the great problems in life — that come from the intersection and blending of the circular and onward movements are solved theoretically by Christianity; and since, through that, you can make the most practically of the interests involved in each movement, the one thing needful for you is to be Christians. At this hour, when you are about to step into active life, and when so many voices are calling you, the one voice which you are to hear is that of Him who says, '*Follow Me.*' Hear that voice, and then you will take your places under his banner by the side of those who are waging with Him the great battle of all time. It is around Him that the thick of this battle has always been. Around Him it always will be. Take, then, your places. You are needed. The veterans are falling. Who shall take their place? The strong men are fainting. Who shall succor them? Go ye, and the earth shall be the better and the happier for your having lived in it. Go; and when the time of your departure shall come, you will be able to say what he said, who has been a standard-bearer in this college for more than forty years, and for whom both its chapel and this desk are now draped in mourning. When consciously dying, and but just able to speak, he said, 'If we view it Scripturally, death is but stepping out of one room in our Father's house into another; and, in this instance, without doubt, into a larger and pleasanter room.'"

Dr. Hopkins's greatest theme was always the universal relations of Christianity. This was the deepest motive of all his eloquence, if I might say so, the pre-moving inspiration of all his public utterances. This gave the peculiar scope and effectiveness to those extemporaneous addresses before the meetings of the American Board which never failed to impress deeply the audiences who heard them. The universality of Christ's love, the all-embracing sweep of his death, found expression in connection with nearly every topic. His preaching was Christian preaching in the broadest and truest sense. In the sermon to the class of 1852, on "Receiving and Giving," he speaks of Christ and his giving in language that rises to a strain of lofty eloquence. "He gave, not as he gives whom giving does not impoverish, but He gave of his heart's blood, till that heart ceased to beat. He planted his cross in the midst of the mad and roaring current of selfishness aggravated to malignity, and uttered from it the mighty cry of expiring love. All the waters heard Him, and from that moment they began to be refluent about his cross. From that moment a current deeper and broader and mightier began to set heavenward, and it will continue to be deeper and broader and mightier, till its glad waters shall encompass the earth and toss themselves as the ocean. And not alone did earth hear that cry. It pierced the regions of immensity. Heaven heard it, and hell heard it, and the remotest star shall hear it, testifying to the love of God in his unspeakable gift, and to the supremacy of that blessedness of giving which could be reached only through death, — the death of the cross. This joy of giving it was that was set before Him, for which He endured the cross, despising the shame."

The sermon to the class of 1856 on "Self-denial" was naturally an exposition of the Christian life. At the very outset of the discourse there is a breaking forth of this thought of wide relations in a comparison of Christianity to the atmosphere. "The atmosphere evaporates water, distributes it, reflects light, bears up birds, wafts ships, supports combustion, conveys sound, is the breath of our life, and the azure of our heavens. So Christianity, while it magnifies the law, and enthrones mercy, and reconciles us to God, and makes known to principalities and powers in the heavenly places his manifold wisdom, is also the regulating and renovating spirit in the relations of time. It alone inspires and guides progress; for the progress of man is movement towards God, and movement towards God will insure a gradual unfolding of all that exalts and adorns man. It excludes malignity, subdues selfishness, regulates the passions, subordinates the appetites, quickens the intellect, exalts the affections. It promotes industry, honesty, truth, purity, kindness. It humbles the proud, exalts the lowly, upholds law, favors liberty, is essential to it, and would unite men in one great brotherhood. It is the breath of life to our social and civil well-being here, and spreads the azure of the heaven into whose unfathomable depths the eye of faith loves to look. All this it does, while yet its great object is in the future. The river passes on, but the trees upon its banks are green and bear fruit."

It was in the addresses to the classes, concluding these sermons, that Dr. Hopkins often expressed plainly the deeper feelings of his nature. There was something in his mind that always recognized and emphasized the dramatic significance of events and crises. The sending forth of a body of young men whose maturer thought he had for a year so closely watched and guided was always to him something more than the simple termination of a college course. It connected itself in his mind, for each graduating student, with all the future, and the final words were always fitly chosen. Sometimes a peculiar relation of the year gave an added interest and depth to his expression, as, for instance, in 1862, when his second son was graduated, who looked forward with some others to immediate service in the war for the Union.

"Are any of you, as some are, in seeking to sustain those 'powers that be,' and that 'are ordained of God,' to encounter the temptations of a camp, the exposure of a southern climate, the hazards of the battlefield? How precious will be the presence and succor of One that sticketh closer than a brother! Are you to bear the responsibilities of life and wage its battles till old age? Little do you know of your weakness and of the besetments and fierce struggles of the long way, if a divine Helper would not be precious to you. He will be precious to you in the final hour. When you shall walk through the valley of the shadow of death, his rod and his staff, they shall comfort you. And when the present order shall come to an end, and that building of God whose stones are now preparing shall go up without the sound of the axe or the hammer, till 'the headstone thereof shall be brought forth with shoutings,' you shall be there, and cry, 'Grace, grace unto it.'"

So there is a touching allusion to the death of a nephew, the son of his brother, who had been for three years a member of the class of 1864, and had fallen a victim to the rebellion at Ashland only a few months previously, in the address to this class.

A peculiar beauty and sweetness is in the farewell words to the class of 1872, the last of thirty-six classes graduated under Dr. Hopkins's presidency. A quotation has already been given from that impressive sermon, and the farewell address follows immediately after the words of that quotation: —

"And now, my beloved friends, the time has come when, in some respects, that which has been is to be no longer. Not only is the peculiar and most pleasant relation which has existed between us the past year to cease, but also the relation which I have so long held to this college. During the thirty-six years of that relation I have failed but twice, once from sickness and once from absence, to address each successive class as I now address you. Hereafter other classes will come, another voice will address them, the circular movement will go on, but you and I pass into the onward movement, you to your work, and I to what remains to me of mine. Behind us is that past, fixed forever, which God will require. Before us — what? Definitely I know not ; but I do know that there is One above us whom we may safely trust. I do know that 'God is love.' Whatever else I hold on to, or give up, I will hold on to that. That I will not give up. To the God of love, therefore, who has hitherto been so much better to me than my fears, do I commit myself;

to the God of love do I commend you, every one of you, praying that in all your pilgrimage He will bless you and keep you; that 'He will make his face shine upon you, and be gracious unto you; that He will lift up his countenance upon you, and give you peace.'"

THE PRESIDENT OF THE AMERICAN BOARD OF COMMISSIONERS FOR FOREIGN MISSIONS.

" Yet there is one I more affect
    Than Jesuit, Hermit, Monk, or Friar:
    'T is an old man of sweet aspect,
    I love him more, I more desire.

" I know him by his head of snow,
    His ready smile, his keen full eye,
    His words which kindle as they flow,
    Save he be rapt in ecstasy."
            CARDINAL NEWMAN, *St. Philip in Himself.*

CHAPTER IX.

DR. HOPKINS became president of the "American Board of Commissioners for Foreign Missions" in 1857, at the meeting in Providence. There was an exceeding fitness in his election to this position. With great dignity of person he combined an effective readiness in extemporaneous speaking and a quickness in discerning the latent tendencies of any movement. His long experience as a teacher qualified him to control discussion to its proper limits, and his sovereign common sense enabled him so to guide the long and often exciting, but often wearisome sessions as to reach the proper result. Had the meetings been purely business meetings, his success might have been less uniform and brilliant. No better presiding officer could have been found for that annual series of meetings, in which instruction, devotion, and business are blended. As has already been stated, the universal relations of Christianity were the inspiring and directing thought of his mind. In the missionary movement, in the contemplation and fulfillment of that last command to "go into all the world and preach the gospel to every creature," the forces of his large nature found a congenial field for activity and expression. He might not have made a successful missionary in the narrow and limited sense in which men commonly use that word. But had he himself gone in the service of his Master to a foreign land, the direction of educational forces, the management of far-reaching and complicated agencies, would surely have come into his hands, and he would have been widely known as the leader and director of movements that might have captured the intellectual men of a refined civilization. For small details of business he was too great, but the wider and far rarer statesmanship which lays down the lines along which the men who attend to details must work was his in abundance. The service which he rendered to the cause of missions in his capacity of presiding officer was great, and for that service the cause of missions and the Congregational churches of our country have abundant reason for thankfulness.

Much of the time at these meetings is given to reports which do not directly arouse enthusiasm. The meetings generally cover a period of three days, and are attended by large throngs of people. Many of these come from points quite distant from the city where the meeting is held, and as the meetings draw to a close, fatigue resulting from the long journey and the constant attention is strongly felt. From the day of his election as president in 1857 until his death in 1887 Dr. Hopkins missed but three of these meetings. On two occasions he was in Europe, in 1861 and 1881, and he was detained at ·home by illness in 1859. As year by year his locks thinned and whitened, he went on his pilgrimage, often several hundred miles, from his mountain home, and endured not simply the ordinary fatigue of the visitor, but, in addition, the fatigue coming from the responsibility for the guidance of the public assemblies. The meetings begin on Tuesday and close Friday noon. On Thursday evening, at least during the later years of his presidency, an address was expected from him. There was something surprising, as the years slipped away, in the ease and strength with which he met this duty. The great audience, which had been wearied by the days of report and discussion, was reanimated and inspired by his words. It was on these occasions that his clear views of the universal relations of Christ and his salvation, of the duties that this salvation imposed on every man who had accepted it, of the claims that all the world had on the follower of Christ, and of the grandeur of following such a Master into missionary work for the most degraded, found their noblest utterance. It seemed that with each succeeding year the power of imparting to others his wide vision and of quickening missionary enthusiasm was increased.

Often he was expected on Friday morning also to extend the thanks of the board for the friendly hospitalities of the city. His addresses were uniformly fitting, and often peculiarly happy.

It would be impossible for any report to do these discourses full justice. As they were generally extemporaneous, they gained much of their effectiveness from the atmosphere of the occasion and the color of the surroundings, which Dr. Hopkins never failed to comprehend fully and to embody adequately in his words.

Although these fugitive elements do not appeal to the reader as to the hearer, there is enough that is characteristic of the speaker in the reports of these addresses which have been preserved to interest the reader. This is true even for those who did not know Dr. Hopkins. For those who did know him, and had heard him speak extemporaneously, which was his usual habit of discourse except on the rarest occasions, these reports will have a peculiar power in bringing up a distinct remembrance of his persuasive and inspiring speech. One might almost say that he never was himself except when making an extemporaneous address before an intelligent audience.

A few extracts may exhibit in a clear way his deep interest in missions, and his admirable service as presiding officer at the meetings in gathering up into one utterance the various lines of thought and emotion that had been developed, and giving to the intellectual men and women who had attended the meeting a final and abiding impression of the nobility of missionary service, and of their direct responsibilities for the work.

At the meeting in Pittsfield in 1866, the following words were used with respect to the desired unity of Christians: —

"Let the whole race fix their eyes upon the North Star and march onwards with steady gaze upon that luminary, and this march will bring them together in one vast multitude, over the centre of which the object of their common regard burns in the firmament. They are brought together not because they planned to meet, but because they had a common object in view, and let the Christians of every name keep their eyes fixed upon Jesus Christ, and the divisions of Christendom will be known no more."

The board met in Pittsburgh in 1869, and from Dr. Hopkins's address at that meeting the following extract is taken. It presents the contrast between the work of God and that of man in his own striking manner, and with simple loyalty to the Master presses home the duty of individual Christians: —

"There is a general pervading persistency increasing the cry of progress, which would almost lead one to believe that the old relations between Christianity and the world were changed. Progress! Yes, there has been progress, and great progress; but progress in what? In Christianity? No; the foundation of Christianity is the same that it was before that last supper which we have celebrated here this afternoon. Another foundation can no man lay. In the requirements of Christianity? No; the strait gate is just as strait, and

the narrow way is just as narrow, as it was of old.
No cry of God's Church can widen the entrance or
the way one hair's breadth. Christianity vindicates
itself as from God by placing itself alongside of its
works. There is no progress in the works of God.
The sun shines no more brightly to-day than it did
six thousand years ago; the seasons come and go
no more perfectly and exactly; the body of man
is nourished and strengthened in no other way than
of old; his heart beats and his blood circulates and
his food digests as it did when Adam was in Eden;
there has been no progress. No; in the structure
of God's works, in their mighty area, in their ceaseless uniformity, there has been no improvement.
When the work of the Lord ceased on the sixth
day it was said, 'Thus the heavens and the earth
were finished, and all the hosts of them,' and there
has been no improvement in anything that God
has made from that time to this. 'What He doeth
is forever,' and so, by a sublime parallelism, I have
no doubt, intended, in that hour of darkness and
of agony, when our Saviour was about to expire
on the cross, He said, 'It is finished.' Yes, 'It is
finished.' All that was necessary for human salvation was completed, and that great work of God
has stood, and stands, and will stand, like the sun
in the heavens, and Christ lifted up on the cross
shall draw all humanity unto Him, and there is
no progress in that because nothing can transcend
it. The relations of Christianity to the civil law
are changed, and everywhere now in the world

evangelical religion turns the world upside down and is everywhere spoken against. Thus it is observed everywhere; thus it is that evangelical religion is persecuted by superstition and paganism in heathen lands. Thus it is that Popery everywhere follows and strikes it; thus it is that ritualism and invention would undermine it; thus it is that in opposing this now as of old Herod and Pilate became friends, and this opposition and just this element our Saviour and his Apostles in their day overcame; this opposition we have to meet. The earth is not yet subdued to God, and the forces are arrayed against the church, and we have precisely the work to do which they laid down their lives for. Did they do it? They did it by love, which was so great that it enjoined them to lay down their lives if it became necessary. And unless we have in us a spirit of love for Christ and love for our fellow-men that shall induce us so far as is necessary to do this same thing, we shall accomplish nothing. Here is our deficiency, here is the thing we need. We need to labor for the single end to make men like Christ. If we labor for that, it is impossible we should have any wrong motive; if we labor for that, we shall be like Christ. It is the greatest blessing we can give to any man to make him like Jesus Christ, and if this purpose and spirit can possess the churches, the missionary boards of the land will need no more money; if it can possess the young men, they will need no more missionaries. I do feel this is a very simple point.

I do feel, fathers and friends, it is of the greatest moment we should labor for Jesus in just this spirit — labor in the spirit of love to make man like Jesus Christ. Thus laboring, if we could but do it, and if others would but work with us, this blessed unity would come of course; our missionary stations, working out from their centres, would blend together as the light of the stars blend together, working for the common object, and in a common spirit all Christians would see eye to eye. The watchmen would see eye to eye, and the Lord would bring again Zion."

The following is an outline of the address delivered at Hartford in 1876 : —

"In passing out of the Opera House the other night, I met a graduate of Williams College who has been greatly successful in winning souls to Christ. The friend asked me if I remembered saying that if they wished success, they must remember how God worked, and then work with Him. I did not remember the allusion, but it occurred to me that it would be true in regard to anything, and that it must especially be true in regard to the great work in which this board is engaged. We are then simply to ask how it is that God works in connection with this work. And it seems to me the essential forces of Christianity through which He works are (1) his righteousness, (2) self-sacrificing love. The righteousness of God is the justice that lies back of all moral government. It lies back of the gospel itself. The gospel is the expression of the law. It makes it honorable. These two, righteousness and love, must work together. Righteousness quickens the moral nature, without which no religion avails. Love touches the heart and brings men to God. These two meeting in the cross, perfect righteousness and perfect love, are as great as they possibly can be. These two uniting like rays of light are the one force by which God draws men to Him. Man's deepest need is the need of reconciliation and pardon from God. Without this need satisfied, man has no peace. These two give reconciliation. The religion of Christ works in man righteousness and self-sacrificing love. Unless these be produced in man, the religion of Christ is a failure. So much righteousness and self-sacrificing love as there is in this house, so much is there of Christianity, and no more. These are the sources of Christianity. When a man has these, he is prepared to work with God in this labor."

The following address is one of the best reported among the papers at the Missionary Rooms. It is given here in full, as it is a good specimen of his peculiarly argumentative and convincing style. It was delivered at Milwaukee in 1878: —

"We are here, fathers and brethren, in the faith that the stone that was cut out of the mountain without hands will become a great mountain and fill the whole earth. This we believe, first, on the ground of supernatural intervention; and second, on that of natural tendency. Of supernatural intervention we can know nothing except by reve-lation. 'The times and the seasons the Father hath put in his own power.' But of natural tendency we can judge. Looking at this we can see no reason why the law of the 'survival of the fittest' should not apply to Christianity as compared with other religions in the same way as to anything else. How then does it apply to anything else? It is supposed by modern science to be a law that regu-lates, without supernatural intervention, the preva-lence and even the existence of the different species of plants and animals on the earth. But how? The survival of the fittest! Fittest for what? Fittest to survive? Does it simply mean that those will survive that are fittest to survive? Or does it mean that those will survive that are fittest for the ends of sensitive life, and especially of man? If it mean the first, it may be a law, but it amounts to nothing. Of course those will survive that are, all things considered, fittest to survive. But if it mean that without the intervention of intelligent will, those will survive that are fittest to meet the wants of man, then it is not a law. The reverse is often true. Left to itself, it is not generally true that that which is fittest to meet the wants of man is fittest to survive.

"When Solomon 'went by the field of the sloth-ful, and by the vineyard of the man void of un-derstanding, and lo! it was all grown over with thorns, and nettles had covered the face thereof,' that was according to the law of the survival of the fittest. The thorns were fittest to survive as compared with the vine, and the strongest nettles as compared with other nettles. As compared with wheat, thistles — Canada thistles — are fittest to survive, and cockle as compared with barley. It may indeed be plausibly said that the things best fitted for the use of man are least fitted to survive. The finest fruits need the most care. Of all grains wheat is best fitted for food, and probably least fitted to survive. No one knows where it is indigenous, and, left to itself, it would soon perish from the earth. It has a natural tendency to survive owing to its environments, but that needs to be supplemented by the intelligence and the toil of man. To us it would seem that that which is fittest for the use of man should be fittest to survive. But in this, Nature seems to be at cross-purposes with herself; and thus do we find, wrought into her very constitution, and proclaimed by science, the elements of that primeval curse: 'In the sweat of thy face shalt thou eat bread.' It is thus that the law applies in nature. And precisely thus does it apply to the different religions of the world. And applying it thus we may affirm of Christianity two propositions : —

"First, that, aside from supernatural intervention, it was, of all known or conceivable religions, the least fitted to survive.

"Second, that, of all known or conceivable religions, it is fittest to meet the wants of men.

"First, then, aside from supernatural intervention, Christianity was, of all known or conceivable religions, least fitted to survive. It had not a single element that the world reckons on for influence. It began in a stable. It was laid in a manger. Place yourselves by the side of that. Follow the infant in his flight into Egypt; in his return to a remote part of a conquered province, and to a disreputable town. See him, without letters, at work as a carpenter. At the age of thirty see him traveling about the country on foot as a teacher, with a few peasant followers. After only three years see him apprehended, tried, condemned, as a malefactor by both Jews and Romans. See him hanging on the cross between two thieves. See him laid in the tomb with a great stone over its mouth, sealed with the seal of authority, and a watch set. Christianity was there. It was in that tomb. Not a person living fully understood it. The words spoken had been dispersed in the air, and no record of them had been left. I ask you if imagination can add a single circumstance to heighten the improbability that a world-wide religion would spring from such a source? But looking at Christianity thus we see but half the improbability of its survival. We need to look also at its nature as a spiritual and holy religion, and at the strength of that which it had to overcome. As spiritual and holy it was aggressive. Its antagonism to all forms of iniquity was uncompromising. It had therefore to overcome not only the aversion of the individual to spirituality and holiness, but also to overcome and displace those organized and deeply imbedded systems of religion and civil government which gave sanction and scope to that aversion.

"If then we mean by the survival of the fittest, that which is fittest to survive, it must be conceded that of all possible religions Christianity was, and I may say even now is, the least fitted to survive. But while we say this, we say again, that of all religions known or conceivable, Christianity is best fitted to meet the wants of man, and so, in the highest sense, best fitted to survive.

"Between Christianity and the wants of man as a sinner, we say that the correspondence is perfect. We say that it is light to the eye, bread to the hungry, cold water to the thirsty soul. We say that it is redemption, deliverance, pardon, peace, eternal life. Coming as tidings — 'good tidings of great joy' — it can be received by all. It implies doctrine, but it is an offer of help; and he who finds himself struggling in the horrible pit and the miry clay has but to reach forth the hand of faith, and he shall be lifted out of it, and he shall find his feet set upon a rock.

"Nor is it merely as a sinner that Christianity corresponds with man. Assuming natural religion, and the revelation of the Old Testament, it meets perfectly every religious want. Is man a creature? It reveals to him an intelligent Creator. 'He that built all things is God.' No atheism, no pantheism, no blind force. As a creature does he need care, sympathy, love? It reveals to him a Father, and says to him that the hairs of his head are all numbered. Does he find himself, through internal struggles and the stepmotherhood of nature, weary and heavy laden? It says, 'Come unto me, and I will give you rest.' Is he called to lay loved ones in the grave? It says to him, 'Thy brother shall rise again.'

"It embosoms within itself the foundation and means of all reforms, individual and social. Beginning with the individual, not with organizations, it places him, whether old or young, rich or poor, educated or uneducated, on the footing of his own moral responsibility and spiritual independence, and then offers him, not only forgiveness, but the aid of the Holy Spirit, that he may become 'a perfect man in Christ Jesus.'

"Passing to society, it lays the foundation of purity in the Christian family. The foundation of peace it lays in the fatherhood of God and the brotherhood of man. If peace is ever to be universal, it will not be from interest or fear, but from a recognition of these. The foundation of civil order it lays in its requirement of subjection to lawful authority. Its guard against tyranny it places in its command to obey God rather than man. Its provision for general enlightenment, at once for conservatism and progress, for reform without revolution, is found in its command to 'prove all things, and hold fast that which is good.' Christianity fittest? Nothing else is fit. It is so fit that, if it were universally and perfectly received, the millennium would have come.

"As the world now is, and left to itself, the thorns, the thistles, the cockle of idolatry, and superstition, and fanaticism, and formalism, and the deadly nightshade of infidelity are fitted to survive. But if the grand ideas of purity and peace and blessedness of which man is capable are to be realized, if the capabilities that are in him as made in the image of God are to be brought out, Christianity alone is fit. It is fittest to live by; it is fittest to die by. Fully received, it can sustain man in death as nothing else can. It can pluck from death its sting, and from the grave its victory. It can take a man once a heathen, cast out by his kindred, and dying in a hut, and enable him to say, when asked how it was with him, 'He has taken all mine and given me all his.' And when asked to explain, to say again, 'He has taken my sin and my death, that is all that was mine, and given me holiness and heaven.' Like wheat, it has a natural tendency to survive; but owing to its environment it needs the constant care of the Great Husbandman, and the prayers and labor of those who work together with Him.

"Prayer and labor, these are the two instrumentalities for us to use. By looking at the first proposition we have considered, we shall see our helplessness and be led to prayer. By looking at the second, we shall see the infinite value of the religion and be led to effort. Such, fathers and brethren,

is the religion we seek to send to those who are des-
titute of it.   Do you think it much that we are
doing to this end?   Do others think of us as fanat-
ical or unwise?   Two considerations set my mind
wholly at rest at this point.   One is that we are
acting under an explicit order, with an explicit
promise of aid.   'Go ye.'   And, 'Lo I am with
you.'   The other is, that that order was given by
One who knew the value of the religion better than
we do; who so knew it that He was willing to die
that we might receive it.   'Thanks be to God for
his unspeakable gift.'   'Freely ye have received,
freely give.'"

This address must have been very effective with
intellectual men.   It was almost as if he were
standing before one of his own classes and considering the claims of Christianity to our consent and
to universal acceptance.   The relation of the whole
discussion to the missionary movement is, however,
most effectively brought out in the concluding sentences.

The address at Lowell in 1880 is less argumentative, but produced a deep impression, and has
touches of that playfulness which often added
beauty to the strength of his discourse.

"Recently, in this country and elsewhere, there
has come up a set of people who call themselves ag-
nostics, by which they would indicate that they are
religious 'know-nothings.'   I agree with those people up to a certain point.   There are many things
connected with religious questions, and connected

with this question of missions, which I do not
know. I don't know why we should be placed
under a general system under which it comes to
pass that so large a portion of the inhabitants of
this globe should be for nearly two thousand years
ignorant of the coming of the Son of God. I do
not know why we are under a general dispensation
in which it comes to pass that so large a portion of
those who know of his coming should reject Him.
This could not have been anticipated; but Christendom is not Christian. I do not know why it
should be that those who are Christians should be
such poor Christians. How can they be? I do
not know; I do not expect to know in this world.
I doubt if I shall ever know why, in a universe
created and governed by a Being of perfect wisdom
and goodness and power, there should be evil at
all.

"But there are some things which I do know. I
am certain of them. I know, however it may have
come, that there is evil both moral and natural;
and I do not believe that there is any agnostic that
does not know this. I know I stand appalled before the varied forms and the vast extent of this
evil. I know that there is a difference between
evil and good, and that good is better than evil. I
know that knowledge is better than ignorance, and
truth than falsehood, and honesty than dishonesty,
and temperance than intemperance, and purity
than impurity, and kindness than cruelty, and love
than hatred. I know that kindness would have

been a more suitable return for what our beloved
Brother Parsons did in Turkey than murder. I
know that the sacrifices of a broken heart are better than human sacrifices. I know that the worship of God, who is a spirit, in spirit and in truth
is better than the worship of idols; and knowing
this, I know — and that is our point here — that
wherever Christianity comes — real Christianity,
not nominal — that which is evil will be displaced
by that which is better: knowledge will take the
place of ignorance, and truth of falsehood, and
temperance of intemperance, and purity of impurity, and kindness of cruelty, and love of hatred,
and peace of war. The savage and the cannibal
will take his place at the feet of Him who was meek
and lowly in heart. Charms, superstitions, the
various forms of witchcraft and idolatry — all that
brood of superstitions which rests with such an in-
cubus, and has for ages rested with such an incu-
bus, upon the race — would flee away as the mists
of the morning. And not only will Christianity
displace that which is evil, but it will displace it by
that which is the very best. I know that it will
displace it by that which is the best possible. I
know this because Christ had a perfect humanity;
and therefore whoever would reach all the possibilities of the nature that is given, be it man or woman, must do it through Christ's likeness.

"I hold that Christ was the second Adam, and represented a perfect, a holy humanity. It is written
in the Scriptures, 'Male and female created He them;

and blessed them, and called *their* name Adam.' This would indicate that humanity is complete only as it includes both man and woman. It may be well to speak of the manhood of Christ, and perhaps to write a book about it; but the distinctive qualities of manhood were no more conspicuous in Him than those supplementary qualities of womanhood which, together with those of manhood, go to make up a perfect humanity. Christ therefore having a perfect humanity, whoever will reach all the possibilities that belong to the nature given to that person must do it through Christlikeness; and Christianity can never be satisfied till each individual follower of Christ comes to be like Him.

"In providing thus for the completeness, the perfection of the individual, Christianity provides for the perfection of society, because the problem of society is the problem of the individual. Christianity knows that, and therefore begins with the individual. Let each individual be perfect, and society, the organization of society, will take on just those forms by themselves spontaneously which are requisite for the perfection of the whole. If, therefore, the possibilities of this race, individual and social, are ever to be reached, I know that the second Adam, the man Christ, must be the model and leader of the race, and that just in proportion as He is thus the model and leader of the race, men will reach their highest possibilities.

"And one point farther. Not only does Christianity thus enable individuals and society to reach their highest possibilities, but it gives the highest conception possible of what those possibilities are. It gives a grandeur to the destiny of man both individual and social which the imagination had never conceived and never could have conceived. In this respect it is analogous to nature, and stands over against nature precisely as nature does over against the unaided thought of man. Not farther does the universe, as revealed by the telescope in its grandeur, and by the microscope in its minuteness and finish. transcend whatever has been conceived by the unaided imagination, than does the Christian heaven transcend in knowledge and purity and glory anything of which the unaided imagination had conceived. It gives us, therefore, the highest conception possible of the grandeur and progress of our nature, the very best.

"Now the difficulty of receiving this lies in its very greatness. What! You take a savage, a cannibal, a drunkard from our streets? Yes, take one of us. What! take such creatures as we are, that are going down into the dust of death, and deliver them from sin and from evil, and raise them up to a dignity and purity and glory like this? Yes, just that. No matter what the incrustations may be upon the diamond; there is power in the glorious gospel of the blessed God to fashion and to polish it, and to set it as a gem in the diadem of the Redeemer. That is what Christianity does. If we look at man, it would seem to be impossible. It is too great to be believed. But if we look at the love of God in Jesus Christ, it could not be believed if it were not so great. It is required by that love and by the grandeur of the system to be so great. 'He that delivered up for us his only begotten Son, how shall He not with Him freely give us all things?'

"We see, then, beloved Christian friends, what that result is towards which God is working, and for which He permits us to work together with Him. We are capable of producing changes. We can cause that to be which but for us would not have been. The changes which the children of this world seek to produce may perhaps all be included in the transfer of matter from one place to another, the transfer of property from man to man. That is all. That is the business of this world. It is a restless sea, always in motion, always the same. But we seek to produce moral and spiritual changes, and we seek to do three things.

"We seek, in the first place, to do for each individual for whom we labor the best thing. We seek to do for him the greatest favor which it is possible for one human being to do for another, — that is to say, to lead him to know and follow Jesus Christ, to lead him to be able to say, as I would humbly say, 'I *know*' — no agnosticism — 'I know whom I have believed, and that He is able to keep that which I have committed unto Him against that day.'

"We wish, in the second place, to found civilizations which shall have so much of intelligence and of principle that they will not collapse by their own want of inherent energy; that there shall be no alternation of civilization as there always has been with barbarism; no alternation of oppression with anarchy. And we wish further to provide material for that higher social state in which there shall be love and purity and joy and peace before the throne of God forever more. This being the work which we have before us, involving the highest social problems, and the highest problems under the government of God, we come to the question which has been so much discussed before this board, What sort of men do we need? And here I must say that I was greatly gratified and in a measure relieved by the remarks which were made by the representative of the Prudential Committee, Mr. Ropes, in regard to that subject. I did feel that we were coming to be one-sided about it. The call was for talent, for the first order of talent, and I would not object to that, perhaps, in a certain sense; but when Christ prayed for his kingdom and for work in it, He prayed for laborers. He did not pray simply for reapers, but He prayed for laborers, for all the kind of labor that is needed; and the kind of labor that is needed in the harvest field is of great variety. I remember the account of a harvest field in old time, and there were reapers there, and then, following them, there were the gleaners; and there was one gleaner named Ruth, who followed the men, and they were directed to let some handfuls fall on purpose, so that she might gather them, and not to reproach her. And now Ruth has been reproduced in these days in the Woman's Board. The Ruths follow the men, and they glean the field; and I suppose, from the amount they gather — there was great surprise expressed at the amount Ruth gathered — that the men sometimes let handfuls drop with purpose, that they may pick them up.

"Now this is a kind of labor that we need, and we are feeling the need of it more and more. And then we need other kinds of labor. I remember having heard (for it was not in my day) that Samuel J. Mills, whom we recognize as having been more efficient in connection with the origination of this missionary enterprise than any other person, was not a distinguished scholar, but rather the reverse. Yet he had his own talent; he had the talent which was needed for stimulation and organization: he had consecration. He could not speak in public, as I understand it, but he went to these distinguished people, these men who need sometimes somebody to direct them, to tell them how to shoot. He went to Dr. Griffin, and I know that Dr. Griffin said (and he was one of the great leading agents in that matter) that whatever he had done he had done at the suggestion of Samuel J. Mills. And a great many cases of this sort occurred. There is talent of all sorts needed; and I agree that there are certain kinds of work (and the highest kinds) for which we do need weak men. But then they are such kind of weak men as the Apostle

Paul was, who said, 'Who is weak and I am not weak?' We need men who feel their own weakness in the face of difficulties which stand in the way of success in this great work, men who feel their absolute nothingness. But then we need men who can also be so much in sympathy with God as to say, 'When I am weak, then am I strong,' — men who are weak in themselves, but strong to take hold of the strength of God; and such men we need because the work which our missionaries do is an apostolic work. That is to say, the first part is precisely what the apostles did.

"That is the theory of our missions. It is to go and plant churches, and to give them that organization which under the circumstances is best for them, and then pass on. Now that is apostolic work, and for it we need the aggressive power of Paul and the firmness of Peter and the love of John. We do need the first talent of our colleges and of our theological seminaries, and I call for it here to-night — the first talent to stand in the front and to organize. Who is there that will hear this call? Who is there that will now in this formative time identify himself with this grandest work of the ages?"

At Portland, in 1882, the distinction between love and duty was admirably made as follows: —

"From the commencement of this meeting there has been evidently a drift in one direction, — an unmistakable drift. It appeared in the reports read by the secretaries Tuesday afternoon; it flamed forth in the sermon; it constituted the substance of the special papers read by the secretaries; it entered into the discussions that followed; it went forth to its culmination in the devotional exercises this morning, when by that inspired and inspiring movement Mr. Dodge offered to double his already large subscription, and that offer was followed by so many who rose successively, and by so many who rose simultaneously to offer the same thing. That drift evidently is toward a decided enlargement of our efforts in all directions. This has been the tendency of the movement of the meeting up to this point, clearly, unmistakably.

"But I have not seemed to see so distinctly expressed, in the speeches which have been made, the motive which is to sustain us in going forward in this movement. In the sermon it seemed to be the presence and power of the Holy Spirit; but then that was for a special purpose with reference to individuals: 'Separate me Saul and Barnabas.' What was to be the motive which was to sustain them during the long years of their labor, and persecutions, and when the hour should come, as come they knew it must, — when they, too, should follow the Master to crucifixion? I have heard three words: one was duty, that is a good word; another was enthusiasm, — missionary enthusiasm, and that is a good word; another was love, — love of the Saviour, and I like that better.

"Some years since there was a woman who had gone out as a missionary to India in connection with the American Board, who brought her children to the coast that she might send them to this country. She put them into the boat that was to carry them out to the steamer that lay in the offing, and watched them until they embarked; then she turned her face away, and with tears streaming down her cheeks she said, 'I do this for thee, Jesus.' Here was a love by this woman of a Being whom she had never seen that was paramount to her natural affection for her children, that was the principle and the spring of her missionary labor. This personal love of the Saviour was long since sanctioned by Him as the motive, not only for missionary, but also for apostolic labor. In the threefold inquiry which our Saviour made of the Apostle Peter after his resurrection, the one thing sought for as a motive for the apostolic labors, labors that were to end in crucifixion, was the personal love of himself. 'Simon, son of Jonas, lovest thou me?' And the one object proposed in the threefold injunction that followed that inquiry was the upbuilding of Christian character: 'Feed my sheep,' 'Feed my lambs.' From this motive and for this object the apostle labored during his whole life. This we know because we hear him saying in his old age, 'The elders which are among you I exhort,'— evidently having reference to this conversation, — 'which am also an elder: feed the flock of God which is among you, taking the oversight thereof, not by constraint, but willingly; not for filthy lucre, but of a ready mind,' — that is from love. As seen in the woman to whom I have referred, this love had in it no touch of earthly passion, it was wholly moral and spiritual; it was the love of One whom she had never seen; it was the love of One whose character was perfect; it was the love of One who had loved her and given himself for her; it was the love of a divine Saviour. Here, then, was the highest possible principle of action; love purged of all selfishness and mingled with complacency and gratitude.

"But then, when you come to this point, what of duty? I said that this love was the highest possible principle of action — what of duty? There are those who say that duty is higher. Now let us look for a moment at the relations of these two to each other. In order to do that I will take as an illustration the man spoken of by Dr. Goodwin in his sermon who, he said, had invested $125,000 in pine lands. If he had asked him for a contribution to the American Board, the man would not have felt pleasantly about it; he would have been reluctant to give it. I did not understand that Dr. Goodwin applied to the man, but suppose now he had applied, and had told this man that it was his duty to give something for the conversion of the heathen, and the man had said that he could not deny the request, and had given him one hundred dollars, glad to get rid of him so. Would it have been the duty of that man to give that one hundred dollars? I shall not discuss that question. Now if the man had gone on making money, and

the year had come around, and Dr. Goodwin or
some other person had gone to him again, and he
had seen him coming, knowing what he wanted,
he would have said, 'There comes that duty again;
I don't like the looks of it; sorry for it, but I
suppose I must do something,' and he gives perhaps two hundred dollars. Now was it the duty
of this man to ask him in that way? I shall not
discuss that question. But suppose he had gone to
this man and told him that it was his duty, not to
give something to the heathen, but to give himself
to Christ; that it was his duty to love God with
all his heart and his neighbor as himself; and suppose the man had asked why he should do this, and
he had been pointed to the cross of Christ, and had
seen 'One hanging on the tree,' and had realized
that He died for him, and had given himself fully
and heartily to Him as the Saviour of sinners, — all
that he was and all that he had, — then, if Dr.
Goodwin had gone to him and asked him for a contribution to the American Board, what would he
have said? Why, perhaps he would have said, 'I
will do as the sainted champion did in the earlier
history of this board, who gave not only his for-
tune but himself, and who said, "Tell me where
the darkest place in this world is, and send me
there," and he went and laid his bones down on
the western coast of Africa.' Perhaps he would
have said that; but he might have said, 'No, I
will give you $1,000, or $5,000, or $10,000;' and
now there would come a voice to him, 'Take care,

what are you doing? Have n't you a family? Don't you know that if a man does n't provide for his own, he is worse than an infidel?' 'Yes,' the man says, 'I have a family, but then I think I have enough for them.' 'Yes,' but this voice says, 'don't you know that presently Brother Clark is coming along, and the home missions will want something?' And he says, 'Let him come, I shall be glad to see him.' And so the repetition comes of the different claims that will be made to him, and now the man looks up and says, 'Who are you that are saying this?' And the voice comes and says, 'I am duty, duty restraining you now. Perhaps you have been hasty, perhaps you have heard Dr. Goodwin's sermon, and are a little over-excited, and it may not be exactly prudent for you to give so much.' And the man says, 'Are you duty? I did not know you, you look so much better than you did.' And now duty comes to regulate the love of the man, and to become the law of his love; and if I understand it, that love is the principle of his action, and the duty is the regulating law of his action. The question is not, how little he shall give, but how much duty will permit him to give. And so, looking over the whole ground under the control and direction of duty, love and duty look into each other's eyes, and they lock arms and move on together. Now when this man was addressed in the first place, when you went to him in the first place, and he gave you one hundred dollars, what did you do? You just took a piece of steel, and you struck a flint rock, and you brought out one bright spark, and then the rock was just as hard and cold as it was before. Now what have you done? You have touched the rock with the rod of God, and there flows out from it constantly a stream of living water that follows the people of God through the desert. And that, as I understand it, is the relation of these two words."

At the age of eighty-three, at the seventy-fifth anniversary of the founding of the board in Boston, in 1885, Dr. Hopkins made the address from which also an extract is given: —

"In addressing you, fathers and brethren, on this seventy-fifth anniversary of the American Board, I desire, first of all, to give thanks to God that I am permitted to be with you. I am older than the American Board, older by eight years. In office I am the oldest corporate member of the board. The board abides in strength, but of those who constituted it when I was elected, in 1838, officers and members, not one remains. Well, then, may I give humble and adoring thanks that I am permitted to be with you. I wish, also, to thank the board for the great honor they have done me in electing me to my present office for these eight and twenty successive years, and for their kindness and forbearance in accepting the imperfect and inadequate service that I have been able to render. Being thus old, having entered upon life at the beginning of the second year of this marvelous century, I have seen all its wonders pass before me. I remember when my lesson in geography in the common school told me there were less than six million inhabitants in these United States. I remember the wars of the first Napoleon, and can feel yet the throb of excitement caused by the tardy news of his great battles. I remember the war of 1812, and the embargo, and the victory of New Orleans. I remember the first steamboat and railroad and power-press, the first photograph and spectroscope, the first telegraph and telephone, and heard the first whisper, and it was but a whisper, of the first Atlantic cable. I remember the first spinning jenny, the first mowing machine and sewing machine and reaper. All these I have seen so extended and applied as to increase the capabilities of the race many fold, and to make of the world that then was quite another world. In common with most of you, I have witnessed the greatest civil war ever known, have seen the dark cloud of slavery pass off and a bow of hope brighter than before span our political heavens. All this I have seen, and, to crown it all, I have seen the missionary spirit coming as the breath of God upon his people, and Christians girding themselves as never before for the conquest of the whole world to Christ.

"The formation of the American Board in 1810 I do not remember, but I do remember the difficulty there was in finding a place for its first missionaries. I remember well the sailing of the first missionaries to the Sandwich Islands, and the exultation there was, when the news came that the natives had already cast their idols to the moles and to the bats. From that time I have been in sympathy with the movements of the board, have known something of its explorations and methods, and have seen the whole heathen world, originally closed, opened to the entrance of the gospel. During this period I have known of the debts of the board, its discouragements, its crises, its deliverances, its triumphs. I have seen the old school Presbyterian brethren part from it; then our Dutch brethren; then our new school Presbyterian brethren, taking with them altogether churches much more numerous and wealthy than our own, and yet I have seen the old board hold on its way with no essential diminution of contributions or of efficiency till now, in its seventy-fifth year, and out of debt, it has expended more than twenty millions of dollars in seeking to spread the gospel, and its missions belt the globe.

"It is nothing to boast of that this vast sum has been expended without loss, and up to the present time with no suspicion of dishonesty. But in times like these it may be well to emphasize the fact, and to ask infidelity, and agnosticism, and all kindred isms, when they propose to show an equal sum, freely given, and intrusted to infidels without security, to be spent for benevolent, or, if they prefer the term, for altruistic purposes."

This was the last meeting but one of the American Board that Dr. Hopkins was permitted to attend. He appeared still vigorous both in mind and in body, and the inspiring retrospect given in the Boston address and the fervid glow of his eloquent faith in the future progress of Christ's kingdom gave hope of years of useful service to the cause of missions. The following year, 1886, at the age of eighty-four, he traveled to Des Moines, Iowa, for the discharge of his duties as presiding officer. He probably went with less joyous energy, with graver resolution, with more solemn thought, than ever before. It was not so much because he discerned that his long period of service was drawing to a close, as it was the knowledge that troublous times had come that sobered the joy of his annual pilgrimage. He had a perfect understanding of the conditions. He knew that the agitation which had arisen in regard to the acceptance or rejection of candidates for missionary labor, though temporary in its peculiar occasion, might arise again and again under other circumstances. He wished a policy to be adopted that would be no temporary expedient, but one that should rest on some principle permanently applicable. With the statesmanlike vision that never failed him in a crisis, and with a bold and heroic fidelity to his convictions, he stood and pleaded at Des Moines for the constitutional in the Congregational polity and the catholic sympathies of an apostolic age. If we consider how busy his life had been and how full of anxieties and problems, how constant had been his training under the hand of the divine Master, it requires no stretch of imagination to conceive that this long training had been largely for this last dramatic appearance of his ever ripening character and powers, for this and what lies beyond. Certainly his best friends, those who knew him best, can only give thanks for the simplicity and firmness, the courtesy and candor, of his words and decisions in that stormy debate. They would not wish one word altered, one expression changed. The significance of his attitude can be explained only by giving an outline of the movements which led to that debate.

THE CRISIS IN THE BOARD OF MISSIONS.

" And last the master-bowman, he
    Would cleave the mark.   A willing ear
    We lent him.   Who, but hung to hear
The rapt oration flowing free
From point to point, with power and grace
    And music in the bounds of law
    To those conclusions when we saw
The God within him light his face,
And seem to lift the form and glow
    In azure orbits heavenly-wise."

TENNYSON, In Memoriam.

CHAPTER X.

THE thirty years of Dr. Hopkins's presidency of the American Board were for the most part years of peaceful and harmonious development of missionary operations. That his influence was not paramount, that he was not able at last to avert dissension and prevent the exhibition to a hostile world of a noble missionary society excluding from its fields young men and women burning with love for the Master, because of their hope in the largeness of God's mercy or their uncertainty as to his final dealing with the heathen, was owing in part to the constitution of the society. He foresaw the perils. Had he been a member of the committee deciding on the applications of candidates for missionary service under the society, as the president has since most reasonably been made, he might have controlled the divisive tendencies, or at least modified certain influences, and perhaps have devised a method of retaining the ardent loyalty of all shades of opinion within the society.

What he could do under the conditions he did, and none of his friends can regret that the closing efforts of his heroic life were made in favor of treating applications for the home and foreign work in precisely the same way.   His attitude and action in this crisis in the history of the Congregational missionary board were a fitting termination to his career.

The Andover Theological Seminary, founded by a coalition of moderate Calvinists and Hopkinsians, has been for several years the centre of extraordinary agitations.   In the judgment of certain friends of the seminary, some of the professors have not taught a theology consistent with the creed which each appointee must sign in order to occupy his professorship.   A number of new professors were appointed in 1882.   The appointment of one of them, the Rev. Newman Smyth, who had been selected by the trustees for the chair of "Christian Theology," was not confirmed by the visitors.   Under the statutes of the seminary the visitors [1] must confirm or reject any nomination to a professorship made by the trustees.   The reason given for the rejection is contained in these words from the record of the visitors' action: "He seems to us a brilliant and eloquent writer rather than a professional theologian:" "of all men a teacher of Sys-

[1] The power of the visitors, and indeed the constitutionality of their original appointment, as limiting the rights of the trustees of Phillips Academy, has been a matter of doubt in the minds of some eminent lawyers.   In the litigation consequent on the exercise of the power of removal in the case of Professor Egbert C. Smyth, the question was debated before the Supreme Court of Massachusetts.   The decision rendered affirmed the constitutionality of their relations.

tematic Theology needs to have profoundness of thought and precision, and these are the very qualities which after all our study we fail to find in Dr. Newman Smyth." Although the visitors distinctly say in their record that his real views upon the themes, "sin, the atonement, and the future state" "are in substantial agreement with the characteristic doctrinal position of the seminary," and reiterate the same assertion in a subsequent minute, it was believed by many that the hostility to his appointment exhibited by conservatives on account of his doctrinal views had great weight with the visitors in leading them to negative his election.

In 1886 "a committee of certain of the alumni" of the seminary preferred charges against five of the professors on distinct grounds, which involve and specify infidelity to some article or articles of the seminary creed. The point of divergence from the belief of the founders which has received greatest attention is what is often erroneously called "future probation," or more exactly the belief that "those who have had no opportunity to learn of a Saviour in this life may be granted such an opportunity in the other life." That several of the professors at Andover held this doctrine is certain, and was well understood for two or three years before the charges were preferred in July, 1886. The visitors took up the charges, and the professors were summoned to answer.

The graduates of the seminary abound in eastern Massachusetts, but are pastors of churches all over the country. All these graduates and the Congregational churches generally were deeply interested in the prosecution. Many eminent men were certain that the professors were not merely heretical, but dishonest. Others held that the duty to the light coming from the Scriptures specifically required in connection with subscription to the creed was paramount. Others believed that articles in the creed were so inconsistent with each other, and that the whole document was so plainly a reconciliation of opposing schools, that the original founders must have put very different constructions upon different parts of it. Others affirmed that there could be nothing dishonorable in the acceptance of an opinion not expressly ruled out, and indeed not even considered, by the "founders" and "associate founders" of the seminary. Many others waited for the issue of the trial. The excitement was probably greater in the Congregational circles in and about Boston than elsewhere. Boston is but twenty-three miles from Andover, and has been the headquarters of the "American Board of Commissioners for Foreign Missions" since its formation. Naturally the managers of this great society were profoundly affected by the movement. The Congregational House at Boston, in which the rooms of the American Board and those of other Congregational benevolent societies as well as the rooms of that newspaper [1] which had been zealous for the prosecution were located, the head-centre of Congrega-

---

[1] *The Congregationalist.*

tionalism, was doubtless a place of constant discussion both before and after the charges weie preferred. The belief in a future opportunity for repentance for those who have had no knowledge of Christ in this life, which belief has seemed generally the most objectionable of the Andover views, had adherents outside of the seminary and its graduates among clergymen and distinguished laymen. Many who would not accept this belief cherished a hope, without laying down any definite mode of divine action, that the issues of the life to come may not in every case have been determined in the present life. Probably views and hopes like these were more generally held by influential Congregationalists in and about Boston in 1886 than elsewhere in our country.

It was perfectly natural that those gentlemen who in important positions looked upon such views as most harmful should do all in their power to discredit them. The cry was early raised that the "Andover hypothesis," as it has been called, which strictly means the belief that an opportunity after death to know Christ and repent may be granted to those who have never heard of Him in this life, and has been held by some of the ablest theologians of this century in England and Germany, and which is certainly as old as the third century of the Christian dispensation, "cuts the nerve of missions." However plausible such a statement may at first seem, there was a revival of missionary zeal in the Andover seminary the year immediately preceding the prosecution. In that same year, 1886, candidates for missionary service presented themselves to the Prudential Committee of the American Board from the Andover seminary. In one or two cases the candidates accepted this hypothesis, or rather refused to deny the possibility of its truth. Other applicants since have looked upon the ultimate destiny of the heathen who have not heard of Christ as involved in mystery, and have had some sympathy with the "Andover" view. The question as to whether those who accepted the belief that for such as had not heard the gospel in this life a knowledge of Christ after death would be given might be sent as missionaries by the American Board arose then of necessity in the committee who decide upon applications. In that committee some went so far in opposition to sending such as to avow that uncertainty in the mind of any candidate as to whether the destiny of every man is irrevocably fixed in this life disqualified the candidate for missionary service.

Perhaps the gravest case of hardship was that of the Rev. Robert A. Hume, a man of singular devotion to his Master and of peculiar efficiency in the Marathi Mission, who, after ten years of service, was enjoying his rest in this country. He expressed himself at the alumni dinner of the Andover seminary as finding some comfort in being able to say to thoughtful heathen that he was not positive that all their ancestors were hopelessly lost, and distinctly intimated that the explanation adopted by some of the Andover professors would make it easier for him to carry on his missionary work. "I can say," are his words, "not only for myself but for a considerable number of workers in the field, that we believe there is light in this matter. It is a practical question, which we believe is going to receive from this source a more Christian and helpful solution." He was the son of missionary parents; he was passionately devoted to his work; his return was longed for by his colleagues; the nerve of his love for the poor Hindoos and for their conversion had not been "cut," but rather stimulated by every step of mental and spiritual growth. A purpose was at once manifested after his frank but tender words at the Andover dinner to resist his return. His request for the privilege of resuming his work, now that his vacation had expired, was answered with evasive postponement.

The applications of the new candidates were practically rejected with the adoption of a resolution that "it is inexpedient to appoint *at present*." Here was certainly a new condition, a crisis in the missionary society of the Congregational churches. Many large contributors regarded this refusal to accept young men who longed to carry "the good news" of God to a dying world, and especially the cruel treatment of Mr. Hume, as certain to do the greatest injury to the kingdom of Christ. On the other hand, many said that these young men, who were ready to leave the brightest prospects in this country to fulfill the Saviour's mission and to partake of his sufferings in benighted foreign lands, did not believe that this *is* "a dying world." To cherish a hope that God in his mercy might make Christ known to those who had not heard of Him in this life seemed to them to disqualify for missionary service a man who was so deeply in earnest to make Christ known to the heathen in this life that he was ready to make the supreme sacrifice in order to go and preach to them the gospel.

In 1871, at Salem, Massachusetts, the following declaration was adopted by the board: —

"Neither this board, nor the Prudential Committee, are in any wise a theological court to settle doctrinal points of belief, but a body instituted by the churches to make known the gospel of Christ among the heathen nations and those who sit in darkness, though nominally Christian, and establish churches among them, maintaining that faith, and that only, which is universally received by those Christian bodies whose agents they are, and who furnish the funds which they administer."

In opposition to this declaration the Prudential Committee of the board had now begun to reject applicants on doctrinal grounds. A disposition was manifest to use this great missionary society for suppressing false doctrine. How much personal antagonism and institutional rivalry mingled with the motives arising from a desire for a pure gospel no one should attempt to say. But it was believed by men of judicial temper that a disposition was shown as early as the meeting in Portland, Maine, in 1884, to marshal the forces of the board against the friends of what has been called "the new departure" in theology.

This was the condition of things in the autumn of 1886, when the board was to convene in Des Moines, Iowa. The venerable chairman [1] of the Prudential Committee, who had been a member of that body for twenty-nine years, was so disheartened by the resolute determination of the committee to exclude from missionary service those whose views were not definitely fixed as to the impossibility for any heathen of repentance after death, that he prepared to resign his position. With him Dr. Hopkins had a warm sympathy. Without any particular interest in the "theory," he felt that the discouragement of these young men was sure to have widespread and disastrous consequences.

The action of the Prudential Committee in rejecting young men, and the whole tendency of the board to constitute itself a theological court to test the soundness of candidates on the most obscure questions of doctrine, Dr. Hopkins fully disapproved. His whole soul condemned the introduction of partisanship into the activities of the board, and his mind eagerly sought for a solution of the difficulties that should enable all shades of belief to work together in harmony for the conversion of the world.

[1] Hon. Alpheus Hardy, of Boston.

The debate that was sure to come at Des Moines opened on the report of the committee to which the Annual Report of the Prudential Committee upon the Home Department had been referred. It was a debate of great interest, in which some of the ablest men of the denomination took part. In the course of the debate an extract from a letter from the newly appointed president of Yale University was read, suggesting the ordinary Congregational council as the proper tribunal for the decision of such questions as the Prudential Committee were considering. It was after that suggestion, which had occurred to many, and seemed to Dr. Hopkins as probably the wisest way out of the difficulties besetting the board, that he made the following address: —

"It will be observed that President Dwight indicates a feeling of fear that there may be certain evils resulting from a reference of this theological question to any other authority than that which is recognized by the Congregational polity. I think that there are such evils, not only to be feared, but are now present in connection with the fact that this board, through its committee, does exercise ecclesiastical functions, or at least that the decision of theological questions is left with the board as it is represented by this committee. That fact does make the board theological in a certain sense, and in a sense in which it seems to me to have already brought with it serious evils, aside from those which have been connected with the discussions in the

Prudential Committee. One of these evils is these theological discussions which we are having to-day. It is a false position of the board in the view of the public. The public do regard the board as a theological body; and in coming here it was in all the papers that the great business of this board was to have a theological discussion. Now, while I agree that the method which has been adopted by this Board in determining the theological fitness of its candidates has worked well, — and I honor the secretaries in having guarded as they have our missions from the entrance of incapable men, and that guardianship is to be maintained, — yet the method by which this Prudential Committee is made also a theological committee, while it did work well for a time while the conditions were favorable, has not worked so well since the conditions were changed. It seems to me that those conditions are changed, and that the method has fallen into a place somewhat like that in which the ship fell that carried the Apostle Paul. That ship got into a place where two seas met, and the only thing to be done with it was to run it aground. Now it seems to me that the method — not the committee, but the method — has come into a place where two seas meet, and it comes to be a serious question whether it can be continued wisely by the board. The board has been placed in that position in the view of the public. Now if the board had originally adopted this policy, or one that is in accord with the resolution that has been read, not referring at all a theological question to the committee, leaving them simply a prudential committee, there would have been no lisp of any difficulty whatever, and all this trouble would have been saved. That is one evil that has arisen; all this difficulty has come simply from the fact that the Prudential Committee have been a theological committee — the whole of it.

"Another difficulty has arisen. Because the board has been considered as a theological body, and a theatre for debating theological questions, and as having the oversight of theological questions, it has been understood, since the time of the meeting of the board in Portland, that the two wings — if I may so express it — of the theological world there at the East have been manœuvring on the one side and on the other — I don't say it is so, but it has been said to be so, and there have been whisperings in the air, and a great evil has arisen in consequence — to make the American Board a makeweight in theological discussions. The American Board ought never to know anything of them. It ought not to be in a position in which that could be possible. But it is done, and in connection with the action of the Prudential Committee there has been a great alienation of feeling in the churches of Boston towards the action of the committee. An officer of one of those churches recently said to me that the churches of Boston would not stand it. Now all this comes from the fact that the decision of theological questions is in the hands of the Prudential Committee, and I agree perfectly with Secretary Clark that, if it were possible, the decision of such points should be removed from that committee. I rather·inferred, from what Dr. Alden [1] said as to the entire unity between himself and Dr. Clark,[1] knowing that Dr. Clark believed that that was the wisest way, that Dr. Alden also knew it and believed it. I was delighted to hear Dr. Alden say that he regarded the Congregational body as thoroughly orthodox, as orthodox as the Presbyterian body; and I could not help feeling, when he said that, that he ought to be entirely content, and rejoice to refer all theological questions to such an orthodox body! I know that there were many things said in Dr. Alden's address that were very encouraging, but there were other things which were not said, — he was not called upon to say them, — namely, that there was any division in the committee. Now, in connection with this theological question, there was a division in the committee, and the chairman of the committee, Mr. Hardy, I know was decidedly and strongly on the other side. There were two members of the committee decidedly and strongly on the other side. Now we do not want divisions in the committee. We know how excited men become in theological discussions, and we do not want anything of this kind in the committee.

"Now I should like to know if it is not in the

---

[1] Secretaries, or managing officers of the work of the Board of Commissioners for Foreign Missions.

scope and power of the Congregational body, of this board, with the Prudential Committee and all its wisdom, to devise some method by which those questions can be taken out of the discussion and leave the Prudential Committee wholly a prudential committee, and not a theological committee. I am inclined to think that if the Congregational polity which has been referred to in the letter of President Dwight is not adequate to the provisions of a fit ministry for the missions, if it is not adequate to secure such orthodoxy as is sufficient and proper in connection with missionaries, I am inclined to think that that polity ought not to be. I believe it is wholly able to secure all that is necessary. There may be modifications desirable, but I know that they can be made, and I trust that this question will not be settled until the question of some method of removing this theological question from the committee and from the board shall be thoroughly debated and thoroughly understood, and if possible settled. Possibly not in this meeting; I do not see that it can be; but I wish to have it come thoroughly before the board and before all these people, so that the condition of the board as a non-theological body shall stand before the country, and that it shall not be considered as a theatre for theological discussion."

This address of Dr. Hopkins was not without great influence upon the members of the board. Conservative men expressed themselves as willing that the experiment should be tried of settling the threatening difficulties by means of councils. The outcome of the entire debate was the passage of the following resolutions, and the fourth resolution may be regarded as largely carried through Dr. Hopkins's influence.

"*Resolved*, That we recognize with profound gratitude the continued marks of favor with which our Lord and Master regards this great work of preaching the gospel to all nations.

"*Resolved*, That the board recognizes and approves the principle upon which the Prudential Committee has continued to act in regard to appointments for missionary service, in strictly conforming to the well understood and permanent basis of doctrinal faith upon which the missions of the board have been steadily conducted, and to which, in the exercise of its sacred trust, the committee had no option but to conform.

"*Resolved*, The board is constrained to look with grave apprehension upon certain tendencies of the doctrine of probation after death which has been recently broached and diligently propagated, that seem divisive and perversive and dangerous to the churches at home and abroad. In view of those tendencies, they do heartily approve of the action of the Prudential Committee in carefully guarding the board from any committal to the approval of that doctrine, and advise a continuance of the caution in time to come.

"*Resolved*, The board recommends to the Prudential Committee to consider in difficult cases, turning upon doctrinal views of candidates for missionary service, the expediency of calling a council of the churches, to be constituted in some manner which may be determined by the good judgment of the committee, to pass upon the theological soundness of the candidate, and the committee is instructed to report on this matter to the board at the next annual meeting."

There was a hopeful feeling in the minds of many members of this great society, when its sessions closed, that the judgment of the president would have weight with the Prudential Committee, but the capital defect of the last resolution was the reference to this committee of the consideration of a method by which the perils into which they had led the society could be averted. They were strongly committed to the policy of excluding from the missionary field of this society all applicants whose views on eschatological questions did not harmonize with those of the majority, and it was a foregone conclusion that they would report adversely to the proposal. The third resolution above quoted commended their zeal in thus guarding the field from these unworthy applicants, and the possibility that by any method any such applicant might enter into this labor was enough to condemn that method.

The resolutions seem to mean that no one having any sympathy with the doctrine of "probation after death" could be appointed, and that, if that result could be secured by councils, the committee might resort to councils.

The council, the highest authority in the Congregational polity, composed generally of two delegates, the pastor and one layman, from each of the churches of a neighborhood invited by the church calling the council, and often also of distinguished ministers and laymen from a distance in addition to those of the vicinity, determines the questions preliminary to the settling and removing of a minister. The questions also on which a church is divided are often solved by a council agreed to by each party. But a council always determines the doctrinal and personal fitness of a minister for his work. Very rarely, when a minister has been invited by a church and parish (two distinct bodies in the Congregational polity, both of which must unite in order that a minister be properly called), does the council invited to examine the candidate declare him doctrinally unfit. Great reluctance is naturally felt to pronouncing a minister unsound in the faith. The Congregational Church in New England has, since the days of Horace Bushnell, been increasingly disposed to grant wide liberty in doctrinal opinions. While her ministry embraces less divergent views than the Church of England, it is probable that individual shades of belief are not less numerous. Of late years there have been many conservative Congregationalists who were inclined to the opinion that a council whose members were judiciously selected, or were taken without selection from the more scholarly communities, would confirm any minister who did not reject the deity of Christ. After the debate at Springfield, Massachusetts, in 1887, on the report made by the Prudential Committee with reference to the final resolution given above, a resolution to the effect that "this board does not discredit the results of councils as representing the doctrinal judgments and fellowship of the Congregational churches" was rejected. This shows how general the feeling had become among Congregationalists that, as Dr. Hopkins put it in his speech, "the Congregational polity is not adequate to secure such orthodoxy as is sufficient and proper." If Dr. Hopkins had been then a member of the Prudential Committee, his influence would have secured at least a minority report in favor of councils which, whatever may be their weakness, are the constitutional court for deciding doctrinal questions in the Congregational Church. The last time his voice was heard in the great meetings of the American Board on any matter of business, it was for the peace and prosperity that can come only by the removal of theological discussions from *all* the meetings of the board; for the concentration of all the forces of the Congregational Church in the prosecution and extension of its great missionary work.

Dr. Hopkins returned from Des Moines to Williamstown somewhat wearied by the long journey and the continuous strain of responsibility for the conduct of the meetings, and by the anxiety for a peaceful issue to the difficult and exciting questions under debate. He was always hopeful that the good sense and reason of men would prevail over prejudice and passion. In his long relations with students he had uniformly relied upon the better elements in their nature. He had always shown a calm and benignant patience, and often that patience had been rewarded by the reëstablishment in a pupil of the earnest purpose to do well that had for a little wavered. He began again after a few days of rest, the work with the Senior class, which he had for so many years conscientiously performed. The period of instruction during the last six years of his life covered something less than four months. generally from the week following the meeting of the American Board in October to a point beyond the middle of February. During this time he taught the Seniors in one division (the classes varied in the Senior year from forty to sixty) first "An Outline Study of Man," and after that "The Law of Love and Love as a Law." He commonly met the class every morning and two afternoons each week, but Saturday morning was given to that study of Vincent on the "Westminster Assembly's Shorter Catechism," which most of his pupils enjoyed supremely. In October, 1886, he began to teach for the fifty-first time the elements of intellectual philosophy to the Senior class of the college. It will be remembered that he became professor of moral philosophy in 1830, so that this was the fifty-seventh year of his instruction in morals. The principles underlying these departments were as familiar and clear to him as ever, and there was no diminution of the vigor with which he announced and enforced his conclusions. The chief change noticeable in his conduct of a class was that occasioned by the gradual failure of his hearing. He was perfectly aware of this loss, and more than once suggested that he was ready to lay down the burden of his teaching if the college could be better served by his doing so. But each entering class looked forward to his instruction. Each graduating class counted it still as the chief advantage of the college course to have sat at his feet. The words from Rev. Dr. Spring's monograph in which he speaks of a visit in this winter to one of his recitations may well be quoted here: —

"If the enthusiasm which burned in Dr. Hopkins's soul was different, it was not less real. It continued for threescore years with no abatement, — at least I could discover none during the last weeks of his work, when after an absence of a quarter of a century I visited his class-room. It was the same gracious and magnificent personality that I had known and revered as a student. When I looked at him, I could see in the deeper furrows that crossed his brow, in the greater deliberation of his movements, in the slight deafness that at times made it difficult for him to catch the answers of the class, that time had touched him, though but tenderly. Yet if I closed my eyes, the old days seemed to have returned. The ear reported that things were as they used to be. He was then eighty-five years old, but his intellectual powers appeared to be as brilliant as ever, and his interest as keen in questions which he had discussed with sixty generations of students."

The months slipped away. His benignant presence moved deliberately about the streets of Williamstown, and while every one saw that his step was less elastic than once, there was no perceptible failure either in mind or body. His interest in the college that he had so long loved and in the Missionary Society of which he was still the head was as keen as ever. He had much comfort in the slow but certain growth of the college in all directions, but the missionary work, or rather the obstacles to expansion of the missionary work, were still a cause of unrest and fear in his mind. An application was made in January, 1887, by another Andover student, the son of a missionary, to the Prudential Committee for permission to go to Japan in the service of the board. The candidate had sympathy with the new views. He was informed that the committee had no option under the Des Moines resolutions, but must decline to appoint any candidate so long as he holds these views. In February, 1887, the pressure for Mr. Hume's reappointment from all sides led the committee to consent to his return to India. Mr. Hume, it should be said, had not committed himself fully to the acceptance of the hypothesis of a probation after death for those who have no knowledge of

Christ in this life.   He had, however, in his speech
at the Andover dinner, shown a friendly interest
and tolerance for that speculation.   But the Prudential Committee made a fine distinction between
one who had been successful as a missionary and
a new applicant for appointment.   A renewed application from two candidates, one of whom had
been refused and the other discouraged, was made
to the committee in April, 1887.   The position
of one of these was identical with that of Mr.
Hume.   Both applications were rejected.

Meanwhile the agitation for and against councils
as the proper tribunal to settle theological questions was continued.   Dr. Hopkins had taken his
stand at Des Moines in favor of the reference of
difficult cases to councils.   Some associations in
the Congregational body had discussed the question, and had arrived at decisions for or against
that reference.   On June 2, 1887, fifteen days before Dr. Hopkins's death, an article appeared in
the editorial columns of the "Independent" headed
"Councils for Foreign Missionary Candidates."
Free quotations are given from that article, as
the last public utterance that Dr. Hopkins made
was in reply to its positions, and appeared in the
"Independent" June 16, the day before his death.
That utterance of Dr. Hopkins must be given entire, and it will be much more intelligible after the
quotations from the paper to which it is an answer.

The editorial in the "Independent" begins as
follows : —

"It is of course natural that those who favor the new and as it seems to us the very dangerous doctrine of a probation after death should be zealous in the effort to substitute scattered occasional councils in place of the Prudential Committee, as primary judges of the theological fitness of candidates for missionary service under the care of the American Board. This gives the only available chance of getting their objectionable hypothesis into missionary fields, and of having it, in an indirect fashion,, practically authorized and indorsed by the board. Their eagerness for it is no more difficult of explanation than the eagerness of a man who has written a book not generally acceptable to get it recommended by those who can secure for it a generous circulation.

"It is almost equally a matter of course that any who, without committing themselves to this particular speculation, are chronically if not constitutionally favorable to whatever is indefinite in theological statement, should be on the same side, ready and eager for any contrivance which they think may open gates and lower bars in the fences which define the orthodox field, and· may leave missionaries and ministers freer for self-approved departures from the faith of the Fathers."

Other quotations necessary to the understanding of Dr. Hopkins's reply are as follows: —

"The man is sent, not to a service likely to be brief, like that of an imperfect pastorate at home, but to one naturally expected and intended to continue for life : only to be terminated, before death, after long inquiry, a long correspondence, a final reluctant action of the committee. Indeed, it does not appear how the committee can properly recall its appointee at all unless another council, sitting somewhere or other, shall have judged him unsound. Even then some are dissatisfied, naturally enough, because he was sent, and so much consecrated money has been wasted. Others are dissatisfied because he has been recalled. The result is inevitable, in diminished contributions, divided churches, hostile parties. The discreet and sagacious system of the board, so carefully framed, so wisely and so safely administered through a long course of years, so successful in its results, is rudely broken up to meet the demand of the rash innovation, — an innovation called for by nothing whatever except the desire to force new theories into the board, and distinctly to remove it from its old and firm basis of doctrine. The effort to make seminaries teach speculative theories contrary to their creeds, which has been partly successful, has its counterpart and its complement in this effort to make the American Board circulate doctrines which most of its members do not believe, and at which its founders would, literally, have stood aghast!

"We quite expect that not only those who favor this latest mischievous theory will be united in effort to displace the established method of the board, but that others will agree with them, as we have suggested, who have themselves some pet speculation not accepted by the churches; who are perhaps Universalists *in petto*, or who deem the Bible a natural product of the religious life of its writers, with no divine guidance and aid to make it the Book of God for the world; those who find the only contents of the Atonement in the coming of Christ and his gracious example, its only virtue in the effect of his mission on human hearts. All such will combine, as a matter of course, to make occasional temporary councils the only judges of theological soundness in missionary candidates, and will regard others as violently 'obstructive' because they oppose it. With them may be united those who hold the old faith, but to whom animated discussion seems a breach of charity, who would like to make all things pleasant to everybody, who particularly desire to exclude debate from the meetings of the board, and to have the entire utterance of those meetings one of profuse and amiable gush."

From this long and able article other quotations would be interesting, but these are the points to which Dr. Hopkins replied. The views expressed are not merely stoutly opposed to councils for the decision of the theological fitness of applicants for missionary work, but present the utility of the council to the Congregational Church generally, as of doubtful value especially in the difficult cases which arise among applicants for pulpits in this country not less frequently, perhaps more frequently, than among applicants for service in the foreign field. Doubtless a machine might be devised that would secure greater uniformity of belief among the ministers of the Congregational body. but Dr. Hopkins did not believe that this is the time for the introduction of such a machine. Nor did he ever assent to the opinion that mathematical orthodoxy is more essential in a young man who invites the ignorant and degraded heathen to "behold the Lamb of God" as the Saviour of his soul than in the American preacher. With a vigor and a positiveness born of a noble liberality and a nobler love of men and Christ as the Redeemer of men he sent the following letter to the "Independent" in reply to its editorial article of June 2. The letter appeared June 16. He died the next morning. It is then at once his valedictory address as the president of the great society for saving the world and his final appeal to the churches.

To the Editor of the Independent: —

In your paper of this week is an editorial on "Councils in Connection with the American Board" which I have just read with surprise and sorrow. So far as it is an argument, and it is an able one, saying, perhaps, all that can be said against councils, I welcome it; but so far as it insinuates looseness of doctrine and heresy on the part of those who favor councils, and imputes to them unworthy motives, both of which it does largely, I deplore it. No man is omniscient, and I had hoped that that mode even of theological controversy had passed away.

I have favored councils, and shall continue to do so if

no better way can be found of obviating the present difficulties of the board. But in doing this I deny that I belong to any one of the classes into which your article divides those who favor them. I deny that I belong to the class " who favor the new, and as it seems to us, very dangerous doctrine of probation after death." I deny that I belong to the class " who, without committing themselves to this particular speculation, are chronically. if not constitutionally favorable to whatever is indefinite in theological statement," and are " ready and eager for any contrivance which they think may open gates and lower bars in the fences which define the orthodox field." I refuse to suffer to pass without challenge the astounding assertion, applicable to all who favor councils, that their introduction would be " an innovation called for by nothing whatever except the desire to force new theories into the board, and distinctly to remove it from its old and firm basis of doctrine." I deny that " the effort to make seminaries teach speculative theories contrary to their creeds, which has been partly successful. has its counterpart and its complement in this effort to make the American Board circulate doctrines which most of its members do not believe, and at which its founders literally would have stood aghast." On the contrary, it has been asserted, and I suppose truly, that the first attempt to use the board as a theological makeweight, or, as I have heard it expressed, to make it a pawn on the chess-board of theological controversy in this country, was made years ago, and has been persistently continued by those who favor the present policy. At this point it seems to me that judicious friends of the board can have but one wish, and that is that it should decline to be used by anybody, should have no partisanship, as far as possible should keep aloof from seminaries and theological controversies, and should steadily pursue its appropriate work of sending out suitable missionaries, dealing directly and fairly with each individual candidate.

I deny again that I can be classed with those "who hold the old faith, but to whom animated discussion seems a breach of charity, who would like to make all things pleasant to everybody, who particularly desire to exclude debate from the meetings of the board, and to have the entire utterance of those meetings one of profuse and amiable gush." It is true that I did object at Des Moines, and should again, to the discussion of the abstract question of the truth of the doctrine of a future probation. This I did because it was not in the line of the proper work of the board; because the decision of such a body on such a question could be of no authority and of no use, and especially because that was not the real question before the board. The real question was either not perceived, or was evaded. It was not, whether the doctrine is true or false, but whether the board would send out men who had doubts respecting it. That question I should like to have discussed. I should be pleased if some one would move at the next meeting of the board that the Prudential Committee be instructed not to send out any one who has any doubt on the subject of a future probation — who is not as certain that there will be no such probation as he is of the being of God. In the discussion of such a motion 'I should expect to hear something besides "gush." If it should pass, as I do not think it should, I should acquiesce cheerfully and wait. I might, perhaps, think the board was composed of old men, but should impute to them no bad motive. If that should not pass, I should be glad if some one would move that the committee be instructed to send out no one who should so hold the doctrine that he would feel obliged to *preach* it; thus leaving each one free to have doubts and form his opinions, and deal with the subject as best he may. For such a motion I would vote. I think it should satisfy the conservatives, and would not be objected to by the progressives. The board should represent its constituency, and I do not believe that any considerable number of them wish to send out men who will preach that doctrine. Perhaps this would be the best way out of the present difficulty. If the board itself would give such instruction, I should be willing to let the matter of councils rest where it is for the present. We should then have a definite policy. Every candidate would know precisely what to expect, and there would be no need to write letters to ascertain what the direction of the board really was. It will be seen, then, that I am in favor of a full discussion of all questions relating to the qualifications of candidates. I am also in favor of such discussion in relation to the constitution and all methods of procedure of the board.

The above denials I make, not solely on my own behalf, but on behalf of the great body of those whose minds have been turned toward councils as a source of relief from the difficulties into which the board has been brought through the policy pursued at the Mission Rooms. These difficulties cannot be denied, though they are wholly ignored in your article. It cannot be denied that the feelings of large numbers of the constituents of the board have been severely tried, if not alienated, by that policy, that their contributions have been given under protest, and that the students of several seminaries have, as a body, felt themselves rebuffed and repelled. It has been solely in view of these, and of other evils that have been mentioned, but of which I need not speak, that my own mind has been led, and as I believe, the minds of ninety-nine hundredths of those who are dissatisfied with the present policy have been led to look to councils for relief. Those who thus look are, in my belief, as earnestly attached to the board, as ready to make sacrifices for missions, and as desirous that the glorious gospel of the blessed God, in all its fullness and power, should be carried to mission fields, as are those who, with whatever good intentions, are constantly making insinuations against them, and substituting these in the place of argument.

You say well in your article that "there is no profit in idealizing councils." I agree with you. There are objections to councils. I have no zeal for them, or for anything else that is simply instrumental. My object in this paper has not been to answer objections to them. If the present policy can be so modified as to produce harmony, I would not disturb it. If not, I believe that we should have, on the whole, as sound, as faithful, and as successful a body of missionaries through the proposed agency of councils as we have now.

But while you say what you do of idealizing councils, I would it had occurred to you to say the same of committees. This might have been hoped for, especially since the following words concerning it of one long chairman of the committee have been so recently and emphatically given to the public. "I believe," he says, " there has been, during the past few years, a divergence in the *practical* management of one part of the board's

work, which has, to some extent, brought the board
from its broad, catholic, ' undenominational' position to
be a partisan in questions that are not within its province, are local, in a measure personal, and divisive."
The committee have done noble work, and are to be
honored. but they are liable to mistakes, and the results
even of their examinations have not always been perfect.
I happen to know that a faithful and successful missionary now in the field held firmly to this doctrine of a
future probation when he passed his examination some
few years since, and yet the subject was either wholly
ignored, or passed by as unessential. If the present
policy were consistently carried out, I suppose this man
and several others would be recalled.

What may be done in the meeting at Springfield I do
not know, but look forward to it with hope. In the
mean time, I heartily join with you, as also, I am sure,
do the great body of those who look toward councils, in
the desire " to save from all complicity with unbelief a
great institution in which, to an important degree, the
life of the Church is involved and revealed, which has
the world for the sphere of its work, and which will
have its grand offices to accomplish for the Lord when
we are gone.

Williams College, *June* 3, 1887.

In answer to this letter in the same number of
the newspaper in which it appeared was another
editorial article. It is not worth while to give its
positions in full, as they did not come under the
eye of Dr. Hopkins, and we are concerned only
with his relations to the crisis. The positions rest
on the assertion that the doctrine of probation after

death for any is a very dangerous heresy, so dangerous, at least, that he who holds it ought not to become a missionary of the cross even from a society in which many large contributors are inclined to look with favor on the doctrine. The positions taken regard the Prudential Committee as especially well adapted to prevent the sending of heretical missionaries, and reiterate the objections to councils previously given, and insist that the change from the old method and reference to a council would be an "innovation called for by nothing whatever but a desire to force new theories into the board."

The last paragraph or two of the article may well be quoted, as illustrating the kind of appeal that was made to Dr. Hopkins during the last months of his life.

"Dr. Hopkins could add no more distinguished and honorable service, crowning the noble work of his life, and making his name illustrious and eminent for all time to come in the history of the American church, than by saying at Springfield: 'This has gone far enough! We are not a theological court, and it is not our function to search out heresies, or to condemn them. But this board was established, and it exists, to proclaim to the world the gospel of salvation by immediate repentance and faith in the Redeemer. Any theory which gives encouragement to delay is outside of our limits, and adverse to our work. It cannot have admission among us. We send the gospel to men in this world, because we do not expect them to receive it after earth shall have closed probation. That is the faith in which our work had its origin. That is the faith now held by our churches; and with that our messengers must be in accord. If others think that they have another scheme of truth, better and larger, to proclaim to mankind, we cannot change, but for them the world is open.'

"Such a word from him would be like Wellington's final command to the unshaken squares on the ridge of Waterloo. Better than that; it would be like Paul's address to the elders, when men were to arise among them speaking perverse things. It would bring such a power from on high upon the assembly as could the word of no other man. We reverently believe that the spirits of those who have given long labor, and life itself, to the service of the Master, in the name of the coöperating churches, and by the proclamation of the one divine message, would hail it with a triumph of gladder praise from thrones amid the heavenly light! We have lived too long to overrate the importance of particular occasions. But it seems to us that no opportunity nobler than this has been offered to man since Mills was touched, almost eighty years since, with the divine fire."

Though Dr. Hopkins did not read this appeal, he had many private letters to the same purport. They struck various notes of admiration, praise, or warning, according to the disposition of the writer. One letter from a well-known clergyman suggested that the close of his administration of the American Board might become like that of James Buchanan's administration of the federal government. The parallel was sufficiently striking, but not very apt.

There is no reason to believe that Dr. Hopkins would have changed his position. When he had once taken a position he was *tenax propositi.* He had a firm faith in the ultimate ascendency of truth and wisdom, and he died in that faith. The exclusion of young men from missionary work because of an unwillingness to assert that the destiny of every one is irrevocably fixed at death he regarded as in direct disobedience to the Master's command, "Go ye into all the world, and preach the gospel to every creature," but independently of that feeling he thought that great harm would come to the missionary cause from the exclusion by one permanent body, even if any candidates ought to be excluded. Less than four months after his death the corporate members of the board at Springfield rejected by an overwhelming majority his parting advice. That was partly because the issue had been rather adroitly shifted, and partly because the liberals, knowing that they were in the minority, preferred to confine their efforts to polling as large a vote as possible in favor of officers who would sympathize with a gentler policy towards the young applicants. The fifty-five votes that were cast for President Angell of Michigan University as the successor to Dr. Hopkins were votes representing largely the educated brain and the tender heart of New England. Many of them were cast with a thought of affectionate honor for Dr. Hopkins's far-sighted and heroic defense of the Congregational polity. His vision was accurate. The troubles are not yet wholly composed. The belief still exists in the minds of able men that to follow his advice would be the safe and happy issue.

THE FRIEND.

"O friend, my bosom said,
  Through thee alone the sky is arched,
  Through thee the rose is red:
  All things through thee take nobler form,
  And look beyond the earth,
  The mill-round of our fate appears
  A sun-path in thy worth.
  Me too thy nobleness has taught
  To master my despair,
  The fountains of my hidden life
  Are through thy friendship fair."
EMERSON, Friendship.

CHAPTER XI.

THE FRIEND.

In 1837 Dr. Hopkins was the orator before the "Porter Rhetorical Society" of the Andover Theological Seminary. That was the summer at the close of his first year's service as president of the college. On this occasion he met for the first time Rev. Ray Palmer, then settled over the Central Church in Bath, Maine, with whom he later formed an intimate friendship, which continued to the end of his life. The attachment was based on strong affinities in taste and work, and was all the more enjoyable that the gifts of the two men were very different.

While Dr. Palmer was for a good deal of his life absorbed in the work of a city pastorate and came more closely into relation with the feelings and wants of ordinary people, he was a scholar in philosophy and ethics, and was wholly able to appreciate Dr. Hopkins's investigations and discussions. When Dr. Palmer reviewed the "Lectures on Moral Science" in the "North American Review," Dr. Hopkins's comment was: "My reviewer understands my system better than I do myself." This bit of pleasantry was more than an expression of affectionate regard. It was a mark of high esteem.

Dr. Hopkins's instrument of expression was prose. His most eloquent passages, full of emotion and beauty as they were, he could not have put into perfect rhythmical form. He had a great admiration of good poetry, and his excellent native judgment was developed by the studies that he made when professor of "Moral Philosophy and Rhetoric." He became familiar with the leading English poets during those six years, and the quotations that he made in his lectures were always appropriate and effective. Mrs. Lesley, in the charming volume containing recollections of her mother Mrs. Judge Lyman, of Northampton, gives a letter from Mrs. Lyman, who heard Dr. Hopkins lecture in Northampton in 1845, and makes this reference to the lecture : "He exemplified his subject by a great many appropriate figures and the introduction of a great deal of fine poetry." He was fond of beautiful hymns, and the contributions that Dr. Palmer made to the hymnology of the churches were undoubtedly an element that promoted the friendship.

The letters that Dr. Hopkins wrote to Dr. Palmer, most frequent between 1860 and 1875, were carefully preserved by Dr. Palmer, and through the kindness of his son, Rev. Dr. Charles Ray Palmer, of Bridgeport, Connecticut, extracts are given from these letters. They illustrate more perfectly what

Dr. Hopkins was in the free familiar movement of social intimacy than any other accessible record.

WILLIAMS COLLEGE, *August* 28, 1874.

Among the first things I do, my dear Doctor, on getting home is to remember my indebtedness to you, and to give some account of myself.

I am just back from your native State, and from within sight of Little Compton.[1] While there I had a call from Mr. Rowland G. Hazard, who wrote a treatise on the Will and some letters to Mill on Cause and Effect. On the Will I think him right as to the fact of liberty, but wrong as to the point where he places it. He says it is at the point of effort, and that choice is wholly an intellectual operation, at which I am surprised. But on Cause and Effect he is able and right and, I think, disposes effectually of both Mill and Hamilton. He spent some days with Mill, and had a long discussion with him. He invited the party — four of us — to dine and to tea, and gave us a ride. He is a business man, a fine mathematician, and I had much pleasure in making his acquaintance, and I dare say you know all about him. He lives at Peacedale, and he and his son have put up a most beautiful Congregational church, they say, the most beautiful in the country.

Charles wrote me that you spoke to him of the English issue of my book, and he offered to procure me a copy. It has just come, and is a decided

1 Dr. Palmer's birthplace.

improvement on the native copy. They are better book-makers over there. The dress of a book does make a difference, and I think it was a mistake not to put it in better shape here.

WILLIAMS COLLEGE, *October* 30, 1874.

On parting from you at Rutland we came directly home. Since that I have been hearing the class, and we have had company most of the time; so that I have done very little. I am just beginning to put something together for my lectures, or rather for my first lecture, at New Haven, but find it slow business. I work alone, and need the stimulus of the interchange of thought.

The meeting at Rutland I enjoyed greatly. The debt was less than I expected, the papers were excellent, and then there was a spirit of quietness and devotedness that seemed deep and earnest, and I cannot but hope great good will follow. The statements were encouraging, but my whole reliance is on the promises. What God has promised He is able to perform, and so I hold myself steady, thanking Him that I may be permitted to do anything.

I supped or rather dined last night with Professor Price, a regular Englishman, and a great talker. He used the expression "A gone coon," and I asked him how he came by it. He said he had known it for thirty years, and then I asked, "What is a coon? Is it a rabbit?" "No, no," said he, "it is an opossum." So I found I knew more than he did on one point, and say again, "Non omnes omnia opossum — us !" This morning he spoke an hour to the Junior class, and pleased them.

New Britain, March 27, 1875.

My lectures at New Haven are over. Tuesday evening next I am to lecture in Hartford, if I can get ready, which I am far from being yet. After that, perhaps next week, perhaps the week after, we propose to go to Washington for a visit.

Of course I went to New Haven with no little diffidence, following such great men, and going among such great men. I endeavored to conduct myself properly, and to say nothing heretical. Judge of my surprise, then, when the lectures were over, at being informed that the theological faculty wanted to see me. I mustered up courage and went. They were all assembled, Dr. Bacon presiding. It was like going before the Sanhedrim. However, they asked me to be seated, and you can imagine my relief when I was informed that their object in wishing to see me was to know whether I would give another course next year. I am to decide within a week. My feeling is against it, but perhaps I ought. I have no idea who it is that makes the provision for the lectures.

Williams College, July 3, 1875.

I have been thinking some about my lectures on "The Scriptural Idea of God," and have fallen into inquiries in regard to the Absolute and Infinite and Unconditioned, and find great disagreement and confusion among writers about them. I am sure nothing can be done for a long time that will bring any uniformity of judgment on those subjects, and it is discouraging to read and think. One trouble is that when men get into the intuitional region they differ about what is known by intuition as much as they do about anything else. I am just looking into Calderwood's "Philosophy of the Infinite," and see that he holds to an immediate and intuitive knowledge of God as a holy God, and thinks that, if we do not accept that, the being of God cannot be proved.

Williams College, *August* 13, 1875.

It is a fortnight to-day since I left home to go to Nahant to preach. I was the guest of my friend Amos A. Lawrence, and had a pleasant time. The congregation is not a promising one to preach to, but I have had evidence in time past that my labor there has not been in vain. The day before I was there, two of the nephews of Mr. Lawrence, one of them the Episcopal minister of Stockbridge, started in their yacht to visit him, and on their way saw the sea-serpent, or sea-monster, whatever it may be, and shot at it with a rifle some twenty times. It has been seen by others, and in such a way that I think we shall have to accept the fact of the existence of some kind of animal hitherto unknown, perhaps the last of a species now nearly extinct. He may be to the ocean what the last mammoth was to the land. Monday I spent at Nahant, except that I went into Boston to look up my overcoat, which I left in the hack in which I crossed the city. I wish all hackmen were as honest as that one, for he called out to me as soon as he saw me and restored the coat.

WILLIAMS COLLEGE, September 2, 1875.

I hasten to assure you that I shall esteem it one of the great honors of my life to have my name associated with yours in such a work as your forthcoming one is to be. It cannot fail to live, and to be an honor to the country and to all connected with it.

What you say of the connection between poetry and philosophy is true. It is true of the lighter kinds of poetry, but especially of all that is of a high and serious character. In fact, much of such poetry is just the flower of which philosophy is the root. The flower has the beauty and the fragrance and is most sought, and sometimes I think we might as well leave the roots of our emotions and actions to take care of themselves, but I remember that roots are more medicinal, and so continue to dig on.

WILLIAMS COLLEGE, November 9, 1875.

Who shall say after this that Friday is an unlucky day? Yesterday afternoon the expressman came with two boxes, both paid in full. One was a small paper box, the other a large one nailed up, and what might be in either I could not conjecture. Opening the smaller one first, there was an appearance of solid gold in the perfectly gilded leaves, and within something more precious than gold. If, as Solomon says, "a word fitly spoken is like apples of gold in pictures of silver," what shall we say of so many words so spoken that not one of them could be changed for another, or changed in place with advantage? The other box was from my friend and classmate Rice, of Cleveland, and contained a dozen bottles of Catawba wine, the pure juice of the grape, old, and with a bouquet like that of the grapes themselves. It was sent, to be sure, more especially for Mrs. Hopkins's health, but as she has hitherto been averse to taking anything of the kind, I hold myself ready, if need be, to encourage her by taking a little myself. If I remember rightly, I encouraged a certain poet once in the same way. Just think of it now — poetry and wine in the same day! was it because poetry is the wine of literature, and that they had an affinity for each other?

Having thus spoken of the boxes together, I turn to the one most precious. And here I may as well say that the first thing I looked at was the inscription. I wanted to see how my name would look embarked on its voyage to posterity between such covers and in such company. Was it vanity? If it was, my vanity was gratified. I could not have wished anything different. I am particularly pleased with the likeness in front. You have reason to congratulate yourself on that because a good likeness is so seldom seen. Of course Mrs. Palmer is not satisfied with it, as what woman ever was in such a case, but I hope she will be resigned when she thinks how much better off she is than some others.

The poems I have not had time to look much at yet, but have read the preface and the notes. There are some things in those that needed to be touched with a delicate hand, and I think you have succeeded perfectly. Everything is in perfect taste.

How you get time for all you do, I do not see, and for work so diversified. I have been reading your article on Longfellow, and do not see what more could be asked. I appreciate him more through you than I have done before, but must confess to a higher estimate of Lowell.

Williams College, February 4, 1876.

Yesterday was my birthday. I was seventy-four years old, almost three quarters of a century. In some respects of my days I can say of them, as Jacob did of his, "few and evil," but in others, and more generally, as David did, "Surely goodness and mercy have followed me all the days of my life," and oh, that I could add with the assurance that he did, "and I shall dwell in the house of the Lord forever"! It seems too much for such a creature as I am, and yet it is not too much for God to give. My health continues good, and I have not as yet missed a recitation since we began last term. We have gone through with the "Outline Study," and

"The Law of Love," and I have now taken up a book on Logic new to me, Jevons. When I get through that with the reviews and examinations, my recitations for the year will be over. Of course we keep up the Catechism, and then I preach. There is more religious interest in the college than for a long time. The meetings are full and earnest, and there are, as we hope, some conversions. I expect to preach to-morrow. It would be a great mercy if we could see a revival such as we have seen here.

Of course in connection with all this my lectures get on slowly; but I think I may be able to prepare them, if not as I wish, yet so that I can give them. I am just now thinking about moral attributes, and whether what are called so are properly attributes at all. Can anything that goes to make up, not characteristics, but character, be properly called an attribute? Whatever belongs to the nature of God may be an attribute, but I suppose the character of God does not belong to his nature. If it grew out of it necessarily, it would not be character. It seems to me distinction enough has not been made between the natural and the moral attributes. Dr. Hodge says the nature of God is the foundation of obligation, and so I suppose he thinks the nature of God is moral.

I hope your poems are continuing their sale and migrations, taking my name over the land in connection with yours. It is after all the poets of a country that are the best known, that is, in a desirable way.

Williams College, *March* 1, 1876.

You are right about the nature. I do not think I ever meant to deny a nature in such a sense that God would have no natural attributes. I remember when that whole thing came to me as in a moment. It was when I was giving the lectures in Boston. I was at the United States, and was in a puzzle about what is ultimate in obligation and the reference of it to the nature of God, when it came to me that in relation to the point that then troubled me God could have no nature, and that is what I hold now. My expressions, I can see, were not guarded as they should have been. It is difficult to know how far we are at liberty to argue from ourselves to God. To some extent we must. It appears to me now that God must not only so have a nature as to have natural attributes, but also that He must have a moral nature as we have — that is, a nature affirming obligation. That would be a necessity to Him, as to us, but He would not be under the necessity of acting, as we are not, according to the affirmation. If any one should say this is making the nature of God the foundation of obligation, I reply it is only making a moral action of any kind possible, and that I mean by the foundation of obligation that in view of which a moral nature is called into action. The moral nature, I suppose, acts by necessity, or it would not be a nature; but that so far as a being is a person and free, and so virtuous or vicious, he has no nature.

There! I have written right along, and cannot go back to read it. I hope it is right. The lectures are getting on so that I think I shall give them, but they will not be as I could wish. The class I have still, and shall have till the middle of the month or after, and then I shall be ready to go to New Haven.

There is a good deal of religious interest here, both in the college and in the town — meetings full and solemn.

BOSTON, April 10, 1876.

I received your note at New Haven last week, just as I was closing up my lectures, which I did Friday, and went the same evening to New Britain. There I spent the night, and the next day came here, as I had engaged to preach for Dr. Webb in the morning, and in the Central Church in the afternoon.

So far as I could judge, the lectures were well received by both the Faculty and students. The students sent me a letter, by vote of the several classes, expressing their interest in them and their desire that they, with those of last year, should be published. Is it possible I am to write another book? I should not wonder, but not yet.

I have had a call, this morning, from Dr. Warren, president of the Boston University, to consult me about coming to Boston and being at the head of the post-graduate department. It seems some gentleman has agreed to give $1,000 a year for five years if I will do it, and President Warren thinks he could get the rest readily. I have declined. Some time since they wrote me, desiring me to give five lectures before their theological students next winter, saying President Woolsey had lectured for them, and also Dr. McCosh. I consented, and gave as my subject, 'The Scriptural Idea of Man,' which was the title of my lectures last year at Yale. It did not occur to me that I should be down in their year book, but I am, and I see am to lecture on Scriptural Anthropology.

Probably I shall be here during the week, as my youngest son is to be married here next week Tuesday. I am appointed to write a centennial discourse for Commencement; it is time I was thinking about it. I wish I could get down and see you.

WILLIAMS COLLEGE, *January* 30, 1877.

I believe I have not written to you since you sent me your letter of advice. That advice was good, and I have followed it, and always mean to. It was that I should do just as I had a mind to. I have always had great respect for your abilities, but must confess it was increased by that letter. I do consider that for a man to say so much and yet say nothing is what very few could do. Probably I ought not to have asked the advice. However, as I said, I took it, and told Mr. Treat I wished he would communicate to the committee my wish to withdraw. He did so, and they desired him to write me a letter, which I have recently received, expressing their unanimous desire that I would let things go on as they are. That letter I have not answered, but in doing so I propose to follow your advice.

We had a pleasant time of it in Boston, wife and I. The Methodists received my orthodox lectures without any wry faces. On returning I took up the studies of the class where we left off, and am now going on with them. The class are doing well, and there is a good deal of religious interest in the college. I preached last Sabbath on the evidence for the Messiahship of Jesus, his own explicit testimony under oath to that point. I do not remember to have seen the subject presented as it struck me, and am inclined to take it up again next Sabbath.

And, by the way, next Sabbath will be my seventy-fifth birthday. Think of that! Yes, and in thinking of it, I find I am in a mistake; I shall be seventy-five years old, and it will be my seventy-sixth birthday. Certainly I have great reason to bless God that I am still able to keep on with my work here in the college, and to preach abroad as usual. I preached twice in the Central Church when in Boston.

WILLIAMS COLLEGE, *December* 18, 1877.

You inquire in your letter, received this morning, whether I find the same interest as formerly in teaching. I think so, and account for it partly from the fact that I teach this system, which expands upon me, as I study it more, and evidently becomes a power in moulding the whole mental life of the class, and often giving bent to their moral and religious life. It commends itself most to the best minds, and they often express their satisfaction in the clearness of insight they gain. I account for it also partly from the manner of my teaching. Nothing pleases me more than to have the class ask questions, and so it sometimes happens that we spend the hour in what is really conversation, making no progress in the book, and the result of that is often most satisfactory. I do not find that impertinent or captious questions are asked. This, of course, causes the recitations to be different every year, according to the minds to be dealt with, and gives nearly as much variety as there would be if it were a new thing. It is really wonderful how new the study is to most young men when they begin it. The first term closes to-day. We have been through the "Outline" and through the first part of "The Law of Love." That is correct, but it seems as if it might be more simply put, and I have hoped to write an article about it for the "International," and still hope to. Some things long in dispute have been settled, and it seems as if that, about the proper adjustment of man's active powers and his moral nature might be.

Williams College, March 6, 1878.

At the same time with this I send the manuscript. If you do not find it convenient to look it over, I will not ask it; but as you have in a sense indorsed what I have said heretofore, I should be glad of your judgment; and as to what you shall do in case of disagreement, I will give you *carte blanche* to make alterations. When I wrote I supposed there would be plenty of time to communicate with you. I have made some references to places in my books where the same subjects are treated of, for I think there are few points, if any, in the article that I have not decided the same way in my books, but for the reasons mentioned in my former letter they have not been so brought together as to be seen in their connection and fully understood. I hope the essential points are clearly as well as continuously presented in the article. I was tempted to some digressions and hits, but concluded to do as I have done. If you approve, I shall be sure what the judgment of the public will be.

WILLIAMS COLLEGE, *March* 14, 1878.

I am greatly obliged to you for reading over my article, and of course am gratified by your approval. If the article had been on an ordinary topic of literature, I should not have asked it, but being on a question that has been discussed for ages, and with the points of which you are probably as familiar as any man in the country, I could not but desire your judgment. Besides, you had expressed approval of my views when they were less distinctly and consecutively put, and I wished to know how this presentation would commend itself to you.

As I said in a former letter, I have been unfortunate in my books from not carrying out in the lectures on moral science my original plan; which was to connect with an exposition of the constitution, that would show the agreement of its law with the revealed law, a practical part. Then when I came to give a practical part in "The Law of Love," I could not use my former work, and so confined myself mainly to the consideration of obligation, in the theoretical part. What I should like to do now is to substitute the substance of the article you have just read for the theoretical part of "The Law of Love." That is right, but it is not a sufficient exposition of the constitution, and besides is too difficult for any but the more advanced classes. When the article comes out, I may want your opinion on this. If that could be done, it seems to me it would give us a real philosophy of conduct and an unanswerable argument for the Scriptures. When the article is published I shall want, and suppose there will be no difficulty in my having, a dozen or so of the separate sheets sent to me. May I ask your kind offices in this?

WILLIAMS COLLEGE, *April* 29, 1878.

Last week I was surprised at receiving some dozen pages of my article in the "International," with a request that I should send them to editors and others. I replied inquiring if there had not been a mistake in sending only a part of the article. This morning I received a card saying they have divided the article for want of space, and adding it will get the advantage of two notices. I have just written them a note complaining of this, but of course it will do no good. It is a kind of thing that would have vexed me a good deal when I was younger. So you see that my article, which you were so kind, I fear in your partiality, as to say would be *the* article of the number, will be no article at all. The article was not over-long, and going off at once might have made a respectable explosion, but divided I fear it will be nothing but two squibs. I think they should have consulted me before taking such a course. They might at least have deferred the whole till the next number, to which I should not have objected.

In all that I see written in opposition to Mill and Harrison, who say that an appeal to our own happiness is an appeal to selfishness, and that action for that is selfishness, it is taken for granted that they are right. That part of my article not to be published as yet takes another view and would probably be attacked, so the evil day is put off. But the idea that men who suppose that death is the end for them can be brought up to an altruism that will lead them to work for a humanity of which they are to form no part is ridiculous.

Have you seen a notice of the death of Mark Hopkins the millionaire, of California? One paper sent me said he was my son. He was a distant relative, though I never saw him. Another paper said he was sixty years old and my *grandson.*

WILLIAMS COLLEGE, *August* 2, 1878.

"What is the use of being a lazy man, if one has to have coals of fire poured on his head? There is no standing that. When I look at your efficiency not only in letter writing, but in writing in all directions, I am ashamed of myself. However, you are a young man yet, and the *vis vivida* is still in full play. Your article on Froude I read, and it is none too severe. My only question is whether it was worth the notice. There is a large amount of that kind of writing now, and will continue to be for some time. There is a piece in the last "Popular Science Monthly," by Lewes, of the same general tenor, but abler and yet showing great want of discrimination. He undertakes to show the difference between the faith of science and of theology, and he knows nothing about it. It is pitiable to find men of reputation blundering along in such a way.

WILLIAMS COLLEGE, *December* 30, 1878.

In losing the old year now about to depart, I feel as if I were losing a friend. The year has been a pleasant one, nor do I find that as the years go on they seem shorter. That you know is often said. One item of pleasantness has been that my work, so far as I can see, continues to be acceptable. I was gratified by your commendation some time ago of my article on "Faith." How singular it is that on a point so central there should still be so much of indefiniteness, and among our foremost thinkers. It seemed to me that I made the subject

plain. However, the world has got along toler-
ably well without clear ideas on that and a good
many other points, and I suppose will continue
to do so. And, by the way, there is a point of less
importance that I should like to consult you about
some time when you are dismounted from your Peg-
asus, and have on your philosopher's cap. It
respects the priority, in the natural history of the
mind, of the ideas of right, and of rights. It is
generally supposed that the idea of right must, as
an original and primitive idea, be first, but right
relates to action, whereas rights belong to us, and
enter into our conception of ourselves. I have long
been inclined to think that the idea of rights is
first. Clearly a being possessed of no rights could
have no idea of anything as right.

WASHINGTON, *April* 9, 1879.

Perhaps, my dear Dr. Palmer, you would like
to know our whereabout and what-about. It is
now two weeks since wife and I came to this capital
of our great country, where we are staying with our
married daughter, Mrs. Nott. I have also a son
married here, which adds to the attraction. The
city is the centre of political movement, but to me
is like the centre of a whirlwind, where they say
there is no movement. I hear less of politics than
at home, and get almost all political news from
New York.

As to my what-about there is little to be said.
I am reading up on the evidences of Christianity,

or rather on the changes in them since my book was published, for I have not kept up with the times in that, and would now like to add a few pages, if I can in that way bring the work down to the present time. The literature on that subject is extensive. The difficulty is to condense and give it point in a form that will be read. There are many pleasant people here to be seen, and numbers of them call upon us. Last evening four members of the class of 1856 came in together, and for one class it was not a bad representation. There was Garfield, the leader of the House on the Republican side; Gilfillan, the treasurer of the United States; Colonel Rockwell, of the regular army, who is stationed here, and has charge of all the government cemeteries; and Newcomb, who has been a number of years at New Haven, but has just been elected to the professorship of intellectual and moral philosophy in the Free College in New York. Two of these brought their wives. Besides these Mr. Bancroft, now in his eightieth year, came in, and also Dr. Peter Parker with his wife. Mr. Bancroft retains his vivacity, rides on horseback a good deal, and works every day so long as to tire out his amanuensis. I had previously dined with him at my son's, where I met also Senator Edmunds and General Sherman. I have just been reading Sherman's "Memoirs," written by himself, written as he talks, and giving a graphic and most interesting account of the scenes he passed through in California and during the war, of which last he has good reason to say *quorum magna pars fui.*

WILLIAMS COLLEGE, *January* 1, 1880.

Here it is — a new year, a new decade, — 1880. That looks like a great deal more than 1879, but I do not know that I feel much older than I did yesterday. Nor does nature seem to be any older. How wonderful that the earth should have gone on for so long with such perfect exactness, and no sign of weariness. How natural it was for Esdras in the Apocrypha to say so long ago that "the world hath lost its youth and the times begin to wax old," and then, "For look how much the world shall be weaker through age, so much the more shall evils increase upon them that dwell therein." How differently we look at it who see the powers of nature just beginning to be found out and subjected to man. I have just seen that conversation has been carried on at the distance of two thousand miles by means of the telegraph wires and the telephone. I wonder what Esdras would have said to that. However, say what we may about this world, it is plain that the kingdom of Christ must consist mainly of those in a condition wholly different from anything we now know with our present liabilities and limitations. And so we look forward to a new heaven and a new earth, and so to the "everlasting kingdom of our Lord and Saviour Jesus Christ." Taking this life by itself, I think it is "worth living" to some, but not to all. To you and me it has been by the mercy of God, and much more.

New York, *April* 29, 1882.

So Emerson is gone. I met him several times, but never had much conversation with him. I was interested in his writings years ago — bought one volume of his "Essays," and then another, but opened to a place in which he spoke of Christ in a manner so distasteful, not to say shocking to me, that I put up the book and have not read him since till just now. He has insight and a charming style. You are enticed along, because you do not know what he will say next. There is no doubt about the wide influence he has exerted and will exert. Probably he may be placed at the head of the modern school of Christianized pagans, who are what Socrates might have been, if he had had the light of Christ's teaching without accepting Him as a Saviour, or acknowledging any personal relation to Him.

Williams College, *July* 17, 1882.

Since dropping you a line from New York on our way home from Washington we have passed through scenes new to us. Soon after reaching home our little granddaughter whom we had with us, a beautiful child, was taken sick, and after between three and four weeks of fever, with constant watching and visits of the doctor once and twice a day, she died. Almost immediately after, Louisa, for whom the child was named, and who was much exhausted by constant care, was taken in much the same way, and with her the fever ran a similar course, medicine seeming to have no control over it, till, on the 4th instant, about five P. M., she left us. She was to us all that a daughter could be, and it had not occurred to me that she could go first. She was perfectly fitted to care for us, if we should fall into that decrepitude of years which, if we live, cannot be far off. But we have great comfort in thinking of what she was, and in the assurance of her acceptance by Him whom she followed. I have known no one who seemed to me to come nearer my conception of a saint. Coming as her extreme sickness and death did, I was unable to take any part in the Commencement, or to be present at the exercises. As you may have seen, Dr. Prime read my discourse on President Garfield. That has been published in full in some papers, but is now being printed as a pamphlet, and I will send you a copy.

I thank you for your letter. Since Louisa's death I have reflected more on the certainty of a future state of blessedness, and the infinite value of the revelations of Christianity respecting it. Without that revelation I must confess I should be greatly in doubt.

WILLIAMS COLLEGE, *January* 20, 1883.

How deeply I am engaged in metaphysics you may judge, when I tell you that I am not only preparing some lectures for metaphysical Princeton, but that I have this morning been hearing a recitation in the Catechism on the decrees of God.

My solution of it was that God decrees to do whatever He does, and to permit whatever He permits,
and that the objection is not so much to the decrees, as to what is decreed, and so if any one
objects, it becomes a direct quarrel with God himself. I suppose every generation will find the same
difficulties, and come up to the same point on this
subject.

WILLIAMS COLLEGE, *May* 16, 1883.

As time goes on I think more of the Bible as
compared with other books, and am satisfied that if
it were read for the purpose of spiritual upbuilding, it would be its own witness. Is not such
reading and study of the Bible the great thing
the church needs?

WILLIAMS COLLEGE, *October* 24, 1883.

Once more I am tied to the college bell-rope,
and fairly started in the routine of recitations, having one every day and part of the time two. I find
myself interested, and the class seem to be. They
are over fifty.

I sent you a copy of the proceedings of the
American Board. I had not seen any one, and
supposed there was an understanding among the
members of the board as to my successor, as I had
given the Prudential Committee notice some months
before, and as my purpose to withdraw was generally known. Any such turn as the matter took was
wholly unthought of by me, till the chairman of
the nominating committee, Dr. Withrow, came to

me Wednesday noon, sent as he said by the committee. He said there had been no prearrangement, and that the members of the committee were not at all agreed, and the committee were unanimous in the opinion that the best interests of the board would be subserved if I would permit my name to be used. I put the matter over till the next morning, and then gave in, having in the mean time seen the secretaries, Colonel Hammond, and some others. Of course I had to explain and defend myself. I have now reason to think that my course is generally approved.

I did not think the meeting as stimulating and spiritually uplifting as some others, but there was clear thinking, principles were established, and the Armenian difficulty harmoniously and, I hope, permanently settled. You were there in your hymns, as you always are in all such meetings, and after all, though business is the object, yet the worship and praise are the best part of it.

So far as I see, my book is well spoken of. One or two of those who have written notices of it I judge have read it, but no one has noticed those distinctions and differences from others in which I think its main value lies. However, those things gradually work their way into the public mind. I have just received an original and valuable little book by Mr. Rowland G. Hazard, whom I suppose you must have known when living in Rhode Island, as the State is so small. It treats of similar topics, and is especially strong on freedom and causation.

My health seems now as good as before I was sick, though with some tendency to cough, and I intend to keep at work while I am able, but happily I have nothing on hand that has to be finished by a specified time. What I shall do just next I do not know. I ought to do some reading. We are rejoicing in the return of Judge Nott and his family, now with us. His health is better. Mr. Denison also, whom Carrie married, is with us, as he preaches for the college, so we have great reason to be thankful and wonder at the forbearance and goodness of God.

May God be with you and yours. My love to them all.

WILLIAMS COLLEGE, *November* 24, 1883.

Preserved in amber — that is what I said to myself as I found your book, the illustrated copy of "My Faith looks up to Thee," on my return from my recitation this morning. However, that is not the kind of amber in which that hymn will be preserved. It will be in the hearts and voices of Christians till the end of time, and I congratulate you on having done such a work that will thus "follow you."

I am much pleased that you are again elected associate pastor, and that you are to continue in a work so congenial to yourself and so profitable to the church. I wish all our churches could have something of the kind.

I see in the "Congregationalist" of this week an

article of yours on companionship with Christ, with which I am much pleased. It is the same idea essentially as that I endeavored to present in my sermon at Great Barrington, a copy of which I sent you. It seems to me that what our Saviour said on that subject has been suffered to lie in a great measure unrecognized, and that it must come up into greater prominence, as you know one doctrine and aspect of the Scriptures does after another, if the Christian life is either to be, or to enjoy what it should. If those passages do not involve mysticism, as we know they do not, they must involve what is most quickening and precious in the Christian life. I agree with you entirely about it, and hope you may follow up the theme.

My health is improved, and I keep at work, but have to be careful.

May the communion of our Lord Jesus Christ be with you more and more.

WILLIAMS COLLEGE, *May* 15, 1884.

Here we are once more, having come home yesterday after an absence of about six weeks, most of the time in Washington. Your good letter reached me there, and should have been answered, but for the most of the time while there I was not good for much. For some years I have had in the spring a cough. It took me this year just before I left home. I had been so well during the winter as to attend all my recitations, not missing one, and, so far as I could judge, with as good acceptance as heretofore. At any rate, when I understood that the class proposed to make me some kind of a present, and I had put a stop to that, they wrote me a letter expressing their thankfulness for what I had done. But to return: just before I left, the cough took me and held on and was wearing me down, but within a week or two I got some essence of pine that came from Switzerland, and by taking it, as put into hot water and through an inhaler, have so broken the cough up that it is almost gone, and now, old as I am, I am permitted to look on this beautiful world in its springtime with a feeling that I am not wholly out of correspondence with it. How wonderful is its beauty! The more I see of it, and the more I reflect upon it, the more I appreciate the marvels of its structure.

I was quiet in Washington, did not go once either to the House or to the Senate; preached once, made one talk before a club, and dined with some of the Judges and great men; though I don't know that I am either wiser or better for that. It was pleasant, however, and Washington is now and is to be not only a beautiful city, but one where the amplest means of social enjoyment may be found.

WILLIAMS COLLEGE, *September* 8, 1884.

You may have seen that I have got into politics, having been nominated as an elector at large on the Blaine ticket. It was known that I was in favor of Blaine, but that was all. As between Blaine and Cleveland, and that is the way it stands,

I say Blaine; and as between the Republican party and the Democratic party, backed up by a solid South, I say the Republican party. I should have preferred not to be put in nomination, but do not think it wise to decline.

The number of letters from which quotations are given is small in comparison with the whole number written. Dr. Palmer died March 29, 1887. There is a letter written by him to Dr. Hopkins dated February 16 of that year, from which a few sentences may well be added: —

"This friendly correspondence has been to me of great interest and profit. It somehow came about as natural growth. It has extended over more than a quarter of a century. I cannot of course hope that it has added much to you except the labor of writing. But to me it has been a material blessing intellectually, socially, spiritually, and in many other ways. We have had many thoughts and sympathies and general lines of life in common, and have never lacked material for letters.

"I think you are right in relation to the A. B. C. F. M. matter. I should hope most for peace, if the method of reference by councils shall be adopted, and think it must come to that. I feel too near the world of love and peace to go into any earthly controversy now, and have carefully avoided this.

"I rejoice that your books have gone into other languages and lands. They will be doing good when you will be with the glorified. I hope my hymns will also."

In a few weeks the writer entered into the land of peace, and in June, less than four months later, was followed by his friend. The friendship had something beautiful in its length and in the naturalness of its close. These aged saints who had grown old together were in their deaths hardly divided, and perhaps soon met again in the Father's house. The last verse of Dr. Palmer's imperishable hymn that they had sung together in public worship, the fervent prayer that in solitude they had often offered, was graciously and abundantly answered.

> " When ends life's transient dream,
>   When death's cold sullen stream
> Shall o'er me roll ;
>   Blest Saviour! then in love
> Fear and distrust remove !
>   Oh, bear me safe above,
> A ransomed soul! "

THE THEOLOGIAN.

" God's Saints are ſhining lights : who ſtays
            Here long must passe
  O're dark hills, ſwift ſtreames, and ſteep ways
            As ſmooth as glasse ;
            But these all night
            Like Candles ſhed
            Their beams, and light
            Us into Bed.

" They are (indeed) our Pillar-fires
            Seen as we go,
  They are that Cities ſhining ſpires
            We travell too ;
            A ſwordlike gleame
            Kept man for ſin
            First *Out ;* This beame
            Will guide him *In.*"
            HENRY VAUGHAN, *Joy of my Life.*

CHAPTER XII.

THE THEOLOGIAN.

DR. HOPKINS was primarily a leader in education. Yet he was in the best sense a religious leader, and few men in his generation in America did more effective service for the Church of Christ. By this it is not meant simply that he trained men for service in the ministry at home and abroad; that he gave inspiration to vast religious assemblies; or that, his unique powers remaining undiminished until all of his contemporaries had fallen, he became by experience and wisdom as well as by gifts a teacher of great influence; but that he left in the conceptions of the Christian Church the definite impress of his own thinking. These conceptions were wider and better, when his work was done, than they would have been, had he not lived. They were better, because they were wider, and as the greatest service of his life was the broadening of men's minds to patient and candid thinking, that greatest service was not confined to the class-room, but was extended to the religious teachers of the age. He was invited to become a professor in different theological seminaries, and pastor of leading churches, but declined with a wise perception of his freedom and of his larger influence. His position as college president was partly what he made it, but the office in those days was one of intellectual leadership, not of administrative sagacity. From that position he could select his themes, and maintain a proportion exactly expressive of his own conceptions. Had he become a theological professor, he would within limits have done the same, but he had the insight to know that he could influence religious thought more efficiently, if not identified with any special or professional school. He was a Puritan. He was a Congregationalist. He was brought up under the Congregational system, and preferred it both for its methods and its principles. Its methods put small value on forms or machinery, and seemed to him to conduce directly to the vital and essential thing, namely, spiritual growth. He inherited the Puritan's dislike of forms of worship, and more particularly in his earlier life he showed that aversion in his sermons, and dwelt upon the danger of appeals to the senses and of superstitious reliance on external rites. He believed that sincerity and purity were of far greater importance in religious worship than anything else could be, and the emphasis laid on minor matters by certain denominations was not in his judgment reasonable. It cannot be denied that this large way of looking at things which found expression in all his teaching and life is in part the explanation of the lofty attitude which he took in later times in reference to the discussions and agitations that invaded the

Congregational body. Singularly enough this largeness of mind and constant attention to the great central ideas broadened at last both into friendliness toward liberal thought, and into courteous recognition of the helpfulness to many of liturgical forms.

The ideas in Congregationalism that appealed most fully to his sympathies were the personal relation to God which it emphasized; the supreme value which it set upon man, made in the image of God, and upon that self-directive power that even the strongest Calvinists claimed to lodge in the human will.

A permanent and uninterrupted movement upward or downward under a primary choice, but a power of choice absolutely free; man a true cause; God a father, as well as a lawgiver; Christ a divine Redeemer; assimilation to Christ by the action of the will under the guidance of the Holy Spirit; the Bible, the infallible rule of faith and practice, — these were the doctrines that were of prime importance in his thought. The great enforcement which he gave them was from analogy. The harmony between nature and revelation; the universal reach of God's laws; the universal character of Christianity, — these were the themes the constant study of which gave to all his thinking a largeness that told strongly on the thought of his time. By as much as he exalted the human will, by so much he exalted the love of God revealed in Christ. For him there was no limitation in the offer of salvation. His whole conception and presentation of God was away from the earlier New England conception of arbitrariness and pure sovereignty. He loved science, and was never afraid of true science.

This is well shown in the following utterance: —

"It is the dignity of science that in it we reach and share the thoughts of God. We may receive them as from a letter unauthenticated, and so have no conscious communion with Him; but we cannot understand them and have a science, a *knowing*, unless they are *thoughts*, and so proofs of an intelligent being who thus expresses them."[1]

He was not afraid of philosophy, but gave his whole life to the teaching of philosophy, and his conception of God as energizing reason in nature was based on these two pillars. The idea of God as redeeming love he found in revelation, and the energizing reason of nature and the love of revelation were brought into harmony in his thought and could not be separated.

Perhaps at times he rested too confidently on a particular analogy. But the habit of looking for analogies based on his faith that God is the author both of nature and of the supernatural gave a remarkable impressiveness to his conceptions. In one of the last magazine articles that he published, that on "Optimism" in the "Andover Review" for March, 1885, he goes back to an analogy laid hold of as early as 1844, and already referred to

---

[1] Sermon before the American Association for the Advancement of Science, delivered at Albany, August 24, 1856.

in the account of the lectures on "The Evidences of Christianity." "Nothing so magnifies the law of gravitation as its grasp on the mote, no less perfect than that on the planet; and nothing so magnifies the law of God as the fact that no least sin of the most insignificant moral agent can escape detection, or be pardoned without an atonement."

The idea that there may be redemption through atonement in other worlds by an incarnate Christ has been a fancy of some. When his mind rose, as it did on one occasion, in the meeting of the American Board at Columbus in 1884, to the thought of moral life in other worlds, the analogy was from the perfection of different forms of vegetable and animal life here to the perfection of different forms of moral life.

"It might seem as if this perfection which can be wrought out in our humanity by Christianity was but one form of that perfection which is to be revealed in the works of God throughout the vast dominion of which I have spoken; throughout that vast system, that moral and social system, which corresponds in extent with that physical system which is revealed; and so I think that while there shall be gathered at last and preserved. as Paul says, a holy church, and every man shall be perfect and the church shall be spotless, without spot or blemish or any such thing. there will be other forms of perfection in other departments of God's universe. And when the great day of restitution of all things shall come and God shall vindicate his government, there may be seen to be coming in from other departments of the universe a long procession of angelic forms, great white legions from Sirius, from Arcturus, and the chambers of the South, gathering around the throne of God and that centre around which the universe revolves."

Here is analogy pushed by imagination to extreme limits, but with a beauty and reasonableness that carry conviction.

That the universe was grounded in reason and governed by reason; that it was equally governed by love and regulated by love; that love and reason must be the same everywhere, — these are the thoughts which his analogies enforce, and these are among the thoughts which he helped to develop in his generation.

In the conversation which he had with the Rev. Robert A. Hume, the missionary to India, on the Sunday previous to his death, this same great illumination by analogy appears.

"Suppose you tried to show that man is a part of a universal and perfect moral system, while himself out of harmony with it. The Hindus can be made to see that the entire universe is controlled by a perfect system, — gravitation and other great laws extending to every atom. Similarly there is doubtless a perfect moral government reaching every part of the system." For the Hindus the great necessity is to show the sinfulness of man and his need of redemption. It was to be done by arguments from the perfect harmony of the work of *one* author, and the contrast between fallen man and the perfection of nature: Such a use of analogy passing over into arguments for the universal presence of God had an immense efficiency in expelling the old deistic conceptions, and presenting God as everywhere immanent. But there is not the slightest loss of transcendence, and indeed transcendence was one thing ardently contended for in the hostility which he evinced to evolution. God as working for ends; God revealed as working for beneficent ends; God as uplifting life by condescension in nature and through grace, — these ideas are as renunciatory of pantheism as of deism. So his "faith is confidence in a personal being." That was his definition of faith in 1850, and probably much earlier, but it is formally enunciated and discussed in the baccalaureate sermon that year. Faith was at once the source and the end of his religious teaching. That men should trust in Christ; that the personal relation to Him should be paramount in every system; that the exaltation of that personal relation would bring the right proportions into a doctrinal system, — these were with him controlling principles. For the true use of creeds and confessions he had great respect. But the law of the conditioning and the conditioned had force in all departments of thought. In his view everything in practical theology was conditioned on the right idea of faith in Christ; on the trust reposed by the individual soul in the divine Saviour, and no creed that did not explicitly exhibit that relation seemed to him rational or clear. Faith in his system did not precede salvation; it is indeed the means of securing salvation, but by the act of faith the believer is saved; by that act he comes into harmony and union with God, becomes the son and heir of God. There was much that was mysterious in God's plan of salvation, but nothing magical about the way of conforming to it. The processes on the part of God were plainly processes of eternal reason and eternal love, and man's response to these processes was wholly rational. The doctrine of ends was equally potent with him in theology and in philosophy. In the chart which accompanied "An Outline Study of Man" worship is presented as the highest outcome of man's complete nature. In any chart that would have expressed his theology, likeness and union with Christ would have been the end of all the powers and activities of man and the key to the whole system.

Dr. Hopkins was not accustomed to dwell much, as do some of the early theologians, notably Edwards, on the awful depravity of man. Least of all did he resort to those descriptions which picture man by the basest of terms and the lowest of figures. These were averse to his mode of presentation. His preaching was encouraging, and hopeful, and inspiring. His students were known in the theological seminaries as "cheerful" Christians, never as pessimists, or gloomy thinkers.

By this it is not meant that there was ever any

palliation of sin in his utterances. Sin was always in his system the abnormal; the discordant; the failure in the noblest being to meet his end; the deliberate and awful choice of evil; "the abominable thing" which God hates. But man was so loved by God in this fallen state that any guilty creature, "however debased and wretched, yea, though he were dyed and steeped in sin," coming with confidence authorized by the death of Christ, would be received as the prodigal son.

The incarnation expressed God's thought of the value of man, and the atonement was the wonderful divine way of purifying those whom God could not let go, and winning back the wanderers to the Father's house. That sons of God, those brought by eternal love once more into sonship, should have a view of sin that increasingly emphasized its sinfulness was reasonable, but that they, the sons of God, should speak of themselves, or be described, as once "worms," or "swine," or "vipers," was not in his style. Perhaps, however, aversion to these epithets common in certain older writers was founded quite as much on their inadequacy to express man's degradation as on the loftiness of his origin. But the degradation implied the loftiness. In a remarkable passage in "The Scriptural Idea of Man," he says: "In that prerogative of man by which he can either accept or reject the law of his being, he differs wholly from any mere animal. No animal can approximate anything of the kind. It lies in a region and sphere of which it knows nothing.

We have here indeed a fundamental, perhaps the most fundamental, difference between man and the brute. By accepting the law of his being, man is capable of rising to a height of knowledge, of goodness, of dominion, which shows *that* in him which must be wholly different in its origin from anything in the brute. Also, by rebelling against God and rejecting the law of his being, he is capable of sinking to a degradation so far below the brute as to show equally that they could not have had a common origin. No brute is any more capable of rebelling against God than of serving Him; is any more capable of sinking below the level of its own nature than of rising to the level of the nature of man. No brute can be either a fool or a fiend."[1]

Election did not mean for him the arbitrary choosing of "worms to be sons;" it meant the acceptance by God of a being made in his image on the ground of trust in the divine Son, and the foreknowledge that certain persons would exercise that trust.

It was a result of Dr. Hopkins's constant study of man's physical, intellectual, and moral nature and of his strong dependence on analogy that spiritual activities and processes were not for him so greatly differentiated in method from other processes as many theologians had made them. This is plainly seen in the following paragraph from "The Scriptural Idea of Man:" —

1 *The Scriptural Idea of Man,* Lecture VI. p. 124.

"And here in the way that sin and corruption come into the spiritual realm we find one of those analogies to what takes place in the lower forms of being that show the unity of the system throughout. All disintegration and corruption of matter is from the domination of a lower over a higher law. The body begins to return to its original elements as the lower chemical and physical forces begin to gain ascendency over the higher force of life. In the same way all sin and corruption in man is from his yielding to a lower law or principle of action in opposition to the demands of one that is higher." [1]

The profound elations and depressions of a spiritual experience, the agonies of conviction, the transports of conversion, that marked the early biographies of New England saints were far more consonant with his brother's ideas than with his. He admitted fully the reality of these extremes, and the diversities of operation by the same Spirit, but the whole influence of his teaching and preaching was to a calmer, more equable, less emotional acceptance and following of Christ. Rarely had any college the two types of religious experience, the fervent emotional and the calm philosophical, at the same time more happily illustrated in its teachers than in these two brothers. The influence of Dr. Hopkins's simple conception and presentation of faith helped largely to a removal of the feeling in the churches that these violent experiences were essential or even desirable in religious life.

<hr>

[1] *The Scriptural Idea of Man,* Lecture VI. p. 123.

His preaching was always so reasonable; every step
urged was so clearly shown to be fit for a reasonable being to take; his pleadings were so cool and
calm, and his exposition of God's relations to men
were so dispassionate and lucid, that the whole
effect was to give tone to the reason and will, and
lead to a manly consecration, rather than to a deep
prostration.

An impression prevailed in certain quarters,
where the doctrine of right advocated by him was
not fully grasped, that this theory was the source
of the doctrine that before a human being could be
finally condemned of God, Christ must have been
preached to him.   That the doctrine that right is
right, not simply because it is right, but because
doing right will promote the happiness of all beings,
the doer included, should be used as a standard to
determine what the infinite God will do with certain classes of men does not seem reasonable.   Dr.
Hopkins believed that God would do and does all
that infinite reason and infinite love can do to win
men back to himself.   But because he believed
this, and further that God has made it plain in the
constitution of things that he who chooses as a
supreme end the blessedness, the well-being of all
beings will do right, and that right action is right
because it conduces to that end, it is certainly a
strange inference that his teaching was preparatory
for the introduction into the thought of this age of
that peculiar, but old doctrine that the heathen will
not be condemned until they have heard the gospel

of Christ; and that if they have not heard it in this world, they must in the next.

The calm, restrained reply to the illogical attack made in the pages of a review was presented in a later number of the same periodical in an article on "The Place of the Sensibility in Morals."[1] This may well be noted as a masterpiece of dispassionate, temperate statement, and it must not be forgotten that he had attained his eighty-fifth year when it was written.

Dr. Hopkins's mind was an open one. The movement in the direction of breadth and charity was very plain the latter part of his life, and made his old age beautiful; and during his entire life he held himself ready to change any view, if new light seemed to make a change reasonable. That was seen in other matters besides his abandonment of the doctrine that right is ultimate.

The statement of Leibnitz that this is "the best possible system," once held by him, was at last wholly abandoned, as is plain from the article on "Optimism" already mentioned. A colloquy once took place in his class-room which brought out objections to that statement by Leibnitz in a striking way. Dr. Hopkins asked a bright student[2] if he did not believe that "this is the best possible system." The student replied that he did not. Thereupon the president said: "Will you please

---

[1] *Homiletical Review*, February, 1887.

[2] James H. Canfield, of the class of 1868, now Chancellor of the University of Nebraska.

tell us in what respects you could improve upon this system?"   "Certainly," was the prompt reply; "I would kill off all the bedbugs, mosquitoes, and fleas, and make oranges and bananas grow farther north."   If the answer seems a little pungent, we have this assurance, that only a student who had been thinking earnestly on the subjects under discussion would have made such a reply.   It was a far more honorable answer to the teacher than a blind affirmation would have been, and was doubtless regarded by Dr. Hopkins himself as an indication that his teaching was not in vain.   I remember distinctly that at the alumni dinner the next summer he spoke most complimentarily of the oration just delivered on the Commencement stage by the keen pupil who made this retort.

He made a good deal of the argument from miracles in the lectures on "The Evidences of Christianity," and never ceased to regard the miracles as a substantial and authoritative support to the claims of Christ.   In the article on "Optimism," one of the ripest and maturest of his discussions, he indicates a change in the proportionate weight which he gave them.

"As compared with the conception of a sinless man as essential to a religious system, and with the presentation of it in real life in its vicissitudes and under its extremest forms of trial, the wonder of miracles is as nothing.   Miracles were needed in the beginning as evidences.   They are needed still, but they will be less needed as the world moves on, and the sinless character of Christ shall take its place and shine with proper effulgence in the Christian system."

At the same time it must not be overlooked that there was a foresightedness and an almost prophetic element in his mind that early seized the points likeliest to be of weight in progress. For this reason the changes in his position were few. For this reason we find in his last and matured utterances points of living contact with the earliest. For this reason, also, in some things he was in advance of his age. He was, I believe, the first in this country to make the study of anatomy and physiology the foundation for the study of mind and morals, and was thus the pioneer in the direction of "Physiological Psychology," which has of late years taken on such large expansion. Indeed the ablest exponent[1] of the new psychology in this country does not exclude, but rather presents Dr. Hopkins's conceptions as expressive of the aims of the new method when he writes: —

"The new psychology which brings simply a new method and a new standpoint to philosophy is, I believe, Christian to its root and centre; and its final mission in the world is not merely to trace petty harmonies and small adjustments between science and religion, but to flood and transfuse the new and vaster conceptions of the universe and of man's place in it — now slowly taking form and giv-

---

[1] President G. Stanley Hall, of Clark University, Worcester, Mass.

ing to reason a new cosmos and involving momentous and far-reaching practical and social consequences — with the old Scriptural sense of unity, rationality, and love beneath and above all with all its wide consequences."[1]   While the pupil would not here claim for his master that he was conversant with the methods or results of the latest physiological investigations, he certainly includes him among the "new" philosophers.   He could not more accurately describe Dr. Hopkins's thought of the mission of psychology than in these words.   He could not more perfectly picture the scope and influence of his teaching.

He stood always for unity, for reason, for love in his philosophy and his theology.   The laws of the conditioning and the conditioned meant unity and reason, and as there was no high end without sensibility, love pervaded the entire system.   The end in morals was the love of man and the love of God.   The end in theology was the same made attainable by faith in Christ.

It is noteworthy that, while his first book was on "The Evidences of Christianity," the last lecture in the last book, "The Scriptural Idea of Man," treats almost wholly of "The Man, Christ Jesus."   The Christocentric trend of modern theology in New England and America was promoted by his utterances.   It would be hard to find a more marked instance of uniformity of exaltation of Christ in all the thought of a thinker.   From the beginning to

[1] *Andover Review*, March, 1885.

the end of his career Christ was the "Sun of Righteousness." He regarded Him as the source of all redemption and inspiring power from the first. His conceptions of Him were enlarged, as were his conceptions of creation, but the authority of his person and the grandeur of his claims and mission always had the relative importance which the last developments in all theology assign them.

Dr. Samuel Hopkins, his great-uncle, defined faith as "an understanding cordial receiving the divine testimony concerning Jesus Christ and the way of salvation by Him in which the heart accords and conforms to the gospel."

The great nephew defined it as "confidence in a personal being." This simplicity and directness of the relation to Christ, the introduction of this conception as the mainspring of all doctrinal statements and movements, was the great contribution of his life to the thought of the churches. It was a contribution that involved many lesser gifts, as, for instance, more rational views of inspiration, and a clearer understanding of the Bible. The whole thought and activity of the churches is now quickened and harmonized by this central and guiding conception, which others indeed before him had dimly perceived, but which he helped to make the luminous centre of modern theology.

THE CLOSING YEARS.

" What wouldst thou have a good great man obtain ?
  Wealth, title, dignity, a golden chain,
  Or heap of corses which his sword hath slain ?
  Goodness and greatness are not means, but ends.
  Hath he not always treasures, always friends,
  The good great man ?   Three treasures — love, and light,
  And calm thoughts, equable as infant's breath ;
  And three fast friends, more sure than day or night —
  Himself, his Maker, and the angel Death."

COLERIDGE, The Good Great Man.

CHAPTER XIII.

THE CLOSING YEARS.

In 1880 Dr. Hopkins was much delighted with
the nomination of General Garfield, who had been
one of his pupils, for the office of President of the
United States. Garfield's entrance of Williams
College had been determined by a kindly letter
and promise of help received from Dr. Hopkins in
reply to an appeal made when he was considering
the means of securing a college education. From
the first the relation was one of cordial and recip-
rocal esteem, which deepened in later years into reverence on Garfield's part for his great teacher, and
admiration on the teacher's part for the brilliant
development of power in the pupil and the steady
promotion which accompanied the development.

In Garfield's volumes of correspondence are
carefully preserved letters from Dr. Hopkins which
were written at various points of advancement in
Garfield's career. The letter of congratulation on
the nomination to the presidency is worthy of the
relation between these distinguished men, and expresses in the frankest and yet most tender way
the joy that a true teacher will feel in the success
of a beloved pupil, — a success won, in this case,
against immense odds.

WILLIAMS COLLEGE, *June* 10, 1880.

MY DEAR GENERAL, — Has the time of telegrams so passed that you can read a letter?

The hour has struck sooner than I thought. You know I thought it would come, and now that it has come I rejoice with you. I congratulate you, not only on your nomination, but on the manner of it, and the enthusiasm with which it is received. The students here are wild over it, and I care not how wild, if they will but learn the lesson there is in it.

It is one reason of my joy that there is a lesson in it. How well I remember those early struggles and your manly bearing under them, the confidence you at once gave your instructors and received from them, and the combination, so apparently easy, and yet so rare among students, of a genial spirit with pure habits and high aims uniformly pursued. That was the beginning of a course in which you have not faltered, and the lesson therefore is, that this honor is the result of no accident, but of achievement by steady work in scholarship and statesmanship, so that when the occasion called, the *man* was there. In this view of it I regard the nomination as an honor to the country and its institutions, no less than to yourself, and if the American people shall ratify it, as I believe they will, I am confident we shall have an administration that will not suffer in comparison with any that has gone before it.

My dear General, I shake hands with you, and beg you to convey my congratulations to Mrs. Garfield and to your honored mother.

When the campaign ended, and the pupil was elected to the highest office in the gift of the people, the teacher, recalling anew all the struggles of the life that had been thus crowned, had great cause for thankfulness that he had been permitted to help make those struggles easier, and to add something by his instruction to the intellectual and moral power of the man. No one could have greater joy in the honor that had come to the once poor and anxious student, now the President-elect of the great republic, than Dr. Hopkins. His brief letter of congratulation expresses this joy.

WILLIAMS COLLEGE, November 3, 1880.

MY DEAR GENERAL, — The news of the morning brings us joy. *You are elected President of these United States by a majority that cannot be questioned.* Thanks be to God for the security and prosperity which this promises to the whole country.

You know, that outside of your own family no one rejoices more in this, your success, than I do. May God be with you.

Please present my best congratulations to Mrs. Garfield and your honored mother.

Dr. Hopkins was in Washington at the time of the inauguration, a guest of his son-in-law, Judge Nott, of the Court of Claims. A meeting of the graduates of the college with their brother alumnus, the newly inaugurated President, and with Dr. Hopkins, was arranged by Colonel A. F. Rockwell, a classmate and intimate friend of Garfield. The following account of that meeting had its origin in the thoughtful kindness, and is given in the words, of Colonel Rockwell. The meeting took place on the afternoon of the inauguration day, March 4, 1881.

"About four o'clock, the alumni with Dr. Hopkins were present in the Executive Mansion, awaiting the President. As soon as he was notified, leaving behind the crowds who were pressing for his attention, attended by Mrs. Garfield, Mrs. Rockwell, and myself, the President proceeded at once to the East Room. On entering, he found the company of a hundred or more arranged in a semicircle. Approaching, he arrested his steps, and, crossing his hands before him, stopped about ten feet away, facing the Doctor. After a moment of silence, Dr. Hopkins began the remarkable address, a faithful copy of which I have the pleasure of inclosing. The emotion of the company was apparent, and, at the moment when 'that venerable and venerated man,' with outstretched hands, 'invoked the blessing of Him who has led you hitherto,' the scene was impressive beyond description.

"The President then began his reply, which, as nearly as I remember, occupied about the same time as the Doctor's address. It is always to be regretted that, in the hurry and confusion of those times, the services of a stenographer were overlooked. To make amends I spared no entreaties to elicit from the eminent men, whose relations on this day were so unique and beautiful, the reproduction by themselves of their words.

"I was more successful in the one case, but only partly so in the other; for the two precious half sheets in my possession, containing the beautiful and touching exordium only of President Garfield's address, were all that my most strenuous efforts could obtain.

"How far, at this late day, the recollections of those present might avail in reproducing the remainder of the President's address is a matter for conjecture."

The following are Dr. Hopkins's words: —

"PRESIDENT GARFIELD, — The alumni of Williams College here gathered, esteem it an honor that they are permitted to be the first to congratulate you in this house, now to be your home, on your accession this day to your great office as President of the United States: and they have deputed me to say a few words in their behalf.

"But, before doing this, I must be permitted to greet and congratulate you personally and on my own behalf. This I venture to do, if for no other reason, because I have been told, and I suppose truly, that I am the only president of a college who has lived to see one, who graduated during his administration, attain to this high honor. This I am now permitted to see, and for it I give thanks to God. In this, with the exception of your honored mother and immediate family, there is no one who rejoices more than I do, and from the bottom of my heart I congratulate you.

"Having thus ventured to say a word for myself, I now speak for the alumni.

"Since your graduation, sir, twenty-four years

ago, your course has been conspicuous, and we have watched it with deep interest. We have seen you passing on and up without defeat, until, by no political manœuvring, but by high statesmanship and continuous public service in the face of the American people, you have attained one of the highest positions this world has to give, — the presidency of the grandest republic hitherto known.

"Well then, sir, may we congratulate you, and I do it in the name of those who hold or have held high positions under the government, in the name of those prominent in the several States from which they come, in the name of your classmates of whom so many are present, in the name of all present, I congratulate you, and assure you that we feel honored in your honor.

"And not in the name of these alone do I congratulate you, but in the name of the college, its trustees, and its alumni, wherever they may be. Standing as I do among the oldest of these alumni, and having taught so many of them, I feel authorized to speak for them. I know that they also feel honored in your honor, and that, as a body, they will be strongly in sympathy with you in your administration.

"To that administration we look forward with confidence. In view of its vast responsibilities and grand opportunities, we invoke upon you the blessing of Him who has led you hitherto; and we trust that in connection with it there will come to yourself still higher honor, and to the whole of this vast country, East. West, North, and South, alike, greater prosperity than it has hitherto known."

In the reply which President Garfield made, it has been related by those who were present, was the distinct assertion that Dr. Hopkins was more truly President than he. Colonel Rockwell's memorandum gives the few words which he secured from the distinguished statesman, and these breathe the spirit of this statement.

"I am deeply grateful to you, and to the alumni of Williams College here assembled, for this cordial greeting.

"It will give me new strength for the duties of this place to know that I am welcomed and supported by this great company of educated men, whose lives illustrate and honor so many professions, and such wide fields of useful activity.

"It is especially gratifying to me that your greetings have been delivered by that venerable and venerated man, who was in our college days and will always be *our* President.

"I hope he will pardon me for a more personal reference. For a quarter of a century Dr. Hopkins has seemed to me a man apart from other men, — standing on a mountain peak, — embodying in himself much of the majesty of earth, and reflecting in his life something of the sunlight and glory of Heaven. His presence here is a benediction " —

. . . .

It was arranged that at the inauguration of Franklin Carter on July 6, 1881, as the sixth president of Williams College, General Garfield, who had represented the alumni at the inauguration of President Chadbourne, Dr. Hopkins's immediate successor, should again speak for the alumni. He was to be the guest of Dr. Hopkins during the Commencement week. He had just started on his journey to Williamstown to fulfill this engagement, when the bullet of the assassin struck him. When the swift telegram on the 2d of July carried the bitter intelligence of his assassination over the land, to no one outside of his own family was the event more distressing than to Dr. Hopkins. The telegrams received by him during the public exercises of the Commencement week and read to the various assemblies always excited deep emotion. There was something strikingly pathetic and representative of the whole people in the eagerness with which the venerable man received these dispatches, in the encouragement which he drew from each favorable sign, and in the anxiety that seemed to underlie all his actions.

Almost immediately after this gloomy Commencement, which was nevertheless brightened by rays of hope, Dr. Hopkins went abroad with his wife and two daughters. Before sailing, he sent a letter to President Garfield, which is here printed.

WILLIAMS COLLEGE, *July* 13, 1881.

MY DEAR PRESIDENT GARFIELD. — We, Mrs. Hopkins, Louisa, Susie, and I, leave to-day for Europe, with hearts lightened and thankful from the hope, now almost reaching assurance, of your recovery. The shock here during Commencement week, the grief, disappointment, and suspense were fearful.

Here the feeling was intensified, but over the whole country it was a wonderful testimony of affectionate regard.

We hope to return in about three months, and God grant that we may find you fully restored.

With affectionate regards from us all to Mrs. Garfield and yourself, I am, with the highest consideration,

Yours.   MARK HOPKINS.

By leaving the country then, Dr. Hopkins escaped in a measure the stress of daily perturbations to which all were subject who honored Garfield and were near enough to read the frequent reports from the room of the sufferer. Still the long, painful illness touched him constantly, and sometimes closely, even in Europe, and the death enveloped foreign lands in shadows hardly less dense than those falling upon our States.

Dr. Hopkins returned from Europe and resumed his work in the college towards the end of November. His health was benefited by the voyage, and seemed very vigorous, when one recalled that he was more than half way through his eighty-first year.

Early in the spring of 1882 he received an invitation from the trustees of the college to deliver a memorial address [1] on President Garfield at

---

[1] This address is published in the book *Teachings and Counsels*, issued in 1884 by Charles Scribner's Sons. It follows the twenty baccalaureate sermons.

Commencement in July of that year. He accepted the invitation, and in the address referred most impressively to the suffering and death of the lamented President.

"I make no attempt to interpret the providence which permitted the death of President Garfield at such a time and in such a manner. To me clouds and darkness are round about it. But that he was eminently fitted in himself and in the circumstances of his death to be the object of a gaze which should illustrate the power of sympathy in the new conditions under which the race is placed will not be denied."

The entire oration was marked by a calm dignity and sagacious insight, but it was not delivered by Dr. Hopkins himself, and for that reason as spoken lost the effectiveness that his venerable presence and his deep, personal feeling would have added. The serious illness of his eldest daughter, Mary Louisa, so saddened and alarmed him that he put the manuscript into the hand of Rev. Dr. S. I. Prime, of New York city, at that time the oldest clerical member of the board of trustees, and it was read by him on July 4, 1882, to a large audience. The circumstances deepened the feeling of solemnity, and the gloom of the previous Commencement occasioned by the startling bullet of Guiteau seemed to return and envelop the community, as the universally beloved daughter slipped away to the unseen world from the home of her father. Her death was a grievous affliction to him

and to all the family. "I have known no one,"
are Dr. Hopkins's touching words in the letter to
Dr. Palmer, "who seemed to me to come nearer
my conception of a saint." With that pathetic
sentence, all who knew her will agree. She was a
symmetrical, lovely character, at once practical and
intellectual, broad-minded and tender, and having
great powers of expression. Somewhat reserved to
strangers, she yet always conveyed a sense of her
goodness, and no one who was privileged to catch
a word from the depths of her life could fail to be
ennobled by it or to remember the moment with
grateful joy. She was like her father in intellectual qualities, and the sympathy between them was
deep.

The next year, 1883, Dr. Hopkins's health was
for a time quite infirm. This was the year in
which the lectures on "The Scriptural Idea of
Man" were delivered at Princeton in the early
spring. It was with considerable heroism that
this honorable duty was discharged. One of the
lectures was read to the audience by Dr. Green, as
Dr. Hopkins was too ill that day to attempt the
labor. One of them he delivered, rising from his
bed for the purpose, and retiring almost immediately after the hour was ended. He returned to
his home in Williamstown late in the spring, but
did not entirely recover from his weakness.

He was annoyed with a cough and with inability
to digest food. He went from his home to the
seaside before Commencement to secure rest and

avoid excitement. His old pupils, to whom the return to Williamstown for the college festivities meant little unless they saw and greeted him and received his greeting, were disappointed to miss his venerable and still stately figure about the college. He returned home late in the summer, greatly refreshed and improved by the change. He looked forward to the meeting of the American Board at Detroit with the determination of there resigning his presidency. He had, however, in October, regained his strength so fully that he endured the fatigue of the meeting with his usual ability, and presided with admirable efficiency. He was finally persuaded to accept the office for another year, to the great satisfaction of the corporate members, and continued president until his death.

He resumed his teaching after the meeting, and did not miss a recitation during the cold weather. Before the spring came the cough returned, and he felt that the visit to his children at Washington might be a help to breaking it up. He left home in the latter part of March and returned about the middle of May, very much improved. At Commencement that year, 1884, he happened to enter the chapel during the alumni meeting at the time when Dr. Stanley Hall, then of the Johns Hopkins University, was reading the report of the committee of the alumni on the state of the college. He had been speaking of the great services of Dr. Hopkins as a teacher of philosophy, just before his old preceptor entered the room. When his familiar and venerable form moved up the aisle, as the thoughts of all were just then fixed upon him, with one accord the whole body of alumni rose to their feet to do him honor.

The gift of $30,000 in seven per cent. bonds made by the Hon. William E. Dodge, in 1867, to the college, inasmuch as the interest was for Dr. Hopkins's use, if he chose to give up his teaching, made it possible for him to withdraw comfortably at any time from his work in the college. At the age of eighty-two, with the consciousness that the passing years gave of declining vigor, there was no disposition on his part to shrink from the resumption of his teaching. The desire to be under his instruction was strong in every class, and in the later years of his life an apprehension was often expressed by members of the lower classes lest when their class reached the Senior year he should have given up his teaching.

In the presidential election of 1884 he was an elector-at-large on the Republican ticket for Massachusetts, and earnestly hoped for the success of Mr. Blaine. When he began teaching that autumn, the class had in it the two elder sons of the lamented President Garfield and sons of other graduates, so that it was with peculiar pleasure that he undertook the instruction of this class.

His speech at the alumni dinner in 1885 was one of his happiest. The American Board met this year at Boston, and the conditions made the labor of attendance and presiding easier than on some previous years, but the anxiety and excitement were wearing. He returned again to his college teaching with joy. It was a calm and beautiful age, honored by his pupils and reverently regarded by all who knew him. Everywhere his name was spoken with affection. The debate at Des Moines in 1886 and the agitations of the American Board have already been discussed. There can be no doubt that these matters occupied his thought and wore upon his strength. But when at the two hundred and fiftieth anniversary of Harvard, in 1886, the degree of Doctor of Laws (Harvard gave him the doctorate of Divinity in 1841) was conferred upon him, and the great audience joined in vigorous applause as he rose before them, he seemed the personification of serene and beautiful old age.

Indeed, when in the spring of 1887, after another winter's teaching, he took his departure for Washington, there seemed no reason to fear that he would not go on with his instruction for a few years longer. He had confidence in his own strength. He had spoken within a year of having delivered an oration at the semi-centennial of the college in 1843, and of his hope to live to hear, or possibly to give, the oration at the centennial in 1893. But on his return in May he was not quite up to his average strength. There seemed to be a little less exuberance of spirit and a little more consciousness of age. It was not until June that he really seemed ill. He took cold, and his strength began to fail. The family physician, Dr. Hubbell, the brother of Mrs. Hopkins, was called in, but there seemed at first to be no cause for alarm. He kept about, went out to ride, and climbed a fence and went up a few rods from the road to the spring which supplies the village only two or three days before his death. This was on Tuesday, June 14. It was the perfect season of the year. I remember his once saying to me at this very season, as we sat in the twilight, and the perfect beauty of June was about us, "This is the most beautiful season of the year. But it passes very quickly." It was in this perfect season that he too was at last swiftly passing. He spoke of death too on that June evening in 1868 (there had recently been a sudden death in the college), and then quoted Professor Kellogg, as having once said to him: "Because I have been so often near death, people think I must know something of it, and what is beyond. But to me, as to all, it is a blank wall." On Wednesday he was no better, but arose and dressed, and on Thursday made himself ready with difficulty for a festival of his grandchildren, whom he tenderly loved. He did not have the strength after dressing to attend the little party. That night he was restless, could not breathe easily, and sat up much of the time. At the coming of dawn he seemed to be aware that his sensations meant something grave. As the birds were singing their morning song, and he was breathing with difficulty, he said to his beloved wife: "Mary, this must be death." As he sat there on the side of the bed, erect, majestic, enduring, his head dropped a little, and his spirit had flown.

With the same courage and faith with which he had met many a crisis, he met death. There is something striking in the fact that he met this last enemy sitting and looking for the dawn. One is tempted to recall Browning's words in "Prospice,"

> "I would hate that death bandaged my eyes and forbore,
>   And bade me creep past.
>   No! let me taste the whole of it, fare like my peers,
>   The heroes of old;
>   Bear the brunt, in a minute pay life's glad arrears
>   Of pain, darkness, and cold."

THE FINAL TRIBUTE.

" There is a stream whose waves divide
    Life from the shady shores beyond ;
And we on this sad side are found,
    Toiling on sandy flats, I ween,
Sighs our one moisture, tears our sheen,
    While the still river flows between.

" And yet, when our belovèd rise
    To gird them for the ford, and pass
From wilderness to springing grass,
    From barren waste to living green,
We weep that they no more are seen,
    And that the river flows between.

" Ah, could we follow where they go
    And pierce the holy shade they find,
One grief were ours — to stay behind !
    One hope — to join the Blest Unseen —
To plant our steps where theirs have been,
    And find no river flows between."
        C. C. FRASER TYTLER, *Crossing the River.*

CHAPTER XIV.

It was on the morning of June 17 that Dr. Hopkins died. On the following Tuesday, June 21, he was buried. The services were conducted by the Rev. A. C. Sewall, of Schenectady, who had been until quite recently for many years pastor of the Congregational church in Williamstown, Professor Edward H. Griffin, then connected with the college as associate professor of philosophy, and later Dr. Hopkins's successor in the professorship of "Intellectual and Moral Philosophy," and the president of the college. Alumni living in remote cities and towns, the officers of various religious and educational institutions, came to pay their last respects to the great teacher. The Senior class, the class of 1887, formed a body-guard accompanying the remains from the church to the peaceful and beautiful cemetery of the college. It was a dark and gloomy day, but at one point during the service gleams of sunlight came through the clouds and, shooting through a window, rested directly upon the coffin. The life had been great and beautiful, and this sunlight seemed like a revelation of the new strength and joy that had come to his departed spirit. There was a feeling of comfort in all hearts in the remembrance of his long and successful labors, and of the deep peace that had marked his later years. As voicing the feelings of those who had known him best, and giving a general statement of the grateful love and honor in which his pupils held him, the discourse which I delivered on that occasion may close this record.

As I passed out of the president's house early last Friday morning in response to the startling message sent by my beloved classmate, the pastor of the college church, I carried in my heart the certainty that the brightest star in the firmament covering these hills had set to rise in the pure ether of heaven. I wondered that nature was still busy with her weaving, her humming, her whispering, her sparrows, and her blades of grass, and did not know and could not know enough to weep for, or even pause to think of, that

> " blossom of the earth
> Which all her harvests were not worth."

But there came another thought: the remembrance that the Prince of Life had assured his disciples that the hairs of their heads were all numbered, that He had told them that not even a sparrow falls to the ground without the Heavenly Father's notice, and had asked the comforting question, "Are not ye of more value than many sparrows?"

And I am sure, as we all have reflected in these intervening days on the life that ended so fittingly, its long and beneficent record, its great powers so wisely used, the benignant and serene atmosphere of these riper years, we must have been deeply impressed with the grandeur and the normal perfection of many of its features, and humbly grateful that God has granted to us to know these features and this life.

This is not the time for the analysis and eulogy of a great intellectual career, but rather to comfort one another with words of gratitude and joyful recognition of what God has given us through this life and in the very taking of it away. And if I call your attention to a few points in it, partly the gift of God and partly the conquest of faith and patience, and our hearts are thus warmed by this contemplation into new love for the Redeemer and new trust in his watchful care of all his saints, it cannot be one side of the true lessons of the hour.

Is it not well to think for a moment of the length and strength of the life of this hero-saint? — of the eighty-five years that he lived, of the sixty years at least of majestic powers fully trained and devoted in calm but ceaseless activity to Christ's service? We recall the declaration of Moses, that man of God, that "if by reason of strength the days of our years be fourscore years, yet is their strength labor and sorrow," and we feel that these words have no application to this life; and that, as it was recorded of Moses himself, so, too, of our teacher it may be said, that when he departed, "his eye was not dim, nor his natural force abated." He was nearly two years old when his great-uncle, Samuel Hopkins, the eminent theologian, died in Newport in December, 1803. Suppose, now, that he had been five years old, and had seen and remembered that illustrious uncle; and then imagine that one of these little grandsons who saw and loved and will remember him should live to the age of eighty, then this life would be the middle link of a chain of three links, covering nearly two hundred and forty years. We see thus how many generations may be linked together, and what a grasp before and behind this life had. He might have been spared a few years more, perhaps, but how much sweeter to remember him as going before "the keepers of the house began to tremble, and the strong men bowed themselves, and those that look out of the windows were darkened."

Is it not comforting, too, to remember, considering simply the relationships of human life, what the prophetic dying Jacob called in the Hebrew idiom "the blessing of the breasts and of the womb," in what tender and gracious ways God blessed our teacher and father and friend? From the earlier years of my knowledge of life in this village nothing is more beautiful to recall than the brotherhood of him who has now gone with that gifted and revered saint, Albert, who died in 1872. The hands that clasped each other affectionately as co-workers and co-educators in this college played with the same playthings and picked the same flowers in childhood. As little boys they were taught and kissed by the same loving mother's lips. As families reproduce in successive or remoter generations their features, I think that the brotherhood of Mark and Albert Hopkins in some measure reproduced that of their great uncle Samuel, the profound leader of New England theologians, with his younger brother, their grandfather, Colonel Mark. The subtle acumen of the great-uncle reappeared in the president, Mark. The soldierly fervor of the grandfather Mark reappeared in Albert. These two men, dealing with the two subjects that filled Kant with wonder, one with the laws and movements of the stars, the other with the laws and movements of the human mind, honored throughout the land, had forty years of brotherhood in the kingdoms of scholarship and of Christ. And if I could speak of that more delicate and tender relation, involving that profounder mystery by which the solitary are set in families, every heart that knows that home would throb with joyful memories of the perfect, the ideal type of union, which, so early formed and continued so long beyond the "golden" day, has been the admiration of all and the inspiration of many. And well might I allude to the chivalrous reverence with which the family relation was always treated; the consummate tact and grace with which every family duty was performed and every family ordinance solemnized; to the numbers of little children (many of them not of his kin) whom he lovingly baptized "into the name of the Father, the Son, and the Holy Ghost."

And then the sons and daughters and grandchildren (almost the last act was to prepare himself for a festival of the little ones), — who can help looking upon all these family conditions as beautiful, and who that knew him can fail to remember him as the beloved head of them all?

Some sorrows came through this organic relation (the thought of the bitter loss of five years ago still causes pangs in many hearts), but how many joys, how many pure and noble lives, how many sweet and winning childhoods, were blest in their claims upon his headship of an ideal family and are to-day blended in the loving union of his memory.

And passing over to what he loved with an almost equally intense affection, the college for which he lived, and which he carried by the sheer weight of his powers for so many years, how inspiring to remember that of the seventeen hundred and fifty living alumni he had taught all but a score or so the principles of mental life and growth, the truths of ethics, and the deeper truths of Christian faith.

His teaching was not perfunctory or mechanical, but was adapted in every case to the conditions. His keen intelligence, his genuine sympathy, his ready wit, his faith in the possibilities of the dullest, made his lecture-room a pleasant place, — the desire of the earlier years, the delight of his class, and the memory of the graduates. Is it not good to remember that for fifty-seven years he moved on as teacher, holding perfectly all the principles and getting constantly a grasp of new ideas, loving each one that showed any love for truth, and leading here and elsewhere by his words and books men and women into purer knowledge and a true faith; and seemed as bright, as clear, as sagacious, as far-sighted the last week that he taught, as when he became president?

He knew the dangers that beset us, his pupils; perils from doubts, and passions, and appetites, æsthetics, and knowledge. He knew how easy it is for the feet of young men to slip downward, and with what clearness, and love, and patience he held up to us "the power of the endless life."

Let me quote here a passage from a poem which has as much fitness for him as for the great teacher to whom his son addressed it: —

> " But thou wouldst not *alone*
> Be saved, my father ! *Alone*
> Conquer and come to thy goal,
> Leaving the rest in the wild.
> We were weary, and we
> Fearful, and we in our march
> Fain to drop down and to die.
> Still thou turnedst, and still
> Gavest the weary thy hand.
> If in the paths of the world,
> Stones might have wounded thy feet,
> Toil or dejection have tried
> Thy spirit, of that we saw
> Nothing — to us thou wast still
> Cheerful, and helpful, and firm !
> Therefore to thee it was given
> Many to save with thyself;
> And at the end of thy day,
> O faithful shepherd ! to come,
> Bringing thy sheep in thy hand."

And so we the alumni of the college come as one great family, looking up to him as our father and head, and praising God for the equable calmness and abundant teaching of his life, for the wideness of his thoughts and charity, for the stamp of manly power that he set on every receptive mind.

This is the last of the examples in New England of the college president as the father, teacher, counselor, and guide. Very different conditions now exist to determine the character of the office; and as it was the last of these presidencies, I think it has also been the most perfect of them all. In him the early system produced a perfect type. In a large college the relation is not so intimate, and as no president ever taught so long, so wisely, with such massive simplicity and condescending aptness, none ever had behind him so large and so loyal a body of grateful and enthusiastic pupils. But the tears that hundreds of educated men shed to-day are tears of gratitude and joy. It is a reverent, believing body who have been taught by him to look up to a personal God, and have seen in him the influence of God's personal abiding presence, and have learned to have faith in immortality for the good, even for him.

What the ongoing of the college will be without his consummate tact, his serene wisdom, the balance and play of his perfect judgment, the colossal solidity of his character, I cannot tell. But let me break the silence of official reserve and say that he has spoken to me only loving words. Never in these six years has he done aught but put the massive force of his reputation and powers most lovingly at the disposition of those intrusted with the dear old college. How desolate the landscape will be without any reappearance of his majestic figure!

A thing most gratefully to be remembered is the childlike responsiveness of his mind that was never more noticeable than in these last years. Every gain for the college in material prosperity moved him deeply. My last talk with him was about a much-needed improvement, and it was with an intense earnestness that he expressed his hope for its accomplishment. It seems strange now that since my last talk with him I should have had a conversation about the deep things of Christ's kingdom only the day before his death with the great son whom Amherst buries to-day, and whose loss seems more inscrutable than that of our master. Amherst and Williams mingle tears to-day over illustrious dead.

Dr. Hopkins had known the struggle of long poverty for the college; of bitter inability to secure for his students the advantages that greater resources would have given, and I am bold enough to say that the full distress of some of those trials no man, not even his brother, fully knew. It was whispered, I doubt not, into the ear of God, and when at last there came in these last years, not opulence, but some additions to our scanty resources, his feeling was purely one of grateful delight. But

his responsiveness was not in the least childish,
only childlike, for his sagacity, his penetration, his
insight, were vigorous to the end, and no member
of the board of trustees had a more perfect appreciation of the changes in the conditions of modern
education, or opened his mind more readily to a
perception of the fact that the college of to-day
could not be the college of fifty years ago. So his
mind was open to every new and true idea, and appreciated with ever-increasing fairness the broadening influence of art, of culture, of literature and
science, as well as of religion. I never expect to
see an instance in which equally to the very end of
a long life the mind turned to the light, and the
man, "like a tree planted by the rivers of water,"
opened sweet flowers of wisdom, justice, and charity in larger and larger proportions and greater and
greater beauty, until the frost came. Beautiful
beyond expression are the declining years of such
a life. Friends, comrades, undergraduates, weep
not, but lift up your hearts to God for the long
expansiveness and the rare fertility of this gifted
and divinely guided mind. What he was to the
family, to the college, that he was to the missionary movement, — always at the head, king of men
by the grace of God, and leader of saints by "the
faith that overcometh."

What he desired was that the church should see
the face and know the mind of the divine Christ.
That Christ's teachers should be more and more
Christlike, that they should not contend about

"tithes of mint, anise, and cummin," or even about the human formulas which can express in but a limited way Christ's divine glory. With what masterly words he would sweep away irrelevant issues, and hold up the true, the vital point in a discussion. With something of the prophetic, statesmanlike power of his brother Albert, refined by his responsibilities and long dealing with minds, he could foresee results; but a joyful optimism, founded on faith in Christ as the head of the universe and on the coming of his kingdom, may sometimes have led him to underrate the power of passion and prejudice in the hearts of even the best men. What schisms of the church he loved, what rupture of institutions dear to him as his life, death may have sealed his eyes from beholding, we know not. But this we do know, that the last year and the last hours of his life his great mind sought with unceasing attention to find and establish an honorable way by which, with unabated zeal, with undiminished resources, with undivided powers, men of varying shades of opinion in all our land might work together as heretofore in the upbuilding of the Redeemer's kingdom, in proclaiming to the outcast and the heathen the gospel of Christ.

What he longed for was the conversion of the world to the divine Christ. If I may read an extract from a letter forwarded to Dr. Denison by Rev. Mr. Hume, who spent Sunday, the 12th of June, with him, it will have intense interest for us all, and especially for the students: —

NEW HAVEN, *June* 19.

MY DEAR DR. DENISON, — A week ago this Sunday, in conversation with Dr. Hopkins, I asked him as to his conception of the best plan for a text-book on theology for the use of preachers in India. On Monday morning he said to me : " I have been thinking over our conversation about a book on theology, and suggest that you begin with the subject of man instead of God. But the crucial point in the system will be how to show man his sinfulness and need of a Saviour. Suppose you tried to show that man is part of a universal and perfect moral system, while himself out of harmony with it. The Hindus' can be made to see that the entire universe is controlled by a perfect system — gravitation and other great laws extending to every atom. Similarly there is doubtless a perfect moral government reaching every part of the system. I expect to preach in the college chapel next Sunday from the text ' There is joy in the presence of the angels of God over one sinner that repenteth.' I shall say : If there is joy in heaven over one sinner that repenteth, then in heaven they know what is taking place here. Also, they know not only the external but the internal life of the world, because repentance is an inward thing. So I could go on to show that *one* system pervades heaven and earth. You can see how this can be followed out."

Very likely no one else knew what plans he had made for the subject of his preaching to-day. This conversation occurred only a week ago. And to-day, instead of preaching in Williamstown, he has gone to serve where he doubtless knows more of that universal and perfect system than even he knew a week ago, and there must be joy in heaven over a ripe saint called to enter into the joy of his Lord.

Thus to the very end the oneness of God's kingdom filled his mind, and he marched from premise to conclusion with clear logic and sublime faith.

The death of a good great man is always impressive, but in this case it cannot be sad. In a perfect poem which our revered teacher loved and once at least repeated, "the good great man" is said to have

"Three fast friends, more sure than day or night —
Himself, his Maker, and the angel, Death."

The man fixes from day to day his character. As life goes on, to the stature of his being something is added; from it something is taken, but the scaffolding of daily relations is there, and hides the figure. Death removes the scaffolding; makes it plain what the man really was; moves out into the bright sunlight and the gaze of all the statue in its calm completeness. Beneath the cross even the centurion said: "Truly this was the son of God." To-day we see clearly what our master was, and we need not wage any "feud with Death" that he has thus made certain the symmetry in which we believed before; that he makes it sure to us that this personality was so rounded in life's struggles as to "become a pillar in the temple of our God and go no more out forever."

What then has Death done to us in this event that we should grieve? Do you say: "He has removed this great teacher so far that we cannot hear him speak?" Is even that true? No. "He being dead yet speaketh," will always speak in the lives of his children and his children's children, in the words of his pupils and of his pupils' pupils; for "God has mercy unto thousands of generations upon them that love Him and keep his commandments."

As we look back then at this life, and see how unique it was in many features, — unique in its lengthened continuance of unabated powers, wonderful in the normal beauty of the family relations, unique in the grandeur of its endowments, unique in the extent and intensity of its personal influence, — so that he, like Abraham, by heroic sainthood became, as it were, the intellectual and spiritual leader of a great race; — unique in the openness and receptivity of his mind, unique in the cordial love that came to him from every side, — could we ask that one feature should be changed? Can we do otherwise than thank God for such an inheritance of faith and love and wisdom which the consecration of his great powers to the Redeemer has secured us? And have not those whose loss is deepest, deepest cause for gratitude? Have we not all profound reason to praise God that his death has been "but a step out of a tent already luminous with light which shone through its transparent walls?" Surely upon him has been fulfilled the prophecy of Jacob: —

"The blessings of thy father have prevailed above the blessings of my progenitors unto the utmost bound of the everlasting hills; they shall be on the head of Joseph and on the crown of the head of him that was separate from his brethren."

None of us will see his like again. God be praised that we have seen *him*, and known *him*, and loved *him*. Amen.

LIST OF REV. DR. MARK HOPKINS'S PUB-
LISHED WRITINGS.

Including, so far as ascertained, Addresses, Sermons, and Magazine Articles.

1. Agricultural Address at Stockbridge. 1826.
2. On Mystery. American Journal of Science and Arts, vol. xiii. No. 2, April, 1828.
3. Argument from Nature for the Divine Existence. The American Quarterly Observer, vol. i. No. 2, October, 1833.
4. On Human Happiness. *Ibid.*, vol. iii. No. 2, October, 1834.
5. On the Adaptation of Christianity to the Moral Nature of Man. The Biblical Repository and Quarterly Observer, vol. v. No. 2, April, 1835.
6. On Originality. *Ibid.*, vol. vi. No. 2, October, 1835.
7. Inaugural Discourse. 1836.
8. Taste and Morals. Two Lectures. 1836.
9. Influence of the Gospel in Liberalizing the Mind. Delivered as an address before the Porter Rhetorical Society of the Andover Theological Seminary, September 5, 1837. The Biblical Repository and Quarterly Observer, vol. x. No. 2, October, 1837.
10. Sermon commemorative of Dr. Griffin. 1837.
11. Election Sermon. 1839.
12. Address before the American Bible Society. 1840.
13. Address at Mount Holyoke Seminary. 1840.
14. Address to the Medical Class at Pittsfield. 1840.
15. Address at the Dedication of Williston Seminary, Easthampton. 1841.
16. Semi-Centennial Address at Williams College. 1843.
17. Sermon before the Pastoral Association of Massachusetts. 1843.
18. Berkshire Jubilee Sermon. 1844.

19. Sermon before the Convention of Congregational Ministers. 1845.

20. Sermon before the American Board of Commissioners for Foreign Missions at Brooklyn. 1845.

21. Sermon commemorative of Professor Ebenezer Kellogg. 1846.

22. Sermon at Plymouth on Forefathers' Day. 1846.

23. Temperance Address to the People of Massachusetts. 1846.

24. Evidences of Christianity. Lowell Lectures. 1846.

25. Sermon before the American and Foreign Sabbath Union. 1847.

26. Miscellaneous Essays and Discourses. Comprising a selection from the above enumerated pamphlets. 1847.

27. Baccalaureate Sermon. Faith, Philosophy, and Reason. 1850.

28. Sermon at Dedication of Congregational Church in Pittsfield. 1850.

29. Sketch of Rev. Dr. Alvan Hyde in Sprague's Annals of the American Pulpit. 1851.

30. Baccalaureate Sermon. Strength and Beauty. 1851.

31. Baccalaureate Sermon. Receiving and Giving. 1852.

32. Address before Society for promoting Collegiate and Theological Education at the West. 1852.

33. Sermon commemorative of Amos Lawrence. 1853.

34. The Central Principle. An oration before the New England Society of New York. 1854.

35. Baccalaureate Sermon. Perfect Love. 1855.

36. Discourse before Congregational Library Association. 1855.

37. Baccalaureate Sermon. Self-Denial. 1856.

38. Science and Religion. Sermon before American Association for the Advancement of Science. 1856.

39. Baccalaureate Sermon. Higher and Lower Good. 1857.

40. Baccalaureate Sermon. Eagles' Wings. Title changed later to " The One Exception." 1858.

41. A Missionary Sermon delivered at Bangor, Me. 1858.

42. Address at the Laying of the Corner Stone at the People's College, Havana, N. Y. 1858.

43. Baccalaureate Sermon. Manifoldness of Man. 1859.

44. Sermon Dedicatory of Williams College Chapel. 1859.

45. Baccalaureate Sermon. Nothing to be Lost. 1860.

46. Sermon at Ordination of Rev. C. M. Hyde at Brimfield. 1862.

47. Baccalaureate Sermon. The Living House, or God's Method of Social Unity. 1862.
48. Lectures on Moral Science. Lowell Lectures. 1862. ———
49. Baccalaureate Sermon. Enlargement. 1863.
50. Discourse commemorative of Nathan Jackson. 1863.
51. The Sabbath and Free Institutions. A paper read before the National Sabbath Convention at Saratoga. 1863.
52. Baccalaureate Sermons, as a volume. 1863.
53. Baccalaureate Sermon. Choice and Service. 1864.
54. Baccalaureate Sermon. Providence and Revelation. 1865.
55. Sermon at Funeral of Rev. Emerson Davis, D. D., Westfield, Massachusetts, 1866.
56. Baccalaureate Sermon. The Bible and Pantheism. 1866.
57. Baccalaureate Sermon. Liberality — its Limits. 1867.
58. Baccalaureate Sermon. Zeal. 1868.
59. Colleges and Stability. A discourse delivered at Marietta College, Marietta, Ohio. 1868.
60. The Law of Love and Love as a Law. Lowell Lectures. 1869. ———
61. Baccalaureate Sermon. Spirit, Soul, and Body. 1869.
62. What must I do to be saved? A Tract. 1870.
63. Baccalaureate Sermon. Life. 1870.
64. Memorial Address at Providence : commemorating the 250th anniversary of Congregationalism in this country. 1870.
65. Baccalaureate Sermon. The Body, the Temple of God. 1871.
66. Address at the Edwards Memorial in Stockbridge. 1871.
67. Baccalaureate Sermon. The Circular and the Onward Movement. 1872.
68. Modern Skepticism in relation to Young Men. An address before Young Men's Christian Associations. 1872.
69. Letter on Education to the Japanese Minister in a volume entitled " Education in Japan." 1873.
70. Prayer and the Prayer Gauge. A Discourse. 1873.
71. Sermon at the Funeral of Rev. John Todd, D. D. 1873.
72. Sunday Legislation. An address before the Evangelical Alliance. 1873.
73. An Outline Study of Man. Lowell Lectures. 1873.
74. Strength and Beauty: Discussions for Young Men. The Baccalaureate Sermons somewhat modified.
75. Temperance and Education. A Tract. 1875.
76. Colportage by Theological Students. Tract Society Address. No date.

77. The Law of Progress. Centennial Discourse before the Alumni of Williams College. 1876.

78. Faith. Princeton Review, 54th year, September, 1878.

79. The Moral Problem. Two articles. International Review, vol. v. Nos. 3 and 4, May and July, 1878.

80. Professor Tyndall upon the Origin of the Cosmos. Princeton Review, 55th year, November, 1879.

81. Grounds of Knowledge and Rules for Belief. *Ibid.*, 57th year, January, 1881.

82. Memorial Discourse on President Garfield. 1882.

83. Personality and Law. The Duke of Argyll. Princeton Review, 58th year, September, 1882.

84. Sermon at the Dedication of the Congregational Church in Great Barrington. 1883.

85. The Scriptural Idea of Man. Lectures before Yale Theological Seminary. 1883.

86. Sermon at the Dedication of the Memorial Church at Hampton Institute, Virginia. 1884.

87. Teachings and Counsels. The Baccalaureates in their original form, except that the addresses to the classes are abridged or omitted. To these is added the Discourse on President Garfield. 1884.

88. Optimism. Andover Review, vol. iii. No. 15, March, 1885.

89. Discourse commemorative of the Fiftieth Anniversary of his election as President of Williams College. 1886.

90. The Place of the Sensibility in Morals. Homiletic Review, vol. xiii. No. 2, February, 1887.

INDEX.

American Religious Leaders.

A Series of Biographies of Men who have had great
influence on Religious Thought and
Life in the United States.

JONATHAN EDWARDS. By Professor A. V. G.
Allen, author of " The Continuity of Christian Thought."

DR. MUHLENBERG. By Rev. William Wilberforce
Newton.

WILBUR FISK. By Professor George Prentice, of
Wesleyan University.

FRANCIS WAYLAND. By Professor J. O. Murray, of Princeton.

CHARLES G. FINNEY. By Professor G. Frederick
Wright.

MARK HOPKINS. By President Franklin Carter,
of Williams College.

In Preparation.

HENRY BOYNTON SMITH. By Professor L. F.
Stearns, of Bangor Theological Seminary, Bangor, Me.

ARCHBISHOP HUGHES. By John G. Shea,
LL. D., author of " The Catholic Authors of America," etc.

CHARLES HODGE. By President Francis L. Patton, of Princeton.

THEODORE PARKER. By John Fiske, author of
" The Idea of God," " Outlines of Cosmic Philosophy," etc.

This series includes biographies of eminent men
who represent the theology and methods of the various religious denominations of America. The Series when completed will not only depict in a clear
and memorable way several great figures in American
religious history, but will indicate the leading characteristics of that history, the progress and process of
religious philosophy in America, the various types of
theology which have shaped or been shaped by the
various churches, and the relation of these to the life
and thought of the Nation.

*Other volumes to be announced hereafter.   Each volume, 16mo,
gill top, $1.25.*

HOUGHTON, MIFFLIN AND COMPANY,
4 Park St., Boston; 11 East 17th St., New York.

American Commonwealths.

Edited by Horace E. Scudder.

VIRGINIA. A History of the People. By John Esten Cooke, author of "Life of Stonewall Jackson," etc.

OREGON. The Struggle for Possession. By William Barrows, D. D.

MARYLAND. The History of a Palatinate. By William Hand Browne, Associate of Johns Hopkins University.

KENTUCKY. A Pioneer Commonwealth. By Nathaniel S. Shaler, S. D., Professor of Palæontology, Harvard University.

MICHIGAN. A History of Governments. By Thomas McIntyre Cooley, LL. D., formerly Chief Justice of Michigan.

KANSAS. The Prelude to the War for the Union. By Leverett W. Spring, formerly Professor in English Literature in the University of Kansas.

CALIFORNIA. From the Conquest in 1846 to the Second Vigilance Committee in San Francisco. A Study of American Character. By Josiah Royce, Assistant Professor of Philosophy in Harvard University, formerly Professor in the University of California.

NEW YORK. The Planting and the Growth of the Empire State. By the Hon. Ellis H. Roberts, Editor of the Utica Herald. In two volumes.

CONNECTICUT. A Study of a Commonwealth Democracy. By Professor Alexander Johnston, author of "American Politics."

MISSOURI. A Bone of Contention. By Lucien Carr, M. A., Assistant Curator of the Peabody Museum of Archæology.

INDIANA. A Redemption from Slavery. By J. P. Dunn, Jr., author of "Massacres of the Mountains."

OHIO. First Fruits of the Ordinance of 1787. By Hon. Rufus King.

VERMONT. By Rowland E. Robinson.

In Preparation.

NEW JERSEY. By Austin Scott, Ph. D.

ILLINOIS. By E. G. Mason.

SOUTH CAROLINA. By Edward McCrady, Jr.

With Maps. Each volume, 16mo, gilt top, $1.25.

HOUGHTON, MIFFLIN AND COMPANY,

4 PARK ST., BOSTON; 11 EAST 17TH ST., NEW YORK.

American Statesmen.

Edited by John T. Morse, Jr.

JOHN QUINCY ADAMS. By John T. Morse, Jr., author of "A Life of Alexander Hamilton," etc.

ALEXANDER HAMILTON. By Henry Cabot Lodge, author of "The English Colonies in America," etc.

JOHN C. CALHOUN. By Dr. H. von Holst, author of the "Constitutional History of the United States."

ANDREW JACKSON. By Prof. William G. Sumner, author of "History of American Currency," etc.

JOHN RANDOLPH. By Henry Adams, author of "New England Federalism," etc.

JAMES MONROE. By D. C. Gilman, President of Johns Hopkins University, Baltimore.

THOMAS JEFFERSON. By John T. Morse, Jr.

DANIEL WEBSTER. By Henry Cabot Lodge.

ALBERT GALLATIN. By John Austin Stevens, recently editor of "The Magazine of American History."

JAMES MADISON. By Sydney Howard Gay, author (with William Cullen Bryant) of "A Popular History of the United States."

JOHN ADAMS. By John T. Morse, Jr.

JOHN MARSHALL. By Allan B. Magruder.

SAMUEL ADAMS. By James K. Hosmer, author of "A Short History of German Literature," etc.

THOMAS HART BENTON. By Theodore Roosevelt, author of "Hunting Trips of a Ranchman," etc.

HENRY CLAY. By Hon. Carl Schurz. 2 vols.

PATRICK HENRY. By Moses Coit Tyler, author of "History of American Literature," etc.

GOUVERNEUR MORRIS. By Theodore Roosevelt.

MARTIN VAN BUREN. By Edward M. Shepard.

GEORGE WASHINGTON. By Hon. Henry Cabot Lodge. In two volumes.

BENJAMIN FRANKLIN. By John T. Morse, Jr.

JOHN JAY. By George Pellew, author of "Woman and the Commonwealth."

LEWIS CASS. By Prof. Andrew C. McLaughlin, of the University of Michigan.

Other volumes to be announced hereafter. Each volume, uniform, 16mo, gilt top, $1.25 ; half morocco, $2.50.

HOUGHTON, MIFFLIN AND COMPANY,

4 PARK ST., BOSTON; 11 EAST 17TH ST., NEW YORK.

American Men of Letters.

Edited by Charles Dudley Warner.

WASHINGTON IRVING. By Charles Dudley Warner, author of "In the Levant," etc.

NOAH WEBSTER. By Horace E. Scudder, author of "Stories and Romances," "A History of the United States of America," etc.

HENRY D. THOREAU. By Frank B. Sanborn.

GEORGE RIPLEY. By Octavius Brooks Frothingham, author of "Transcendentalism in New England."

JAMES FENIMORE COOPER. By Thomas R. Lounsbury, Professor of English in the Scientific School of Yale College.

MARGARET FULLER OSSOLI. By Thomas Wentworth Higginson, author of "Malbone," "Oldport Days," etc.

RALPH WALDO EMERSON. By Oliver Wendell Holmes, author of "The Autocrat of the Breakfast-Table," etc.

EDGAR ALLAN POE. By George E. Woodberry, author of "A History of Wood Engraving."

NATHANIEL PARKER WILLIS. By Henry A. Beers, Professor of English Literature in Yale College.

BENJAMIN FRANKLIN. By John Bach McMaster, author of "History of the People of the United States."

WILLIAM CULLEN BRYANT. By John Bigelow, author of "Molinos the Quietist," etc.

WILLIAM GILMORE SIMMS. By William P. Trent, Professor of English Literature in the University of the South, Sewanee, Tenn.

Other volumes to be announced hereafter. Each volume, with Portrait, 16mo, gilt top, $1.25 ; half morocco, $2.50.

HOUGHTON, MIFFLIN AND COMPANY.

4 PARK ST., BOSTON; 11 EAST 17TH ST., NEW YORK.